The Story of the Secret Team That Defeated
South African Urban Terrorism

African
perspectives
· PUBLISHING ·

www.africanperspectives.co.za

African Perspectives Publishing
PO Box 95342, Grant Park 2051,
Johannesburg, South Africa
www.africanperspectives.co.za

ISBN PRINT: 978-1-0370-2164-0
ISBN DIGITAL: 978-1-0370-2270-8

Editor: Tumelo Motaung
Proofreader: Joe Latakgomo
Typesetter: Phumzile Mondlani
Cover Image: Zubair Sayed
Cover Design: Jenilee Prinsloo – Ryzenberg

To my old man, Stanley Africa, who bestowed his love of books upon me; and to the liberation struggle – which encouraged me to develop the liberating art of writing, and introduced me to the honourable craft of intelligence.

Contents

Acknowledgements

This book started as a dry analytic tome, and was well on its way when I realised that the value and ideas I wanted to transmit would be lost if only a few academics got sight of it. My friend, Marianne Merten, must take the blame for convincing me to write a more accessible memoir from my insights, reflections and recollections. For this, I am very grateful.

Various people have commented on the manuscript, and I am thankful for their insight, whether critical or otherwise. Jeremy Vearey, who has seamlessly transitioned from spy to author, was a great help with checking facts, reviewing balance in my judgement of people, and providing input on using various literary devices to enhance the storytelling. Pinto and Ricardo gave exceptional feedback on intelligence tradecraft. They often challenged my own views on things and forced me to rethink issues. They are the sort of spies South Africa needs.

Rose Francis, my publisher and fellow Pan-Africanist, has been a pleasure to work with and a bright beacon in an industry both institutionally and mentally dominated by whiteness. Most importantly, I have my lovely daughter to thank for her daily and forceful invocation of 'Papa, how many words have you written thus far?'

Foreword

It is not every day that a book of this nature makes the shelves of bookstores. It tells the story of how a small group of committed intelligence officers neutralised the vigilante organisation People Against Gangsterism and Drugs (Pagad) in the late 1990s and early 2000s. David Africa tells the story from the inner sanctum of the state security apparatus that initially failed, but eventually succeeded against Pagad's paramilitary G-Force. This successful intelligence operation, a testament to the power of strategic thinking and commitment, provides noteworthy insights that significantly contribute to our knowledge on the subject.

South Africa and the world at large confront a series of polycrises, the details of which are drip-fed to us through a daily dose of catastrophe, mismanagement, and poor governance. This book offers us a glimpse into the possibility of producing excellent outcomes if we care to be thoughtful, committed, and strategic. Africa has written a book on the successful intelligence operation that neutralised the threat of Pagad's urban terrorism, allowing us to imagine police and intelligence services known for the efficiency and innovation that existed at the time.

One of the reasons for this is the limits on political interference in the intelligence structures' work, and the consistent support and strategic direction they received from above. The lessons contained in this book are essential food for thought for anyone interested in the development of capable state institutions and the safety of our communities. The book takes you on a journey of commitment to service and the application of one of the oldest crafts in the world of strategy.

In July 2021, South Africa exploded into devastating violence as crowds attacked and destroyed public and commercial infrastructure in response to the arrest of former president Jacob Zuma. The lack of preparedness and the absence of a coherent political response at the apex of government decision-making betrayed a lack of foresight and political leadership that ignored the warnings emanating from the security community. If intelligence capabilities so carefully constructed in the struggle against Pagad were nurtured and sustained, the likelihood of such a security and political disaster would have been greatly reduced.

In Africa, the reader encounters a narrator who speaks with authority based on his deep experience with the Pagad troubles of the late 1990s. He somehow introduces wit and humour into a serious, often traumatic, but ultimately victorious story. The narrative alternates between the high-tension drama typical of espionage operations and a reflexivity that draws lessons amid all the drama.

Africa and his comrades in the team at the story's centre integrated into the post-Apartheid intelligence structures after the election of the first democratic government in 1994. Here, they exploit the lessons learned from their days in the liberation movement, from using politics to isolate an adversary to applying their training in secret work gained from years in the political and military underground. Typical of political activists turned intelligence operatives, the team never forgot that the success of any underground operation lies in your relationship with the people, who become your eyes and ears. This was the training inculcated in those of us as we were being prepared for infiltration back into the country, and these lessons were subsequently imparted to those trusted internal operatives of the struggle like the author, David Africa.

Two recurring themes of the book are the value of critical reflection and an obsession with learning to improve how they confronted what seemed to many like an invincible adversary. Lives on the Line is not merely a narration of events but has a profoundly personal thread running through it. We are exposed to the author's struggles with demanding responsibility, the building of camaraderie between old comrades and former enemies, the physical dangers of intelligence work and the personal toll all of this has on the people who do this work, and their families who witness them go through this turmoil in silence.

Africa wears his politics on his sleeve and is not shy about politically interpreting events and decisions. The internal confrontations with some old guard security police receive some of this treatment, as does the democratic government's initial failure to comprehend the potential of the Pagad threat. This personal narrative invites the reader to empathise with the sacrifices and challenges faced by those in the intelligence community.

The lens through which events are interpreted and narrated is unapologetically Black, partially because the struggle between Pagad and the intelligence operation against it was fought out mainly between Black protagonists. But the book also narrates something rarely publicised: an example of Black excellence in the complex world of intelligence and statecraft. The covert intelligence team that Africa was part of is characterised by innovation, strategic sophistication, and exceptional leadership, all sorely lacking in our security and political institutions today.

Lives on the Line achieves a delicate balance between exploring intelligence tradecraft, the political management of security threats, internecine battles in the security establishment, and the personal highs and lows of its protagonists, both spy and terrorist. It concludes with valuable lessons for intelligence practitioners globally, providing a unique and insightful perspective. It is, in equal parts, riveting and enlightening. It is a book many, not only in the intelligence and related communities, have been waiting for.

Ayanda Dlodlo
Former Minister of State Security, South Africa

Introduction

Few things are brought to a successful issue by impetuous desire, but most by calm and prudent forethought.
—Thucydides

The mid-winter evening of Sunday, 4 August 1996, was chilly. The skies were clear with a slight breeze. Several thousand members of the vigilante group People Against Gangsterism and Drugs (Pagad) had gathered at the house of notorious Cape Town gangster Rashied Staggie in Salt River to protest against gangsterism. Amongst the crowd were two undercover intelligence officers, Chris Martin and myself.

Formerly the textile hub of South Africa, Salt River was an established, predominantly Muslim suburb at the foot of Table Mountain. It would become a feature in the South African and international media for the few days that followed. What started as another one of Pagad's frequent protest marches ended with the brutal lynching of Rashied's twin brother, Rashaad Staggie, in full glare of the media.

The otherwise ordinary house was distinguished from its neighbours only by the heavy security and permanent presence of several armed men – members of the infamous Hard Livings gang. Even though we had sent a warning alert to the police and intelligence management on the Friday, we did not expect the night's events to turn out as violently and dramatically as they did.

Martin and I found ourselves amid a crowd that fired several thousand rounds of ammunition at Staggie's house while the small contingent of police on the scene stood by helplessly. Trained in the adversarial structures of the Apartheid Security Branch and the African National Congress (ANC), both of us responded instinctively, taking cover as bullets flew above our heads. At the subsequent court inquest into Staggie's death, Martin described the shooting frenzy as akin to 'the breaking out of a small war.' If only we knew then that the country had just entered the most dangerous phase of a battle between Pagad terrorists and the State, one that would span over the next five years. What had begun as a cold night transcended into five years of scorching conflict, sometimes in the open and often in the shadows.

Staggie's lynching was one of the most dramatic in a series of traumatic and violent events that played out in Cape Town between 1995 and 2001. These incidents had a fundamental impact on the conduct of policing and intelligence in the nascent democracy, which was struggling to shed its Apartheid skin and embrace the constitutional freedoms for which so many South Africans had died. It was a time when the social movement turned terrorist organisation Pagad unleashed an orgy of violence upon the city, its citizens, businesses, and government. In the end, its violent campaign targeted whoever opposed it, challenged its ideological position or methods, or refused to submit to its intimidation and financial extortion.

By 1998, the State had officially categorised its campaign as Urban Terrorism, a designation the United States government adopted as it added Pagad to its Terrorism Exclusion List. By 2000, Pagad operated with impunity and expansive freedom of movement, able to deploy more than 200 members of its paramilitary G-Force in attacks against drug dealers, gang leaders, police and judicial officers, academics, business people, and entities representing Western interests in South Africa. Shopping malls and places of entertainment became deserted as tourists and locals alike, expecting a shooting or bombing to take place at any given moment, avoided becoming another name on Pagad's growing list of maimed or murdered victims.

All the while, the State seemed either unwilling or unable to bring this reign of terror to an end. The new South Africa appeared to have faltered in confronting its first major National Security challenge. No matter how well-intentioned, effort after effort in the State's response fell short of achieving a decisive breakthrough against Pagad. However, by late 2000, a sudden break in the Pagad campaign of terror occurred, leading to the relatively rapid decapitation of the organisation's armed capability. What appeared like a bolt out of the blue was the sharp edge of six years' worth of painstaking, stubborn, and innovative intelligence work by a team of which I am proud to have been a part.

The book is the story of the intelligence team that whittled away at Pagad until we brought down a seemingly invincible colossus. It is a narrative of six intense and dangerous years spent at the coalface of the struggle to neutralise Pagad, bring its terrorist campaign to a swift end, and bring the perpetrators of murder and mayhem to justice. The results of our work surprised Pagad as much as the general public. It baffled even well-informed observers of the organisation's meteoric rise to infamy and the State's serial failure to counter them. The fatal blows were as decisive as they were swift, and the long-lasting results are a testament to intelligence deployment that achieved decisive, optimal, and sustained effects. The example of the intelligence operation against Pagad stands out as a singular, exceptional success of post-Apartheid counter-terrorism and intelligence. Some involved in this operation became prominent figures in the South African National Security community.

I left government service in 2001 after spending almost all my time as an operational coordinator of a covert intelligence unit focusing on the Pagad threat. This book has been brewing since. The unintended slow writing has allowed me to appreciate the enormous effort and spectacular outcome achieved through the work of a small group of intelligence officers and those who constitute the lifeblood of any intelligence organisation, its sources, and agents. Twenty years of slow writing has also allowed me to see the events of those intense six years at the dawn of our democracy in a greater context, infusing the writing with a subtle but unique flavour. I hope it has produced something the reader can consume and find in good taste.

Like the many narratives of the South African condition, this work is intensely political yet deeply personal. The milieu in which the operation to combat Pagad took place, the increasingly aggressive nature of its assault on the young democracy, and the political histories of many of the key role-players in this narrative (on both sides of the equation) have defined its character. Pagad emerged onto the South African scene just as the country held its first democratic election and voted in its first Black President. The election of Nelson Mandela as the founding President of the democratic order was a fundamental break with the country's autocratic past. Yet, perhaps paradoxically, Pagad was partially an expression of a political rebellion against the negotiated settlement that brought Mandela and the ANC to power.

Its emergence and initial popularity constituted a rejection of the new political dispensation, which Pagad's founders viewed as fundamentally immoral. A rejection that turned out to have very few limits and in whose name its proponents would unleash a reign of terror that no one in the new government foresaw as we embarked on the endeavour to transform the South African nation and society. While the early approaches to dealing with the Pagad issue swung between ham-fisted and ignorant, the State and its intelligence apparatus gradually developed a political strategy for Pagad that was as successful as the law-enforcement efforts to arrest, prosecute, and convict Pagad members engaged in acts of terrorism.

Given the political context from which Pagad surfaced and its essential objectives, our intelligence strategy embraced diplomatic and ideological work as a prerequisite to defeating Pagad. We discredited its anti-state ideology and ensured its eventual defeat would be sustainable. Many intelligence operatives working against Pagad had experience working in anti-state organisations during the 1980s. This experience informed the political and ideological approach we adopted. Many of the central characters in the intelligence community were in dual political and military roles of the national liberation movement and, therefore, developed a fine appreciation of the relationship between mass mobilisation and armed action.

Those who operated in the ANC underground also understood the mechanisms of resistance and secret work. This discernment allowed us to think like our adversaries and imagine their next steps as if we were alongside them. Our involvement in the liberation movement also gave us access to established and deep networks in the Muslim community, from academia to business, religious leaders to social movements. Where these networks did not exist, the liberation struggle had sufficiently skilled and prepared us to build networks from scratch. These networks would become a pool of intelligence, a great source of insight into the politico-ideological dynamics that drove Pagad, and an ideological weapon against them. It enabled us to approach Pagad and its terrorism as a whole systemic problem instead of trying to bite off small chunks of it.

The story of both Pagad and how the State responded to it is mainly, though not exclusively, a story of a violent struggle carried out by Black South

Africans at great pain to all involved. During the apartheid era, the leaders of the movement behind Pagad's formation, Qibla, had spent time in prison alongside political activists and leaders of the ANC, some of whom were intelligence operatives and would play an essential role in the struggle against Pagad. As a social movement, Pagad was embedded in Cape Town's Black community. The intelligence operatives leading the charge against them, on the other hand, were predominantly Black operatives of the ANC who had integrated into the civilian, military, or police intelligence structures after the establishment of the democratic government in 1994.

While others have written often insightful commentary, academic articles, and at least two books on this subject, I believe that those of us who were at its centre should own it, narrate it, and ensure that our voices are heard in the first person and not as subjects of someone's research. I believe that telling the story of Pagad and the effort to neutralise it from the perspective of a Black intelligence officer who grew up in a community ravaged by the very gangs and drugs that Pagad used to legitimise its violence adds a valuable angle to the understanding of the twin phenomena. This book will hopefully make a contribution to that effort.

A book on clandestine work poses many dilemmas for an author. Chief is whether the author's knowledge, some of which comes from work in a controlled intelligence environment, should be placed in the public domain. To many spies, the default response would be a resolute and unqualified no. However, I disagree with applying a blanket ban on writing about sensitive issues such as those explored in this book. The events narrated here occurred more than 20 years ago and have been told in bits and pieces in several fora and formats, all militating against the blanket ban approach. Articles and books have been written, conferences addressed, and testimonies given in open court.

The story of Pagad and the intelligence effort to decimate their terrorist infrastructure is no longer the secret it was at the beginning of the millennium. Perhaps most importantly, those Pagad members who have been the involuntary beneficiaries of long periods of incarceration have a decent idea of how they came to tumble down from their pedestals. It is also true that the South African intelligence community, like similar organisations elsewhere, suffers from the maladies of overclassification and an obsession with secrecy that often bears no relation to the actual origin, sensitivity, or unique value of information.

The book explores sensitive topics and draws upon experiences confined to a few people. Its publication adds significant value to our understanding of the period covered at no risk to any individual or institution. Of course, no one is exempt from the embarrassment of their ineptitude or lack of commitment. Secrecy often protects such characters but has no applicability here. It is almost comical that several police officers have risen to the top of their profession either in part or in full based on claims that they were centrally involved in the effort against Pagad. One such example is the incumbent national police commissioner. A reference to his supposedly significant role in the operation against Pagad accompanied his appointment, apparently indicating his leadership ability. In his case, as in some others, these claims of involvement are often pure fantasy manufactured by opportunists who have seized the evident value of the exercise and used it to promote themselves.

And yet nobody involved in the assignment against Pagad has written an authoritative account of what we did, the struggles encountered, and the results of our efforts. I have taken great care to mask the names and identities of people, except where their role is public knowledge. The reader will forgive me for a certain measure of deception to shield those who need to be protected and have earned that protection by the quality of their service to the State and people of South Africa. In substance, this story is factual, to the extent that it is my recollection of an experience that stretched over a traumatic and intense six years.

Where I had doubts about details, I consulted with those who could shed light on events or correct any misunderstanding I might have formed of events, personalities, and outcomes. I am acutely aware that my recollection, shaped into narrative, does not constitute the entirety of the Pagad experience and the intelligence efforts against them. Many others played a central role in that struggle, and Pagad's defeat would have been unattainable without their contribution. They, too, should tell their stories (in one form or another) so that – as it always is with history – the tapestry that represents the more-or-less complete story of that fascinating, dangerous, and complex period in South Africa's history can be illuminated for our and future generations.

Thirty years into our democracy we have matured as a nation, often pessimistically and cynically. The reality of a shattered dream for whom many of my contemporaries struggled, suffered, and sometimes paid with their lives should not escape any sensible South African. With the receding idealism occasioned by the many challenges of state-building and societal transformation, many of us have taken to extreme scepticism that plays into racist tropes about Black South Africans, highlighting our alleged inability to govern, to build anything, or to engage in the sort of complex work previously reserved for white South Africans under Apartheid.

While the challenges of our country are expansive, this story is a tale of Black South Africans building a world-class intelligence capability under the most adverse circumstances, deploying it with great precision, and achieving outcomes beyond what anyone could have expected. We faced not only the risk of being killed but also the constant assault on our efforts by some of our colleagues – many of whom were leftovers of the Ancien Régime. The success of the intelligence operation against Pagad's campaign of terror should serve as an example of what is possible when commitment, dynamic leadership, and a refusal to submit to the naysayers intersect. It is a combination that can make great things happen under the most trying circumstances.

As South Africa grapples with a wide range of complex national security challenges, from organised crime to corruption and the lack of economic development, I am baffled by the fact that we did not dedicate the required time to study the Pagad experience and the intelligence successes outlined in this book. Reflecting on its many varied lessons could provide insight for the national security leadership and the young officers who will follow in their place. I fear that we have become blind to our successes, and that our failures consume us. The case of the intelligence work against Pagad deserves recognition. It also warrants integration into our strategy, doctrine, and modus operandi. Why would we obsess with teaching our intelligence officers about terrorism and counter-terrorism in far-off countries while ignoring the rich and insightful experience we have at home?

I find this even more perplexing because institutions worldwide have invited me to teach and speak on this experience precisely because they recognise the actual value of what we managed to build and achieve in South Africa. Our success and its sustainability starkly contrast the litany of counter-terrorism disasters that have befallen even the most powerful states. Our continent has felt the effects of disastrous and ill-conceived counter-terrorism policies, often destroying the social fabric of countries.

Though this work is my own, and I claim to speak for no other individuals or collective, an important motivating factor for writing it was to give recognition to people who cannot or do not want to be named and have yet to have their names publicly attached to their roles in defeating the terror unleashed by Pagad. Some exist to the public through pseudonyms, while others were known even to the tiny community of intelligence officers by alphanumeric codes. They know who they are, and I remain grateful for their camaraderie, exceptional commitment to our work, and singular dedication to bringing down what many thought to be an invincible adversary. They succeeded, and we are all the better off for their effort.

CHAPTER 1

Illusions Shattered and the Cape Set Ablaze

The true facts are not always obvious. They often have to be looked for.
—**Oliver Tambo**

The events that led to the public lynching of notorious Cape Town gang leader Rashaad Staggie on 4 August 1996 started as a march, a lot like many others that had preceded it. Pagad marches had become an institution on the city's landscape, occurring with a regularity that deceived many into accepting them as part of the usual protest routine. They were, however, growing into more of a concern for those of us in the intelligence community who had a deeper insight into the strategic line along which Pagad was marching.

By August 1996, the marches had developed a familiar flow and protocol. Pagad supporters would gather at Masjidul Quds, a mosque in the middle-class suburb of Gatesville – where many Pagad members lived.The mosque was also proximate to many of the gang bases and drug outlets that littered the working-class townships on the Cape Flats – making a march or short ride to these locations very convenient and easy to organise.

Although Pagad claimed to be a non-sectarian movement, a strong Islamic identity had always characterised its activities, starting with prayers at the mosque, followed by a march on foot or a cavalcade to the target location. There, the group would protest with placards, singing songs, and shouting slogans demanding that the drug dealer cease activities or face the wrath of the community. What would begin as peaceful protests gradually escalated in both their rhetoric (Death to Gangsters!) and action. Petrol or pipe bomb attacks or shootings shortly after a Pagad march were commonplace. This trajectory, evident from the information we had gathered since late 1995, was a clear sign for some of us in intelligence. Pagad and Qibla members were actively seeking illegal firearms, materials for explosive devices, and military-grade explosives – specifically hand grenades.

This context is critical to understanding the complete failure of policing that led to the disastrous and fateful events of that Sunday in 1996 when Pagad supporters marched to Staggie's house in Salt River. To assess the risk and potential scale of violence during this event we had to consider two factors. First, we had to evaluate the capability of Pagad's paramilitary wing, the G-Force, to carry out a significant attack. In the preceding months, they had amply demonstrated such ability, increasing the number of attacks and introducing hand grenades to their arsenal. By then, it was also evident that the G-Force had established a clear and well-oiled command and control system that allowed the deployment of well-coordinated violence during and shortly after marches.

Secondly, we had to consider the Staggie brothers as the primary target. The twin brothers were notorious figures in the Cape Town underworld, having risen to the pinnacle of the gang world as leaders of the Hard Livings gang. The gang was involved in a range of criminal activities, including a widespread drug distribution and dealing network. The twins also had a public profile, transforming them into larger-than-life characters. They fit the profile of those Pagad would typically target and take down, which would significantly increase the movement's public appeal and prestige in the anti-gang community. The brothers represented what would be referred to as high-value targets in today's intelligence and targeting parlance. A public march organised by an increasingly violent organisation targeting a high-value target should have raised a general level of concern amongst the local police.

These risk factors led me to write an intelligence alert late on the Friday afternoon of 2 August. I warned that the above indicators, coupled with specific intelligence we had received from sources in the days leading up to the march, led me to believe the planned march to Staggie's house constituted a higher-than-usual risk of violence. I specifically asked that sufficient police resources be deployed on the evening of the march to minimise the potential for violence during the event. I sent the report to Western Cape Crime Intelligence management and the Public Order Policing Unit – which was responsible for maintaining law and order at high-risk public events. Alas, the combination of a lack of trust in our intelligence and the failure to appreciate the logic of escalation resulted in an event that would end in Staggie's lynching and a devastating exposé of the police's incompetence.

Having finished their meeting at Masjidul Quds, Pagad members moved by cavalcade to Salt River. A solitary police vehicle with two junior officers was there to observe them. Martin and I joined the group in an unmarked car, our faces covered in the traditional Palestinian *keffiyeh* like most other men present. The procession stopped as we entered Salt River, and the group disembarked. Then, we started marching towards 20 London Road, the target house. We found ourselves amongst a few thousand Pagad members, many with guns, and we suspected a few also had explosive devices. Pagad marches were characterised by the recital of Islamic religious phrases mixed with slogans against the twin evils of gangsterism and drugs. Having participated in many anti-Apartheid marches during the 1980s, I was familiar with the almost hypnotic effect that group solidarity and identity, coupled with chanting slogans and singing, could have.

That night, I was among a group that displayed all these attributes. The fact that most of them were armed elevated the situation to explosive levels. Martin's proverbial 'small war' broke out soon after. Without warning, someone from the crowd fired a volley of shots towards the Staggie house. Everyone else more or less joined in and fired indiscriminately in the general direction of the house. We took cover to avoid joining the other eighteen participants wounded during the entirely uncoordinated and undirected shooting, then hastily withdrew from the scene to communicate with my commander, Johan Maree.

As luck would have it, our cell phone batteries had died, so we were compelled to go to the local police station to contact Maree. We briefed him on the developments in Salt River, and he agreed to meet us back at the scene. He would also contact the police so they could send reinforcements and take control of the situation. Returning to Salt River, we established that Rashaad Staggie had arrived at the scene and had somehow been allowed to pass through the police roadblock and head for his house, which remained under siege from Pagad members. The group effortlessly identified Staggie and a few of them surrounded his vehicle for a confrontation. In the brief encounter, a shot was fired while Staggie still sat inside his Nissan Sani van.

If one watches the video now, it is clear that one of the four or five men who were part of the confrontation shot him. He somehow manages to get out of the van, at which point medical personnel intervene and try to provide medical assistance. To their credit and as a testament to their dedication, they do this while surrounded by the armed Pagad group.

Shortly after, an individual in the group shouts, 'he's the man that killed the children,' after which someone throws a petrol bomb onto Staggie, setting him alight. As the notorious gang leader burns, shouts of *'Allahu Akbar,'* god is great, punctuate the air. He is shot multiple times in the minutes that follow, set upon, and beaten by the crowd as he stumbles towards his house, where he falls into the gutter and dies. News of Staggie's murder spread like wildfire through Cape Town, both to the many gangs in the city as well as Pagad sympathisers who welcomed the news. Maree and I decided to focus on preventing a further escalation of the violence on the night. Pagad's morale was sky-high. They had tasted blood and taken a prized scalp in their fight with the gangs, and the potential for further violence was very real.

If they could brazenly kill Staggie in the way they did, Pagad could go for anyone they wanted, and that was precisely what many of them felt was needed that very night. We decided to intervene and engage their leadership at Masjidul Quds, where they had retreated after Staggie's murder. The Pagad-supporting Radio 786 had started broadcasting continuous updates on that evening's developments and were calling on the Muslim community to gather at the mosque, claiming it was under imminent threat of attack. As the crowd at the mosque grew, so did the number of firearms. Some of the gatherers honestly believed they'd come to protect the mosque from a potential retaliatory strike, while others came to join further action that might have developed.

Before that night's events, Maree and I had worked together for a year. We came from very different backgrounds and now had the joint task of halting violent action that ran the real risk of escalating. He was a relatively young officer, having joined the police's Security Branch late in the 1980s. Afrikaner to the core, Maree was a precise character who had the refreshing quality of not taking life too seriously. In the short time we had been working together, he distinguished himself from his contemporaries in the bureaucratic police force by being a supportive leader. Maree provided cover for his team when they were under pressure, engaged in a hazardous operation, or had committed a mistake. He was also clearly more politically enlightened than many of his old police Security Branch colleagues.

Between myself – the 'former ANC terrorist,' and him – the 'racist Security Branch cop,' we developed an excellent working relationship amidst the increasingly grave and dangerous growth of Pagad. That night, we entered the mosque and requested a meeting with their leadership. Walking through a crowd of armed G-Force members, we found Farouk Jaffer, Pagad's National Coordinator. After introducing ourselves, we asked him to join us outside to discuss letting the steam out of the very explosive situation. Jaffer was a more moderate member of the Pagad leadership and was aware of the danger that any further action would trigger. If Pagad decided to engage further on the night, they would be dealing with what had by then become a sizable and well-armed police contingent, not gangs.

Speaking with Jaffer, we reminded him that they had, on their terms, achieved a significant victory that evening. Our appeal was that there was no further need for a dramatic showdown with the police. He took our concerns to the Pagad leadership gathered inside the mosque; they decided to call it a night and asked their members to leave the area and return to their homes. Relieved that matters appeared to have settled for the night, we had to return to our offices, write up reports, update the higher-ups, and prepare for what was bound to be a chaotic and uncertain week ahead. One thing was sure: the coming days would be defined by allegations of incompetence, denial, obfuscation, and discrediting intelligence that should have led to a stern police response on that Sunday.

The events of that night removed any doubt I still had that we had to prepare for a series of impending battles, both against the narrative of what happened that fateful night and how to deal with an emboldened Pagad. This battle, which would consume almost all my time, intellectual effort, and emotional energy over the next six years, was the first significant challenge in my role as an intelligence officer with the police's Crime Intelligence (CI) Division, which had started 17 months earlier. On Monday, 3 April 1995, I joined twenty fellow ANC intelligence officers across the Western Cape to do what would have been unthinkable five years earlier. We joined the South African Police Service's Crime Intelligence division.

Almost without exception, we were previously targets of the same division, then known as the notorious Security Branch. Amongst us were Peter Jacobs, Jeremy Vearey, and Anwa Dramat, who had been arrested and tortured by the Security Branch in 1987 and subsequently convicted for activities in the ANC's military wing, Umkhonto we Sizwe (Spear of the Nation – MK). Others like Yasser Splinters, a fellow communist from Manenberg, suffered prolonged detention and torture for their activities in student organisations.

I had been on the run from the Branch for most of the 1988 to 1990 period, with officers regularly raiding my parents' house searching for me. The Branch's threat to kill their 'terrorist bast*rd son' had a traumatic effect on my parents, especially my mother, who suffered two strokes during this time. This improbable journey started during the turbulent 1985 national uprising when my fourteen-year-old self became active in high school student politics. I was an active figure in student politics through the late 1980s. I was recruited into the ANC underground in 1988. I undertook two years of military training in Uganda until I returned to South Africa after the first democratic election and the ANC-led Government of National Unity installation in 1994.

That journey of activism ultimately led me to a 5th floor conference room at the notorious old Branch operational centre, 112 Loop Street, central Cape Town. Here, we met many of those who had hunted, arrested, tortured, and sent some of us to prison. Some of those around the imposing mahogany conference table were responsible for the deaths of dear comrades who did not live to see the fruits of their sacrifice in the form of a democratic South Africa. By the same token, MK cadres targeted at least one of the Branch officers present for elimination, and he narrowly escaped with his life. After the formal introductions we overcame the mutual awkwardness and apprehension between former enemies with a braai (South African parlance for barbeque, though no self-respecting South African would use that term). Here, people who had previously plotted each other's demise made fire and grilled meat together. The Boers might have run the country into the ground, but they knew how to braai, and we thought that it was a good start to what would hopefully turn into a very smooth and productive integration process.

My decision to join the intelligence services took a different path to many of my fellow ANC intelligence operatives who stepped into the former lion's den in Loop Street. While I underwent conventional military training in Uganda, many already worked in the ANC's Department of Intelligence and Security (DIS). They spent a year or more preparing for this integration. Given my training in conventional warfare, I was meant to join the new South African National Defence Force when I returned home. Upon my arrival, however, I decided not to take this option and returned to civilian life in Cape Town. Like many ANC members, I was an unlikely soldier, and my motivation to join the liberation army was also politically motivated. The regimentation of military life was something I found completely unappealing.

I was willing to serve the struggle, but our newfound democracy allowed me the freedom to explore other professional options, like finding a job working at a newly established youth centre in one of the African townships, where I managed a youth leadership programme. Nonetheless, Bulla, a persistent and dear comrade from my Manenberg student activist days, convinced me that doing intelligence work in the new government was a better use for my skills. Initially reluctant, many chats and teas at my office in New Crossroads culminated in me agreeing to join the team integrating into Crime Intelligence (CI). While we ended up working in separate intelligence organisations, we were both pioneers in the state's efforts against Pagad.

My decision to then join the intelligence services was also political and aligned with that of many of my fellow ANC intelligence operatives. When we achieved the democratic breakthrough, I felt I could make a contribution to building a transformed and accountable national security community. It was also clear that if we wanted to secure the democratic government that our party now headed, we could not leave the instruments of coercive power in the hands of the very people who had gone to the ends of the earth to prevent the emergence of the new political order.

Our continent was rife with intelligence and military officers from old regimes who were instrumentalised by external powers to overthrow progressive governments. We were also all brought up on a healthy diet exposing the litany of US-supported coups against leftist governments in Latin America. The overthrow and subsequent murder of Salvador Allende were the most prominent of these. Even though we were small in number, we believed our mere presence within the state's intelligence structures would enable us to play at least a delaying and, at best, a preventative role against any rearguard action by old Apartheid securocrats to undermine, sabotage, or overthrow the democratic government.

Intelligence work also appealed to a young person like myself for various personal reasons. The political activism of the 1980s in South Africa was a high-risk activity, and even at the tender age of 14 or 15, to stay out of the hands of our adversaries, young activists had to learn the basics of information and personal security. To understand the art of counter-surveillance, meeting security, non-personal communication, and the basic signs of detecting enemy infiltration in our ranks, we studied 'How to Master Secret Work,' a Communist Party pamphlet on the conduct of secure underground work. More notable training in military combat work followed when I graduated into the ANC underground. There, and in the student organisation where I was active, I investigated fellow activists who engaged in suspicious behaviour. We later confirmed that the enemy's intelligence structures handled our supposed comrades in at least two cases.

The training also exposed us to a long and storied history of communist intelligence, ranging from our own Dieter Gerhardt, a senior South African navy officer who spied for the Soviet Union until his arrest in 1983, to Richard Sorge, the Cambridge Five, and Leopold Trepper – all outstanding intelligence officers who worked at the coalface of international intelligence during World War 2 and the Cold War. With that background, I found the prospect of the more thrilling aspects of intelligence work quite appealing. However, as a bookish teenager interested in history, warfare, politics, and philosophy, I wanted to explore the analytical work central to modern intelligence.

During the struggle, I shied away from making myself available for executive positions that drew too much public attention. Being on a stage addressing large crowds didn't fit the shy David of the time. While I could not entirely avoid the limelight, I much preferred working behind the scenes with small groups of comrades, running covert study groups, and discreetly distributing banned literature to fellow activists. This combination of experience, personal disposition, and skills would naturally lead me to a position where I would be most impactful in Crime Intelligence, its Western Cape Undercover Operations Unit.

Jeremy Vearey, a member of the ANC military wing imprisoned for MK activities in 1988, headed the Western Cape Group after his release from Robben Island. The ANC's Department of Intelligence and Security appointed him to its leadership, where he would lead the integration of the DIS Western Cape contingent into Crime Intelligence. Vearey, a self-described dialectical cop, had the persona of a spy, dressed the part, and was an excellent transmitter of intelligence knowledge. The latter might have something to do with the fact that he was a teacher before his rather abrupt relocation to the Security Branch's Culemborg detention and torture facility and, subsequently, Robben Island – in which some of the very officers we were now joining played no small part.

In the months before our integration into Crime Intelligence, he presented a series of workshops on intelligence tradecraft to our group. Integrating theory with demanding practical exercises would prepare those amongst us who had yet to be exposed to such training and boost the skills level of those who had prior exposure. Everyone benefited from his engaging and animated facilitation style and deep insight into intelligence tradecraft. Vearey had the unenviable task of ensuring that our integration was smooth and, perhaps most importantly, that we did not let our side down but delivered exceptional quality work. Some of us were militant and had thought integrating into Crime Intelligence meant storming the Bastille. On the contrary, we found it meant labouring away discreetly, building influence, and asserting leadership over people and the institution.

The organisation I was joining had a disreputable history. It had yet to change its leadership or institutional culture between the opening of the South African political space in February 1990 and the day of our integration in April 1995. It remained a white Afrikaner-dominated institution beholden to ideas of the white Christian civilising mission at the southern tip of the African continent. Meetings opened with a Christian prayer, and many of its leaders continued to wear their false religious morality on their sleeves. An atheist like myself found this fake moralism quite irritating, given the institution's well-known role in the brutal suppression of Black South Africans. Our group of twenty was a drop in the ocean of the established institution we integrated into.

At the point of our integration, we constituted less than 15 percent of the Western Cape staff and commanded none of the units. Aside from the smaller offices in the rural towns across the province, Crime Intelligence had four significant capabilities. The first was the provincial office, headed by Louis Du Plessis, referred to as Dup by his subordinates.

Du Plessis managed the administration, the division's provincial analysis, and information management capability. He oversaw the province's entire collection and analysis capability, guiding all his subordinate units, maintaining standards, and building new capabilities. I had known him from a distance during my days in student politics, circa 1987, when comrades coming out of detention reported the arrival of a new 'huge boer from the Free State province' in the Cape Town Security Branch. His primary skill seemed to be the ability to swing chairs and other sorts of furniture at detained students. None of them reported any interesting or probing interrogation by Du Plessis. It seems that he was the physical one and left the more cognitive work of probing and recruitment to his colleagues.

My experience with Du Plessis over the next six years only confirmed this perception, which had taken shape in the minds of teenage activists in the late 1980s. I cannot recall one meeting or personal conversation (and there were many) where he provided unusual insight, offered an innovative solution to a problem, or even acted in defence of his staff. He certainly was no Trepper or Sorge (the respective heads of the two most effective Red Army spy networks in occupied Europe and Japan during World War 2). He contributed nothing to the struggle against Pagad despite being the head of a sizable intelligence apparatus for most of the time the organisation was engaged in its campaign of terror.

The seven-story Loop Street building in central Cape Town was an operational hub in the Apartheid police's intelligence and torture apparatus. Until 1994, this facility was divided into sections working on a wide range of target groups: student and youth organisations, the ANC and South African Communist Party (SACP), trade unions, other left-wing organisations, and after 1990/ the increasingly dangerous white right-wing. Every morning, the teams gathered in the fifth-floor conference room, and section heads would present the daily incoming intelligence, report new or expected developments, and plan the day. The commander of this centre, always a white man, occupied a large office on the same floor. The morning conference kept the same format when we integrated, except that the ANC and SACP desks no longer existed. These parties constituted the dominant force in the Government of National Unity, and all the integrated officers were ANC or SACP members.

The majority of our DIS contingent, myself included, would be based at the Loop Street centre and deployed to the various thematic desks. I needed to navigate my way around the Loop Street centre. We quickly tried to figure out who was who in the Loop Street zoo, who we could speak to, who we needed to avoid, and who we might have had to confront. I found three types of security policemen at Loop Street (including the Afrikaner women who referred to themselves as policemen). The first type was the reactionary holdovers from the old days, who were insufficiently skilled to move on elsewhere and thus remained in their jobs. They often were the ones trying to spoil our integration process. The second type, usually the younger ones such as Maree, were more open to welcoming the new entrants and saw the possibility of building something new together.

Then there were the few Black staffers, almost all at the lower levels of the hierarchy, who approached our integration with trepidation. They were all uncertain how their new Black colleagues and former foes would treat them. Until then, we regarded them as traitors to their own people. During Apartheid, they had expended the most effort in combating us when they lived amongst us, and we faced off as adversaries. Now, they had to work alongside us, too. We entered the service laterally, and the organisation ranked most of us higher than them, even though many had ten or more years of experience in the Branch. Martin was one of them. He was directly involved in efforts to track and detain me during the 1980s and ended up working as my subordinate on the Pagad team.

Manie Viktor, an affable middle-aged Afrikaner who held the rank of Major, headed the Loop Street centre. Viktor was an operational man at heart, but it turned out that he also had exceptional people management skills. Having had the task of integrating us dropped into his lap, he managed the situation relatively well, despite the occasional (and one could say unavoidable) clashes between ourselves and some of his old Branch colleagues. He did not take the side of his old allies during these clashes. Viktor was a good listener and a soft-spoken man who tried to develop personal relations with many of our team who worked under his command.

Unlike Du Plessis, he was open about intervening on behalf of his team members if they needed management support or backup in a conflict with other elements within the police. I experienced this first-hand when he took my side in a clash with Leonard Knipe, one of the most influential policemen in the province and Viktor's senior by some distance. Viktor started integrating us into the Loop Street centre and, a year later, had done much to establish functional teams and a sense of belonging for many of us. He was, unfortunately, transferred to the head office in Pretoria, where he continued to do good work. The centre lost not only operational experience and skill due to his departure but also his engaging personality. In the next few years, his replacements comprised a succession of relatively nondescript characters with no significant impact.

A discreet but critical component in Crime Intelligence was the Technical Support Unit (TSU). An ageing Len Nel headed it then but left most of the operational work to his more dynamic and competent deputy. The TSU was the only unit without ANC officers, as, for some strange reason, none of our group integrated into this very sensitive and critical unit. Given that it conducted technical operations ranging from the monitoring and interception of communications to physical surveillance of targets, it was to play a critical role in the fight against crime and, in our specific case, terrorism. Dramat and I frequently engaged the TSU; most of our encounters were frustrating, but some were showcases of creativity and led to some of our most impressive successes. The chance of failure or success, we figured out later, came down to which individual we worked with. Once we figured out that magic formula, we stuck to the ones where we knew we had a higher chance of success.

The Branch had a long history of covert operations against the liberation movement and had established many covert structures across the country and abroad for this purpose. Some were classic intelligence collection structures, while others dabbled in a spectrum of active measures – from propaganda to false flag attacks and, most notoriously, the murder of activists. By 1995, there were only a few covert intelligence units in the major metropolitan areas, including Cape Town, with a formal mandate reduced to intelligence collection. However, some continued to engage in influence operations, primarily due to the quality and positioning of sources the covert units tended to recruit.

The police covert units operated at arm's length from the other crime intelligence capabilities, such as the Loop Street centre, though the level of distance varied from province to province. They typically operated from discreet premises, sometimes in a commercial building, other times larger houses in residential areas, and always under a cover name. While covert intelligence units would classically operate undercover with several layers of backstopping (traceable backup information that supports its cover story), the Branch units operated much closer to their overt counterparts than, for example, those of the National Intelligence Service or Military Intelligence. The latter two agencies, even by 1995, had covert units operating with much more substantial cover than the Branch units.

At our integration, Gordon Brookbanks headed the Western Cape covert unit. Brookbanks was an unlikely character for the Branch because he was an English-speaking South African with a more enlightened worldview than many of his Afrikaner contemporaries. The hard-drinking and chain-smoking Brookbanks was a world-wise officer. He spent some years amongst progressive student activists at the liberal Rhodes University at the beginning of his spy career and subsequently in London, where he managed front companies and handled sources reporting on the ANC and SACP. In the period leading up to our integration, Brookbanks and his covert unit collaborated with the DIS team in the province, cooperating on areas such as gang and transport-related violence, as well as community conflict. Unlike Viktor at Loop Street, Brookbanks ran a much smaller unit with fewer DIS operatives integrating into the covert unit.

A year or so later, after Brookbanks departed to head up the Provincial Intelligence Coordinating Committee (PICOC) located with the National Intelligence Agency (NIA, his deputy and former Branch colleague, Kallie Calitz, took command of the unit. However, Calitz's tenure at the covert unit was short-lived for reasons that became apparent once the next commander and first DIS person was appointed. By the time Calitz left the covert unit in 1997, it was a shell of its former self and firmly on its way to being phased out of existence. Its diminished capability and influence must have been one of the key reasons Du Plessis saw it fit to hand over command to Mzwandile Petros.

Petros's meteoric rise to fame and leadership in the South African Police Service (SAPS) started with his adventure at the covert unit, where the law of unintended consequences, the support of a spectacular team, and a significant amount of luck ultimately saw him take up the position of Provincial police commissioner, first in the Western Cape and then Gauteng. Like Vearey, Petros was a teacher and also served as a manager at Matla Trust – a voter education project leading to South Africa's first democratic election in 1994. By the time he was appointed to head the covert unit, a caucus consisting of the majority of DIS members who integrated into the police had decided, using whatever political influence we had, to make Petros our centrifugal figure in a long-term project to elevate him to the most senior position in the province. His rise to police leadership is a testament to his ability to substitute a shortcoming in operational savvy with a mixture of technical management skills, gravitas and political manoeuvrability.

More significant national dynamics, both political and institutional, shaped the integration of our DIS team in Cape Town. At the political level, the advent of democracy and the election of an ANC government ushered in a fundamental transformation of the country's national security apparatus. The history of Apartheid, and specifically the rise of a securocratic state after the 1978 elevation of PW Botha to the position of Prime Minister, compelled the new democratic government to effect significant changes in this community.

In the policing domain, a consultative process culminated in the adoption of the National Crime Prevention Strategy (NCPS) in 1996. A demilitarisation strategy, codified in the South African Police Service Act of 1995, envisaged a police institution transformed from a paramilitary force to a public service, a commitment to the new constitution, and building an accountable relationship with local communities.

In 1994, Mandela had appointed Fholisani Sydney Mufamadi as Minister of Safety and Security. In the five years he served as minister, Mufamadi would shepherd the new police service through the complex terrain of policy renewal and institutional transformation. Like the Branch before, Crime Intelligence existed within a unique and paradoxical reality, with one foot in the policing and the other in the intelligence domain. Therefore, two very different cultures, institutional dynamics, and rules of behaviour shaped its doctrine, structures, and modus operandi. For those of us integrating from DIS, this dynamic often presented a challenge. Attempting to transform CI in the context of these two parallel sets of evolving architectural and policy environments would be a challenging task.

We integrated when the government published the first White Paper on Intelligence, pivoting the intelligence community from an autocratic orientation to defending the new democratic constitutional order. Of all the security agencies, the police service was the largest, yet contained the smallest number of ANC officers integrating into its ranks. While thousands of MK soldiers integrated into the new National Defence Force, the DIS contingent deployed to CI numbered around one hundred. Most of the ANC's intelligence personnel had assimilated into the two new civilian intelligence services, the NIA and the South African Secret Service (SASS). Crime Intelligence headquarters in Pretoria had a smattering of DIS officers amidst a large Branch contingent. Though the ANC's Nceba Radu commanded it, old Branch hands supervised the key capabilities, two of whom I got to know very well when I transferred there.

National security threats do not wait for states to develop appropriate policies, institutions, or capabilities before appearing and often proliferating in those less-governed spaces that are the hallmarks of transitional societies. Whilst states and societies are trying to find their feet, as we were doing in post-1994 South Africa, transnational organised crime, corruption, and all sorts of extremisms quietly and deliberately embedded themselves into the country's political and societal fabric. We had to build intelligence capability on the fly, as it were, unable to wait for tedious bureaucratic processes to play out. Given the fundamental differences in the strategic and legislative environment in which we now operated, we had no roadmap from which to draw. It was a situation in which the bold would confront the biggest risks and potentially achieve the most remarkable results. The innovation required would, by necessity, be faltering, often painful, and sometimes plainly fail.

Back at the Loop Street operational centre, we were building intelligence capability. Alongside an old comrade from a suburb bordering Manenberg, Pete Arendse, I was deployed to what was known as the extremism desk. He was a quiet and thoughtful character with a knack for conceptualising systems. Explain anything to him, and he'd be on a board or scrap of paper drawing blocks and organograms explaining away systems theory. Arendse and I worked with three former Branch members, one of whom, Johan Maree, was our unit commander. The other two were pleasant individuals, too, so they gravitated to the jovial Maree. One was hardworking, while the other mainly occupied himself with private business and building a new property in Cape Town's northern suburbs. Like many of the old Branch Officers at Loop Street, he had lost the urge to do intelligence work now that the organisation served the constitutional government instead of the Apartheid regime.

Like Arendse, I initially worked on the minor but concerning right-wing threat amongst coloured members of the old South African Defence Force. Some of them had developed a close working relationship with the white extremist right wing in the Western Cape. They had the skills that could cause serious mayhem unless reined in before they succeeded in establishing a foothold amongst Cape Town's so-called coloured community. As fate would have it, my move from investigating right-wing extremism to emerging Islamic extremism would come one Monday morning while I sat at my desk on the seventh floor of the Loop Street operational centre. I had no idea what effect an investigation into a newspaper article would have on my career and life that morning in late 1995 when Maree dropped a brief newspaper report on my desk.

The report related to a protest march in the central Cape Town suburb of Bo-Kaap. The Bo-Kaap is a small, predominantly Muslim community. Most of its residents were descendants of Muslim exiles who settled in the Cape in the late eighteenth-century from Southeast Asia. Maree's request was simple. His 'David, please have a look at this and find out what lies behind it' would take me on a path to encountering, investigating, and ultimately being a central figure in the destruction of South Africa's most significant terrorist threat in the democratic era. Not expecting anything earth-shattering from investigating a mere protest march, I started working on investigating the protest march and maybe took the request too seriously. Maree had noticed something uncanny with the march, making it stand out from the many marches in the city every week. I, too, was now intrigued.

Fortunately, I felt equipped to take on the task. Even as a twenty-four-year-old, I had been active in the liberation movement since high school. I had been recruited into the ANC underground and trained in Military Combat Work, the art of working underground. It was a skill set that would come in handy in trying to draw links between what is and what appears to be. Between 1989 and 1991, I was involved in an investigation and reported to the ANC and the Communist Party on someone I had worked with in the ANC underground. During this time, I gained the discreet investigative skills I could apply to figure out what Pagad was all about. Vearey's intelligence training contributed considerably to my ability to peel back the layers of what appeared to be just another march.

As I delved deeper into what lay behind the march, it became clear that it was part of a concerted ideological project to delegitimise the new government. Like Alice in Wonderland, Maree's newspaper article sent me tumbling down a rabbit hole from which I would emerge six years later, having learned many fascinating things, including the highs and lows of building and deploying an intelligence capability from scratch.

CHAPTER 2

Puzzles and Mysteries: Making Sense of Pagad's Genesis

A riddle wrapped in a mystery inside an enigma.
—Winston Churchill

The arrival of democracy in 1994 restored Black South Africans' right to govern themselves but left the country's fundamental socio-economic challenges more or less untouched. The incoming administration prioritised the establishment of a functioning government, a task of immense complexity and difficulty, given the fact that colonialism and Apartheid had carved up the country into many small ethnic enclaves with varying levels of institutional capability. The establishment of nine new provincial governments, each with its bureaucracy and legislature, further complicated the merging of more than ten different administrative systems into one national government.

This intricate structure, while a testament to the diversity of the nation, also became a source of conflict within the police and between them and the executive, adding to the complexity of governance in the post-apartheid era. It quickly became apparent that where one level of government failed, the automatic response was to blame another. This dynamic applied to crime and gangs in Cape Town and the battle against Pagad. While the police reported to both the provincial and national governments, our key interlocutors in the intelligence community had to account for their actions only at the national level. This aberration would also affect the relationship we had with our closest partners.

For many, the formation of Pagad remains, to this day, shrouded in mystery. The popular narrative and widespread understanding of the organisation's genesis was that it was a concerned community group that had gone vigilante and then took a further leap toward terrorism. Whatever narrative one adopts, what is indisputable is that the gang and drug pandemic in Cape Town provided a critical platform for its emergence, mobilisation of popular community support, and launching of a terror campaign that targeted gangs. The logical next step was for Pagad to turn to direct anti-state terrorism.

The movement had conducted what intelligence analysts call a classic case of incipient warfare: the slight, hardly perceptible, but constant shifting of a target or community from where they are to where you want them to be. The propaganda it created, as well as the fact that the media adopted its portrayal as 'the good anti-gang guys', masked its transition from a supposed concerned community group to a terrorist threat.

Breaking this conceptual stranglehold regarding Pagad's genesis was one of the first significant battles we needed to tackle. Our ability to accurately characterise Pagad would shape our strategy, the resources we committed to the fight, and the selection of capabilities most suitable for the specific type of struggle we intended to wage. By the time Pagad emerged, Cape Town already boasted of a long history and entrenched culture of gangs. By the mid-1990s, gang membership in the city approached one hundred thousand, and the context of an opening society, economy, and trade caused an explosion in the drug trade.

Gangs were a prominent feature of everyday life for a kid growing up in Manenberg in the 1970s and 80s, but their influence and societal effect were not nearly as deep as during the 1990s. Gang fights were limited in scope, frequency, and lethality, and the casualties were confined to combating gangsters. The latter was partially due to the weapons at the disposal of gangs – mainly knives, pangas, and other kinds of blunt instruments. The level of firearm violence that later characterised gang violence was something relatively unfamiliar in Manenberg at the time. There seems to have been a sudden proliferation of firearms and a commensurate increase in fatalities from gang violence by the early nineties.

During this period, the expansion (both in scope and product variety) of the South African drug market had a devastating effect on communities in the Cape Flats – that desolate windswept space where the State consigned Cape Town's poor Black populace, usually through forced removals from areas that Apartheid legislation had proclaimed white. Manenberg was my home from the time my family moved there when I was three years old. I can still clearly remember, as more areas were declared white and their Black inhabitants issued notices to pack up and leave, the constant stream of 'newcomers' into the township.

These forced removals continued into the mid-1980s when the last people removed from Cape Town's leafy suburb of Harfield Village settled (or perhaps more aptly unsettled) in Manenberg and other townships across the Cape Flats. The city continued to feel the effect of this pernicious practice of ethnic cleansing, and it played a central role in the condition in which her so-called coloured communities found themselves during the hopeful democratic transition. The violent tearing asunder of social bonds and family relations that had sustained Black communities in the Cape for decades (and sometimes centuries) and the random displacement of people to desolate newly built townships on the Cape Flats was bound to have an impact that was as traumatic as it was sustained.

The mushrooming of gangs across Cape Town was not merely a response to economic marginalisation and inequality but, in large part, also a survivalist response to the alienation of entire communities from their historical roots, mutually supportive community relationships and sense of space. The growth of gangs and the uptick of the drug trade in Cape Town was an issue of great concern for the ANC, even before it came to power. As activists in Manenberg during the late 1980s, gang violence consumed a significant amount of our time and political effort. The local United Democratic Front (UDF) area committee served as the de facto peacemaking organ in the township, and in 1991 the local ANC branch took a proactive step by leading the establishment of one of the first community police forums in the country.

I served as one of the organisation's representatives on the forum for a while. In the forum, I met someone who would play a role in the police and its struggle against Pagad, then Captain Arno Lamoer. Lamoer was the deputy station commander at Manenberg police station and, unlike his seniors and peers, was a progressive cop who had already come to terms with the need to transform the police. He would later rise to the rank of provincial police commissioner for the Western Cape.

While the ANC had relationships with some of the gangs during the anti-Apartheid struggle, the State utilised other gangs against the liberation movement – to the point of incorporating them into the regime's covert death squads. The ANC, constantly vigilant towards potential threats to the democratic government, was concerned by the dangerous role this historic collaboration of gangs with the Apartheid security forces could play in a potential rearguard action by Apartheid securocrats against the democratic government. Vearey was central to the work done by the Department of Intelligence and Security to infiltrate and influence gangs in the lead-up to the first democratic elections.

Between the opening of the political space in 1990 and our integration into crime intelligence in 1995, the government and civil society launched many initiatives to combat crime, improve and transform policing, and mitigate the devastating drug pandemic. Cape Town, where the gang problem was most entrenched, served as the focus of many of these measures. Non-Governmental Organisations obtained funding from foreign donors for anti-crime or policing projects, the government adopted a multidisciplinary approach to combating crime, and neighbourhood watch groups flourished across Cape Town's townships and middle-class suburbs. While community organisations such as the Western Cape Anti-Crime Forum had done sterling work to mobilise communities against crime, neighbourhood watches emerged in the early 1990s.

Pagad's successful explosion onto the scene was evidence of an increasingly impatient populace that denied the new government the 'honeymoon' period to resolve the crime problem. This set of circumstances created by illegality, gangs, and drugs was the perfect cocktail of issues around which to launch a campaign of vigilantism and terror.

Intelligence is not merely an information-gathering activity but, in essence, a sense-making one. The dramatic stuff of spies, wiretaps, and raids constitute an important, but only partial, element of intelligence tradecraft. To make sense of Pagad meant pursuing Maree's initial 'What lies behind it?' question to its logical conclusion. Intelligence sense-making is the process of identifying and understanding the underlying factors that drive the emergence of an organisation or threat. This is a crucial aspect of intelligence analysis, as it allows national security professionals and policymakers to form a comprehensive understanding of the threats they are dealing with. These key factors are not always evident to the casual or semi-informed observer. They can remain equally elusive to the professional tasked with the sense-making or the policy-maker if they suffer from the wide range of analytic pathologies that often afflict intelligence professionals or their policy-making consumers.

We would find out, to our chagrin, that these cognitive pathologies, which are mental barriers that hinder effective analysis, were common among national security professionals and the political elite. Sense-making demanded painstaking work to build a picture that enabled the national security professional and the policy-maker to understand what they were dealing with and identify opportunities for advantageous decision-making. In short, we had to discern the nature of the threat and then develop the path to its neutralisation.

Information is the elementary building block of intelligence. Without concrete data, the 'intelligence' produced remained guesswork – a gamble that might be right on some occasions but wrong on others. Such an approach would essentially amount to playing the lottery with the country's national security. In the case of Pagad, the challenge of intelligence sense-making was compounded by the classical problems of deceptive, dispersed and denied information. As Carl von Clausewitz, the 19th-century Prussian general and strategist, aptly put it, 'War is the realm of uncertainty; three-quarters of the factors on which action in war is based are wrapped in a fog of greater or lesser uncertainty.'

Pagad took great pains to obscure its strategic aims and tactical modus operandi. This information complexity would only worsen because I worked in an institution not geared for the type of challenge Pagad presented – a rapidly evolving, innovative, and mobile adversary with a low tolerance for security breaches. Information on Pagad did not exist in one neat box, where unlocking it would magically bring all the organisation's secrets to light; it was dispersed through multiple entities, personal relationships, and collaborative partnerships.

The public membership of Pagad was several thousand strong. It involved a range of social and political activities, from running a drug rehabilitation centre and organising protest marches to raising funds for imprisoned members. It boasted a sizable executive committee that conducted dealings with other fraternal organisations. Then, its paramilitary G-Force (consisting of various cells) with a Security Council that allocated targets and tasks to its subordinate cells. All these entities held information critical to developing our understanding of Pagad's intent, capabilities, activities, and internal frictions. Its organisational size and division of labour were so vast and complex that even the most senior Pagad members did not have insight into all the activities or people engaged across the organisation. We had to follow crumbs of information, accumulate these, and hope they contributed to our understanding of the organisation.

Violent or disruptive social movements take measures to deny the State access to some of their activities and information. They do this either as a defensive measure to protect their members from a repressive regime or to achieve surprise when launching an action. Established organisations such as Greenpeace have developed this scheme into a fine art, using precise intelligence and information denial to execute well-planned and often spectacular operations. An even more significant need for such denial existed in a paramilitary organisation such as the G-Force, which needed to protect the security of its members and activities. Failure to do so could have resulted in the loss of operational efficiency, arrest, imprisonment, or death – especially in cases where they intended to attack armed targets such as police officers or gangsters.

G-Force members were made aware of the need for operational and information security and the consequences should this rule be breached. A punishment of death awaited those who actively divulged information to the intelligence or policing agencies, a fate suffered by several Pagad members. Pagad's deception at the strategic level must be judged as exceptional, succeeding in concealing its intent and origin not merely at the start but several years into its campaign. The myth of a community pressure group turned vigilante was the conventional wisdom accepted by society, the media, and the State until 1998.

This confused the State's response to Pagad, and they fumbled along as they incrementally realised what they were dealing with. It affected the allocation of resources, the crafting of counter-strategy, the creation of structures, and the appointment of suitable leadership to counter Pagad. More importantly, it provided Pagad with a three-year period to exploit this combination of confusion and intransigence. It used this time to embed itself in communities, build its cell structure, and run an ideological training programme that sought to transform members from 'mere' anti-gang activists into ideologically committed terrorists.

The effort to undo this stunning accomplishment in deception required precise information, exceptional analytic work, and the ability to argue convincingly for an alternative perspective. In 'Crises of the Republic", the political philosopher Hannah Arendt writes, 'Half of politics is "image-making," the other half is the art of making people believe the image.' So, in late 1995, I set off on a journey of image-making, and by 1998, it had transformed into a mission to convince others to believe our characterisation of Pagad. We had to look beyond the obvious and find what else could have driven this movement that most daringly emerged out of the blue.

The first crumbs of information I followed led me to an organisation that had called for a campaign against gangsterism and drugs, the Islamic Unity Convention (IUC). The group led a non-sectarian campaign, welcoming all Cape Town citizens opposed to the scourge of gangsterism and drugs. Established in March 1994, shortly before the country's first democratic elections, the IUC claimed to represent nearly three hundred constituent organisations from across South Africa. These were mostly small, locally based organisations, including mosques, youth and women's organisations, charities, and other social movements.

At its inaugural conference in Cape Town, the IUC elected Imam Achmat Cassiem as its leader. He was an old anti-Apartheid activist and member of the Pan Africanist Congress (PAC) of Azania, one of the recognised liberation movements in the country. Cassiem had an exceptional political pedigree, having been one of the youngest political prisoners to serve time on Robben Island under Apartheid. He read philosophy during those years and was an eloquent speaker with a sharp mind and a long history of militant political activity.

Cassiem was also the leader of Qibla, a fringe Islamist militant movement inspired by and established after the 1979 Iranian Islamic Revolution. Qibla never developed a mass following amongst South African Muslims and remained a relatively small, closely-knit organisation. The realisation of Cassiem's leading role in the IUC was a significant breakthrough. It led us to reconsider the nature of the IUC, especially when we noted that several other Qibla members were on its executive committee. This suggested that the IUC might not be a broad, run-of-the-mill social movement but a front for Qibla. However, this was still just a hunch at this stage.

Our investigation required direct access to Qibla and the IUC to comprehensively understand their respective platforms. This access was crucial to transforming our initial hunch into actionable intelligence. We also needed to determine the direction of influence between the two entities, answering the key question of whether the IUC was a consumer of Qibla's influence, or if the relationship was reciprocally balanced. Qibla was notoriously secretive, and accessing its closed deliberations required a somewhat circuitous route. Still, in the end, we gained sufficient access to determine the relationship between Qibla and the IUC. Simply put, the IUC was a front for Qibla, but only in the sense that Qibla exercised a discreet ideological leadership role over the IUC. The vast majority of IUC affiliate organisations or members had no idea that this was the case.

Qibla's modus operandi emitted a familiar scent, particularly for someone who cut his political teeth in the ANC and Communist Party. It was that of a Leninist organisational strategy, a strategy I didn't just know but deeply understood. In a sense, Qibla operated as a numerically small vanguard organisation of ideologically conscious individuals, much in the mould of the classical Leninist parties. In their case, it would be Muslims with a high level of political understanding of and commitment to a particular militant interpretation of Islam. Qibla's ultimate goal was to establish an Islamic State in South Africa, despite the Muslim community constituting only about two per cent of the national population. This community is concentrated in a few provinces and does not constitute a majority in any of South Africa's nine provinces.

Muslims are an integral part of the community in Cape Town, and even using the word integrated would be both an insult and a complete mischaracterization of the role of Muslims in society. Growing up on the Cape Flats, we didn't just coexist with our Muslim friends; we celebrated the Eid festivals, the holy month of Ramadan, and Christmas together. We intermarried without the slight blink of an eye. When I joined Crime Intelligence, I was married to a woman of the Muslim faith, something completely natural in the communities where we grew up. As we developed our image of Qibla and its role in establishing Pagad, we began to characterise its six-stage operational approach to building militant political power.

Creating awareness of a particular social or political issue of concern amongst the Muslim community constituted the launching stage and was followed by active mobilisation. The third stage conscientised the group to the relationship between the specific problem and the more general, national, and global struggle for an Islamic State. How this played out in the case of Pagad was in the form of its leap from targeting gangsters to expanding the label to include academics or religious leaders who were critical of Pagad, state officials, and politicians.

This transition from the particular to the general – conducted and calibrated as the organisation grew in numbers, stature, and capability was very familiar to those who worked in the ANC underground and quasi-legal mass organisations during the 1980s. It was a tactic that the ANC and Communist Party had perfected during that time, driven by the perspective that 'we always proceed from the real to the possible.' Like many who ended up in the ANC underground or Communist Party, I had made that transition from a student concerned with democratic decision-making at school to general resistance against the socio-political system.

Once a sufficient number of people adopted the premise that resolving the particular concern they grappled with could only come with a more general struggle against the status quo, the fourth stage involved challenging the authority of the State with mass mobilisation, protest action, and the gradual introduction of armed violence. This incremental approach has multiple benefits. It allows the organisation to cautiously build its capability, test its members, assess who to recruit for armed activity, and desensitise those not directly involved in violence to its devastating effects.

This stage culminated on the night Pagad members murdered Rashaad Staggie. After Staggie's lynching, Qibla (with Pagad as its instrument) felt bold enough to ramp up its activity to the fifth stage, an armed revolution against the existing order. This armed revolution aims to overthrow the current social order and replace it with an Islamic State. The fact that South Africa is a democracy and the political system enjoys the support of a majority of citizens is a non-factor in how Qibla views its legitimacy.

The Islamic revolution's armed defence follows the revolution's success and constitutes the sixth and final stage of its strategy. Despite its relative obscurity and unpopularity among South African Muslims, Qibla has a long-standing strategy of operating behind the facade of ad-hoc committees or front organisations. This approach is evident in its association with several ad-hoc international solidarity committees, such as the Bosnia Support Group and Muslims Against Global Oppression (MAGO), and more established fronts, such as the IQRAA Foundation and the Islamic Unity Convention (IUC).

Neither does Qibla divulge details of its members nor declare membership figures. The general belief is that its core membership is less than fifty, with a broader circle of active supporters and sympathisers. The primary aim of refusing to make its membership public is to create the impression that Qibla is not an organisation in the strict sense of the word but rather a broad social movement. The value of Qibla's covert modus operandi and the use of front organisations become evident from this perspective. This method of organisation allows Qibla to maintain distance and claim plausible deniability when its members or front organisations commit acts of violence or intimidation. It provides Qibla with legal cover and maintains its legitimacy as an organisation in the Muslim community.

Since the advent of South African democracy, Qibla had considerably expanded its political and organisational activities. This development was partly due to the opportunities offered by an open society and the attendant ability to freely organise, raise funds and network. As with any transitional society, the new government inherited socio-political issues from the past that were not easily solved and new problems that arose due to the transition. These were issues that Qibla used to mobilise political support.

Under Apartheid, topics such as high levels of crime played second fiddle to the political struggle between the two primary protagonists in South Africa, which were the ruling National Party and the African National Congress. In the new dispensation, a free press and social movements brought this and other issues to public attention. Therefore, they became apparent issues around mobilising support and potent tools in the hands of those intending to weaponise society's general disenchantment with how the government was dealing with it. It was clear that the IUC and other Qibla fronts were attempts at contesting hegemony for political leadership in the South African Muslim community, particularly from the community's traditional, often conservative religious leadership. Cape Town became the laboratory where the effect of this strategy played out after 1994.

Despite Qibla's repeated and energetic efforts, its initiatives to establish popular front organisations have been met with limited success and short-lived victories. The group has faced significant challenges, particularly in gaining popularity among South Africa's predominantly Sunni Muslims due to its hostility towards the recognised Muslim clergy and Qibla's perceived association with Iran. Traditionally, when Qibla established front organisations, it did not maintain a sufficient distance from these organisations so that they could operate with at least a semblance of independence. Being confronted with Pagad, the first Qibla initiative to gain widespread popular support amongst Muslims and non-Muslims alike, was our misfortune.

According to Pagad's constitution, its main declared objective was to 'serve as a broad front against gangs and drugs and to act as a pressure group to force the government and its agencies to deal with the problem of drugs and gangsters.' Despite its predominantly Muslim character, Qibla initially brought together a broad spectrum of organisations and individuals with diverse political persuasions. This diversity was reflected in the leadership, which included some pro-government elements, members of the ruling ANC and a Roman Catholic priest from Mitchells Plain in Cape Town, Father Christopher Cleohessy.

Despite the strenuous effort of creating a public image of a broad-based organisation, Qibla members dominated the critical positions within Pagad. Even as the organisation promoted cooperation with the government during its initial phase of mobilisation, some key members were actively acquiring illegal firearms and explosives, as well as the training of Pagad members in the use of these materials. We can attribute the initial popularity of the Pagad front to two key factors.

First, Pagad addressed the issues of gangsterism and drug abuse that affected almost every household in Cape Town's poverty-ridden Cape Flats. By 1995, the new government had been unable to make a dent in the scale and impact of gangsterism in the Western Cape. The police were at the beginning of a painful organisational transformation, and this process logically impeded its competence. The vast capabilities developed before 1994 were unsuited to combating crime in a democratic society.

Yet, the communities of the Western Cape were tired of gang violence and drug abuse and vulnerable to Pagad's vigilantism. At this stage, Pagad had not openly opposed the government, only its policies on combating gangsterism. The nifty sleight of hand netted thousands of unlikely supporters and a few hundred hardcore militants from which it could construct a terrorist infrastructure.

The second reason for Pagad's initial success was its strategic distancing from Qibla. The Qibla members who conceptualised Pagad took the campaign's formal launch through a process called whitewashing. They introduced the idea to some Qibla and non-Qibla leaders in the IUC, who took up the campaign and invited Muslim communities from various townships across Cape Town to participate. There was no mention of Qibla, lest it scare off those who may have worked with the broad front IUC but would not touch Qibla with a bargepole. Before long, Pagad was a campaign with broad base organisational support. The concept was 'washed' clean and good enough to present to the public.

The organisation burst into the public spotlight in February 1996 when its members marched on the residence of the Minister of Justice Dullah Omar. Omar was a Pagad target because he was a Muslim serving in what Qibla regarded as an illegitimate ANC government. The march to Omar's residence turned violent and was the first occasion police intervened in Pagad activity. Unlike most cabinet ministers, Omar had chosen to continue living in his house in the Black suburb of Rylands instead of moving into one of the secure and more comfortable ministerial residential estates at the foot of Table Mountain. Rylands was a predominantly Muslim community; many of Omar's neighbours were active Pagad and Qibla members.

This incident should have set alarm bells ringing, but neither the senior police, intelligence management nor the political leadership thought much of it then. Omar himself, whom I knew as a political leader and activist lawyer from my days as a student activist, had faced rather more serious personal attacks from the Apartheid regime, which included multiple assassination attempts. Ironically, in the context of the supposedly anti-gangsterism banner under which Pagad targeted him, the most publicised attempt on his life came from Cape Town gangsters who were in the pay of the Apartheid state's notorious and euphemistically named assassination unit, the Civil Cooperation Bureau.

First targeted by state-funded gangsters and then by the self-proclaimed anti-gangster vigilantes, Omar adopted a relatively sanguine attitude toward the latter incident, perhaps because of this prior experience and the support from Aunty Farida – his powerful wife and partner of many decades. The incident at Omar's house was a harbinger of what would come. Pagad's publicity following the escapade created an attention-seeking template of disruptive, violent protest that gave them the propaganda value most protest movements craved. That episode was the embryonic representation of the anti-state violence organisation into which Pagad would later morph.

Inside Crime Intelligence, I struggled to convince my seniors that we were not dealing with merely a passing combination of protest and vigilantism but a potentially severe security threat. As frustrating as it was, I took Winnie the Pooh's sage advice: 'If the person you are talking to doesn't appear to be listening, be patient. It may simply be that he has a small piece of fluff in his ear.' I hoped the fluff would dissipate and the recipients of my reporting would take in what I was saying, emphasising the potential threat of Pagad to invoke a sense of concern.

After the incident at Omar's house, my one-man Pagad intelligence unit doubled in size with the addition of a character with whom I had a long and adversarial relationship but who would prove a reliable colleague and partner. Martin served in the Branch and was a central player in its operations against the Western Cape Students Congress (Wecsco), for which I played a small backroom role in the late 1980s. Although not a member of the Wecsco executive committee, by 1987, my focus was on building the influence of a small pro-ANC caucus within the student movement. Together with other student leaders, I sought to transform Wecsco from a contested ideological space into an ANC bulwark amongst Cape Town students.

Apart from the public activities in which Wecsco engaged – protest marches, awareness-raising programmes at schools, and working with other progressive organisations under the umbrella of the United Democratic Front (UDF) – our small group established underground reading groups, where student leaders delved into revolutionary theory, strategy, and tactics. It also provided a platform for distributing banned ANC and SACP literature. Wecsco, at large, and the small group I was part of were significant headaches to the Security Branch. Our disruptive activities raised the profile of the outlawed ANC across the high schools in Cape Town. Still, more disconcerting to them, we were preparing young students for recruitment into the ANC underground, including its armed wing.

Martin, then working under the Du Plessis of 'beating up students' fame, was personally involved in tracking me when I was on the run from around January 1988, after the Branch arrested a number of my close comrades. Martin and two other Branch officers, then Warrant Officers Johan Cronje and Piet Taljaard, were regular visitors at my house. He also recruited a Wecsco activist who participated in one of the underground reading groups I facilitated and pressured him to tell them where I was. The comrade misinformed him that the ANC had sent me to Palestine, and there ensued a great deal of consternation as the Branch and their Israeli allies tried to track me down in Palestine.

It was the time of the first Palestinian intifada, and I'm still not sure if I was supposed to be in Palestine to learn from our Palestinian friends or whether I went there to transmit the lessons of the South African uprising to them. In reality, of course, it was neither of the two. Together with two other Wecsco comrades who were also on the run, I lived in a defunct, vacant school building owned by a private developer – the father of a white student activist. The building was right in the centre of Cape Town, a stone's throw from the very Loop Street operational centre where Martin and I later made each other's formal acquaintance. Captain Africa and Sergeant Martin became the forerunners of Crime Intelligence's work against Pagad.

I found Martin to be a fascinating, if contradictory character. The contrast was perhaps because he must have realised that he had been aggressively fighting, with aplomb, for a white supremacist regime against an adversary to which they not only lost but, he belatedly discovered, was constituted by decent people who only had the best interest of the country and her people at heart. What must have made things more difficult for him, and it came through often enough, was that the people he was hunting just a few years prior now all held ranks senior to himself. At the same time, white Branch officers of evidently lesser quality than him were promoted to positions on par with the incoming DIS officers.

Recruited into the Branch while still a university student in the mid-80s, Martin came from a family that supported the anti-Apartheid struggle. Though he would never say exactly why he agreed to join the Branch, I suspect it might have had something to do with getting married and starting a family and the commensurate demands this places on anyone. If I had any doubt about his willingness to work under my direction and serve the new government, it didn't take long before it would dissipate. We developed an excellent relationship, found ourselves in many hazardous situations together, and conducted several decisive source recruitments jointly.

Yet, given our history, how my wife received him would be the real test of whether Martin and I would be good colleagues. He was involved in her detention in the mid-1980s while she was a student activist. In 1987, he was somehow involved in her sister's arrest for activities related to her ANC membership, and late in 1989, he endeavoured the arrest of her youngest sister, who was also a Wecsco leader. Once, as he dropped me at home on the day we celebrated the Eid al Fitr festival, I invited him to join the family (including all the sisters mentioned above) for lunch, as is customary. For a man who had hunted so-called terrorists, participated in brutal interrogations, and was now a democratic-era counter-terrorism officer, Martin was terrified at the prospect of having lunch with my wife and her sisters. What played out next was as unlikely as it would be liberating for him.

'David, are you crazy? These women are going to kill me. They might even poison my food.' My jocular reply was, 'They should do exactly that, but they won't do it today because it's Eid, so come inside.' As we entered the house, I announced his presence to my wife and the family. They all remembered him well. Without missing a beat, my wife said, 'Come in, have a seat, and have some food,' and instructed someone to fetch him a plate. 'Add some poison,' she went on to say, which broke the ice and opened the door for him to pop in frequently when we worked together. We often worked sixteen or more hours per day and would eat wherever we could get cheap fast food or had a moment to pop into one of our houses, where the family would quickly throw together some ingredients and feed us. It was comforting that any colleague, regardless of his institutional origin, would be welcome to join.

While Martin and I found ourselves running around and scheming to recruit sources within Qibla and Pagad, the other function in our sense-making apparatus rested with Crime Intelligence's information management unit, which was formally responsible for analysing the activities of both organisations. The innocuous, friendly, and hardworking Gerrie Strydom headed this team. Strydom's main shortcoming was that he did not regard information management as analytical work but more or less as that of a postman, transmitting reports upwards and information requests downwards across the hierarchy. The net effect was that his team added less value than they could in enhancing our human intelligence reporting.

He had the misfortune of working under the direct management of our inept provincial commander, Du Plessis, which would not have made his task any easier. The longer I worked in CI, the more I realised that the postman role was not something Strydom had invented but that he was merely mirroring the standard practice across Crime Intelligence, from the provincial level up to the headquarters. When I worked at the headquarters at the end of 1996, I found that the analytic desks more or less took raw human source and operational reports, wrote some generic commentary that masqueraded as analysis, and passed it on to the most apparent consumer – usually the person one level above in the hierarchy.

This practice was so widespread that I concluded that the Apartheid security agencies, with the possible exception of the National Intelligence Service (NIS), had worked along these lines when we were on opposite sides of the battleground. This would have explained their lack of insight and their proffering of inevitably failing solutions to the national crisis that confronted the country in the 1980s. They could not make sense of the assortment of information provided by an expansive source and technical capability. In turn, they could not translate the details into sense-making for the decision-maker. Most disconcerting was that no one seemed to care enough to do anything about it.

While working at a so-called analysis desk at the head office, I proposed an analytic workshop on the Qibla-Pagad threat. The idea was so unusual that there was no prescribed procedure for how to go about arranging it. I might as well have proposed a moon landing. The analytic doctrine, analysis training, and integration of analytic methodology into crafting reports were lacking. We merely passed on reports with the occasional comment of 'this is now the 5th or 10th incident of this type' – Commentary masqueraded as intelligence analysis.

Unsurprisingly, the first significant analytic contributions on the Pagad threat came from Vearey and myself, two former DIS officers. I started working on a lengthy analysis of Qibla and Pagad, the evolution of the threat posed by these organisations, their modus operandi, and their targeting approach. Parts of this report found their way into the National Intelligence Estimate, the collective intelligence community's authoritative analysis of a threat. This led Strydom to write a glowing letter of commendation highlighting the insightfulness of the review and how unique such a contribution was. All the while, I thought that this constituted intelligence officers' day-to-day work.

Vearey had, in the interim, left the covert unit and was appointed as Du Plessis' deputy, taking command of the CI intelligence coordination unit. He became the point man in our analytical and production relationship with our sister organisations, the National Intelligence Agency (NIA) and Military Intelligence, where he worked with the provincial inter-agency intelligence coordinator, Gordon Brookbanks. In his new role, Vearey regularly crafted analyses on issues ranging from Pagad to gangs and organised crime. Even though the expectation was that Strydom's team carry out the analytic work, they couldn't produce consequential inputs. Vearey was innovative and filled a gaping hole in our function, something we would feel pressured to continue doing in the face of an inert institution that contained many incapable people.

With the introduction of the term 'Urban Terrorism' to describe Pagad's violent activities and intent, Vearey would make a seminal contribution to our characterisation of the threat. There we were, alas, two ANC 'terrorists' defining Pagad's actions as terrorism. We, at last, started doing the essential work of sense-making.

CHAPTER 3

A Soaring G-Force, Saboteurs and Sleepwalkers

He who closes his eyes sees nothing, even in the full light of day.
—Leopold Trepper, chief of the Soviet Red Orchestra intelligence network

In retrospect, the curve mapping Pagad's transition was a steady and almost inevitable development. From a protest movement to a vigilante group and ultimately a terrorist organisation, a turn to terrorism was always a distinct possibility, given the manner of its birth and the motive behind its establishment. However, no one in Crime Intelligence could have foretold the scale and effect of Pagad's actions. It was beyond what I had expected, even though I had, by the middle of 1996, been studying the organisation and Qibla for a year. The growth curve and its seemingly endless escalation were partially on account of how it mobilised support and established its structures. It was also due to the dismal failure and criminal negligence of the police in the Western Cape.

The initial months of mobilisation were done discreetly. Qibla members representing the campaign against gangsterism and drugs visited areas across the Cape Flats where these issues were rampant. They met with mosques, churches, and community organisations in Manenberg, Retreat, Mitchells Plain, Hanover Park, and Kensington to advocate for an extensive city-wide campaign. The campaigners found a welcome reception almost everywhere they went. In Mitchells Plain, they were given a receptive ear by Father Christopher Clohessy. An unconventional Roman Catholic priest, Father Clohessy was close to members of his community and actively engaged in dealing with the myriad of social ills.

Community neighbourhood watches, which had battled gangs across the Cape Flats, and members of community policing forums who had confronted the often incompetent and corrupt local police, were natural recruiting grounds for Pagad. These organisations had established networks in the preceding decade, derived their legitimacy from many years of community service, and had intimate knowledge of the local gang and drug networks. Given how the government was struggling to come to grips with the gang and drug pandemic on the Cape Flats, these kinds of organisations and the individuals associated with them were a godsend to Pagad. They transferred their extant legitimacy onto Pagad.

The neighbourhood watches were essential to how Pagad's paramilitary structure evolved. They comprised organised community members, were trained to respond to crises, had granular knowledge of their local communities, and, most importantly, were armed. By capturing these structures, Pagad created an army out of nothing. Allie Parker and Nadthmie Ederies, who, by the winter of 1996, had respectively risen to the positions of Security Chief and National Coordinator at Pagad, came to join the organisation through the Surrey Estate neighbourhood watch.

The Qibla core attended the mobilisation meetings and stayed behind to speak to individuals they considered recruiting into their paramilitary structure. This core, central to developing Pagad, consisted of Ebrahim, Salie Abader, Rushdien Abrahams, Shahied and Nazier Mathey brothers. Late in 1995, they established contacts with criminal networks and started to gather a small arsenal of what they called '*haraam-ies*,' code for illegal firearms. They also explored networks that could facilitate access to military explosives at the local Denel Swartklip arms manufacturer.

The core group met regularly at a hardware store in central Cape Town owned by Ebrahim's brother, just a stone's throw from the inner city's central police station. Here, they designed the contours of a campaign that would mobilise sizable popular support for Qibla and allow them the opportunity to build and unleash a potent paramilitary capability. Initially, their targets were the gangs, but the new government became their ultimate target. In contrast to the defensive security force headed by Parker, this group constituted Pagad's offensive paramilitary capability. In time, they consumed the defensive security force and turned it into an entirely offensive instrument of terror.

Ebrahim lived in the middle-class, historically coloured suburb of Lansdowne, on the same street where Qibla leader Achmat Cassiem lived. Ebrahim had a close and affectionate relationship with his leader. He came from a trading family who owned businesses in the city centre and the bustling commercial suburb of Gatesville, where many working-class Capetonians did their weekly shopping and the average household could get their hands on any spices.

Abader was tall and carried himself with a certain gravitas, exhibiting a more composed presence than the perennially agitated Ebrahim. While Ebrahim seemed to get along better with the more aggressive G-Force members as the organisation evolved, Abader connected better with those who played a crucial role in its bombing campaign, the more ideologically driven types. He resided in Walmer Estate at the foot of Table Mountain, a mere seven-minute drive from the spot where the organisation claimed its first major scalp in Rashaad Staggie. He would also shepherd his son into the ranks of the G-Force.

Abrahams, who went by the nom de guerre Abu Jihad, was the only one in the core group who came from working-class origins and led a precarious existence, living off odd jobs and the charity of friends and family. His role in a 1985 Qibla operation, where they killed and disarmed a security guard at the Lincoln Tavern in Cape Town's Belgravia, made Abrahams a figure of repute within Qibla circles. He had subsequently gone into exile in London, from where he travelled to Afghanistan and fought alongside the Afghan mujahideen against the Soviet army. A battle-hardened combatant with an extremist ideological position, Abrahams now planned to deploy his skills against Cape Town's gangsters and the government.

Since the fateful Saturday of 30 November 1985, when Nazier Mathey gathered a team of Qibla members, including his younger brother Shahied Mathey, Abrahams and his younger cousin, to carry out the Lincoln Tavern operation, the Mathey brothers operated like conjoined twins. They had spent several years in prison after their conviction for the attack. Both received amnesty in the early 1990s as part of the negotiated political settlement by the very ANC they now sought to overthrow. They lived a comfortable middle-class existence in Rylands, a suburb designated as 'Indian' under the Apartheid Group Areas Act. They became the axis upon which the G-Force's bombing campaign centred, forming the core of an innovative team of bomb makers.

Pagad gained the confidence of very contrasting characters, Parker and Ederies. The two would play an essential role in the organisation as it publicly launched its campaign and entered the grey zone of popular mobilisation mixed with increasingly violent actions against gang leaders and drug dealers. They brought a wealth of experience organising armed groups and deploying them against gangs in the Surrey Estate suburb. In their previous roles in neighbourhood watches, they stopped short of violent attacks, but there was no shortage of intimidating gangsters and drug dealers. They were also actively engaged in mobilising popular support for their neighbourhood watch.

Parker and Ederies, in many ways, mirrored the personality differences between Ebrahim and Abader, aggressive in tone and disposition versus soft-spoken and more considered in argument. Ederies, who had strong links with the local ANC branch where he lived, was a curiosity within Pagad. His affiliation started affecting his loyalty to Pagad once the ANC began to view the organisation as a threat to the government instead of only to gangsters. This dynamic played no small role in his break from Pagad.

My first source inside the G-Force, let's call him Beachwalker, was a problematic and ill-disciplined character. He was impulsive and failed to heed the basic rules of secrecy, yet desperate beggars can't be choosers. He was an easy catch and gave me essential insight into the organisation's structure and leadership. He was capable of swiftly reporting actions taken during or shortly after marches. With a combination of pressure and guidance, he started delivering early warning information that allowed us to tip off the police of intended attacks by the G-Force or impending violence during Pagad protest marches.

Mobile phones were not that common in 1996. I had to develop elaborate reporting routines for Beachwalker that would allow me to submit reports and commentary on the evening's developments before Viktor's 7:30 a.m. debrief meeting at Loop Street. Beachwalker might have been impulsive, but he had an eye for detail and greatly assisted in developing our understanding of the tensions between the Qibla core and other Pagad leaders, such as Ederies and Jaffer, then still simmering below the surface. This intelligence came in handy later when the possibility of creating a breach in Pagad arose. Beachwalker was also the source who provided us with the information that led to my compilation of the critical warning alert two days before Pagad's march to Staggie's house, where members of the group lynched him.

By June 1996, I had recruited a source inside Qibla, who had access to the organisation's assessment of Pagad. Qibla was astonished by the rapidity with which Pagad had emerged to become a powerful organisation, attracting thousands to its marches and meetings. What surprised them most was the consistently high public support and participation levels and the speed with which Pagad had established and expanded its G-Force. Whoever in Pagad's ranks decided to base their paramilitary capacity on the small cadre of Qibla loyalists, bolstered by mass recruiting from neighbourhood watches, had effected a tactical masterstroke. In combat, commanders always look for the opportunity to create a compound effect, defined by Darren Hardy as 'the principle of reaping huge rewards from a series of small, smart choices.' Qibla's cadres in Pagad had unlocked a capability beyond their wildest dreams.

Although not directly involved in Pagad, my source was quick to notice the strategic foresight of the Qibla core. They demanded that Pagad maintain a high level of operational autonomy. They were not content with being mere implementers of decisions by Qibla's leader. This autonomy enabled them to swiftly adjust their tactics and organisation without needing approval from the Qibla leadership. Though heavily influenced by the machinations of the Qibla core, Pagad's turn to violence gained additional impetus from the inflammatory language used by speakers at Pagad meetings and marches. A young and impressive student of Islam, Abdurrazak Ebrahim, who held the title of *amir* (leader or commander) of Pagad, would speak at most meetings and marches, almost inevitably invoking the global struggle of Muslims against oppression, and likening the condition of South African Muslims to those in Algeria, Bosnia and Egypt, where Muslims were either oppressed by autocratic regimes or under attack as part of military conflict.

The equation of the democratic South African State to Arab autocracies was a clear signal that Pagad had established itself as an anti-state instrument from the word go. The fact that the young Pagad *amir* was a leader in the IUC and close to the Qibla leadership also did not escape me. The violent mood within Pagad was not confined to Qibla or its associates. At the height of its popularity in the latter half of 1996, Ali Parker was as belligerent as any Qibla member, as were people like Jaffer and Ederies. The milieu was one of frustration, intolerance, and the need for cathartic violence. Some wanted to exploit this mood in a limited fashion, only directing it to the criminal underworld.

The Qibla core, in contrast, wished to apply it to the expansive targeting of opponents and the State. This did not bode well for us because it opened the gap for many Pagad members to take that small leap from anti-gang to anti-state violence. By late 1996, it was clear that many Pagad members had already made the jump.

Martin and I attended many of the Pagad protest marches. I observed from the sidelines, trying to mark faces, notice serial participants, and listen to who had said what. This was part of building an intelligence picture of Pagad and developing a sense of the mood that is often difficult to extract from a sterile source report.

The mood within Pagad at the time was a critical factor, and we, as intelligence, had to develop a good sense of it. This mood determined how much space non-Qibla members within Pagad would give the government to show movement in dealing with their concerns. Once a group is sufficiently tilted to the side of impatience and aggression, it can be challenging to roll back the sentiment, even if addressing the immediate issues raised by the group. By mid-1996, the mood was clearly not on the side of the government.

It was, however, equally important to note the clusters that formed during Pagad meetings and protest marches. I knew from my experience in the mass democratic movement and the ANC underground that such huddles often provided good indicators of new targets for recruitment or structures being established. The one obvious observation was the coalescing of a certain group of people around Ebrahim. These were the individuals that constituted the Qibla core. I also noticed some fleeting huddles. A member of the Qibla core with a group from Kensington or with one or two individuals from the rural town of Paarl just outside Cape Town, which historically has a solid, if small, Qibla presence. These were the interesting ones and must have been fleeting and furtive for a reason. The only explanation I could think of was that they were actively avoiding coming to the attention of fellow Pagad members and whoever was watching.

Yet, the ANC cadres amongst us had been in that position before and knew what it meant. These were old networks being re-established in the context of an immense political opportunity or new relationships being discreetly cultivated, with the aim of new recruitments into the Qibla core. The pot boiled over, and the situation turned openly violent in the middle of 1996 when Pagad members marched to prominent gang leader Richard Stemmet's house and attacked it while people were still inside. The transition from protest and shouting anti-gang slogans to attacking an occupied house was uncontroversial and seamless for Pagad members. With this attack, they crossed a seemingly insignificant but critical line.

The murder of Rashaad Staggie was a watershed moment. It had a profound psychological effect, somewhat akin to the impact the ANC's 1980s armed propaganda campaign had on the political situation in South Africa. This event marked a significant shift in the dynamics of Pagad, bolstering its public protests while emboldening the G-Force to more aggressive action. The old adage that war is the continuation of politics by violent means was starkly evident in post-Apartheid South Africa. The post-Staggie moment was an important juncture for the

Qibla core to assert its dominance over Pagad. The decision to seize control at this precise moment was not arbitrary. It was a calculated move, driven by the convergence of an unprecedented political opportunity and the necessity to employ violent means to exploit it.

Pagad's 11 August 1996 rally at Vygieskraal stadium in Athlone was a significant event in the organisation's history. While it may have appeared conservative to some, it was a joyous day for the Qibla core. They not only celebrated Staggie's execution but also marked the pinnacle of Qibla's public popularity. The Imam, which was how Qibla members fondly referred to Cassiem, was addressing a crowd of twenty thousand. He wasted no time in drawing the ideological links between Pagad and Qibla. Arguing that there was 'no peace without justice,' Cassiem legitimised Pagad's violent actions and denounced the democratic government as the product of an immoral sell-out deal with the Apartheid regime.

In one speech, Cassiem solidified Pagad's ideology as anti-state, anti-democratic, and legitimising violence. The sentiment was echoed by Pagad's *amir*, Abdurrazak Ebrahim, who invoked the Quranic phrase 'to those against whom war is made, permission is given to fight because they are wronged,' followed by the slogan 'one gangster, one bullet!' The crowd met these messages with thunderous applause, a clear sign of their resonance. Even the moderate Muslim Judicial Council (MJC) leaders, instead of voicing disagreement, chose to remain silent. Qibla's ideological hegemony over Pagad became irreversible at this point.

The following day, at a Pagad meeting at Masjidul Quds, Pagad leaders declared jihad – in Islamic scripture a call to struggle or exertion, but in the context of Pagad it constituted a call to armed action - not just against gangs but the government as well. To carry out this jihad, Pagad members were called upon to establish armed underground units. The remaining task for the Qibla core was to cement control of the organisational apparatus, specifically the G-Force, and decisively marginalised non-Qibla leaders. While the execution of Staggie propelled Pagad into the national and international spotlight, it also marked the beginning of the first significant fissure within the organisation.

The Qibla core was in an intense contest for control of the Pagad security operation. They set out to wrestle power from Parker, who had acquired legendary status due to the militancy of his speeches and the wounds he had sustained when Staggie was murdered. Parker had no intention of ceding control of the organisation's security apparatus without a fight. He had no moral objection to using the G-Force to launch attacks on gang leaders and drug merchants but sought to maintain distance between Pagad's offensive and defensive operations. The Qibla core now rushed to integrate these two streams of armed force into one offensive instrument. The first objective of this seizure of control was to multiply the G-Force's ability to use violence, while the second was to deny the non-Qibla faction a paramilitary capacity to defend themselves in the event of a violent breakup between the factions.

The collapse of Pagad's internal unity was precipitated by Qibla's move to openly assert its control of the organisation and facilitated by the arrest of the three non-Qibla leaders, Parker, Jaffer, and Ederies. The arrests left a temporary gap immediately filled by the Qibla core. Given the increasingly extremist anti-state rhetoric driving Pagad, external political actors pressured Ederies, Parker, and Jaffer to disassociate themselves from Pagad. Despite the brief but intense battle for control that played out during September 1996, the Qibla core emerged victorious. They successfully withstood interventions by religious leaders associated with the MJC, some intelligence officials in Cape Town, and a range of community anti-crime leaders, and by the last quarter of 1996, their control of Pagad was complete.

This false view held by many, that Pagad had to return to its supposedly original aims of fighting gangsterism and drug abuse, led to a miscalculation of the balance of forces within the organisation, with many underestimating the level of control Qibla already had over the organisation. Admitting that Qibla was in control of Pagad, was engaged in extortion against Muslim businesspeople, and planned to overthrow the democratic government, Parker conceded defeat on 20 September of that year. The expulsion of the defeated leaders simply formalised a balance of forces and an organisational trajectory that had been clear since the murder of Staggie.

The shift in power dynamics within Pagad, with Qibla's control becoming more pronounced, significantly altered our intelligence operations. We were now facing a more unified adversary, devoid of the internal divisions that typically provide intelligence access and influence opportunities. This required us to identify and leverage alternative motivators for source recruitment. In short, the new openly Qibla-oriented Pagad would be a much tougher nut to crack than the more diluted Pagad ever was. We embraced the task with determination and a readiness to face the challenges it presented. Recognising that our loyal but peripheral Qibla source and the few Pagad sources we had recruited would no longer suffice in underground cell-based operations, we set our sights on gaining direct access to the Qibla core. This was crucial as they now controlled the G-Force. We understood the urgency of a breakthrough before the new cell structures became entrenched, less penetrable and developed capability beyond the small Qibla core.

I found Khalid Johnson (pseudonym) emaciated and cold in the Table View police cells on a wet day in September 1996. It was early evening when a colleague from the investigation team at the Loop Street centre requested that I accompany him to see Johnson, who had been arrested a week earlier. Johnson was angry and desperate. Infuriated, he claimed, because the cops had refused to provide him with the halaal meals delivered by his family. Desperate because the police cells were still cold in the early Spring, and the absence of food had weakened him physically.

'Let's get this guy some fresh air and decent food,' I told my colleague. Johnson smiled an awkward, almost childlike smile, something that would become common in our interactions. We checked him out of his uncomfortable police accommodations and drove to the nearby Blouberg beach, where one has the most spectacular view of Table Mountain. We stopped at a halaal takeaway shop on the way to the beach and bought some warm food and tea. I knew the food quality from my days as a student activist, and was sure a near-starving Johnson would consider it food fit for kings.

'Bismillah my brother. Have something to eat,' I said to Johnson, and so began a relationship that would prove to be of immense intelligence value despite the serial attempts by police investigators to sabotage us and the eventual tragic outcome. As Johnson and I walked on the beach, with my Afrikaner colleague not far behind, it was clear that he had spent the week in the police cells reflecting on his situation and was eager to escape it. As an old Qibla man, he was fully aware of the risks but seized the opportunity I offered him with both hands. At the end of that beach walk, Johnson committed his services to Crime Intelligence.

Our relationship with Johnson was to become a crucial element in our intelligence operations. We agreed to work to our mutual benefit in ending what he referred to as a ticking time bomb that would create absolute madness once it exploded. We made arrangements for meetings and communications once he was out on bail and temporarily said goodbye when we dropped him off and checked him back into his police cell. We made sure to leave instructions for the cops to ensure he received the meals brought by his family.

Our new contact within the G-Force opened up new avenues of pursuit that we had not previously been able to pursue. He provided us with insights into the first fully constituted G-Force underground cell. The cell was made up of at least three Qibla members from the 1980s and one fresh recruit, Afzal Karriem, who would later become notorious for his alleged involvement in the murder of witnesses in Pagad-related cases. This was the first cell we neutralised, using a combination of recruitment inside the cell, creating an untenable operational situation using aggressive surveillance and the harassment of members. The cell disintegrated, even though Karriem would retain the connection to the G-Force through the Qibla core network he was inducted into.

One of Karriem's interlocutors was a new Qibla recruit who went by the alias Pretty Boy. Another member of the Kensington G-Force cell was a desperate Qibla member in dire financial straits who ended up offering his services to all and sundry in the intelligence world, ourselves included. We cut him off after a few weeks.

Given his background with Qibla, the information Johnson shared held value beyond successfully infiltrating the Kensington cell. It took us right into the two places we were desperate to get our eyes, ears, and heads into at the time: the Qibla core, by then firmly in command of the G-Force, and the individuals responsible for the construction of the

Pagad pipe bombs. Johnson, who was respected within the G-Force, had intimate knowledge of Qibla and was involved in planning Pagad's bombing campaign. He provided the type of intelligence access that enabled us to shut down the G-Force early on if we played our cards right. All we had to do was retain his cooperation, handle him with the security that someone of his stature demanded, and deploy his intelligence judiciously.

We could not rush into the sudden arrest of people close to him. It would take some time to test the quality and integrity of his reporting and design an approach that allowed us to bring down the G-Force while protecting his identity as a source. But I can state, without any doubt, that he had access and reported all of it to the point where the demise of the G-Force was simply a matter of time and method. Johnson was a gold mine, but our challenge was to exploit his access to optimal effect without blowing his cover.

The conduct of an intelligence operation of the sort we now conceived is like arranging a museum exhibition. Everything has its place, and nothing in the arrangement is accidental. Anyone walking through the exhibition must exit with a particular feeling created by carefully curating objects and ideas, the distance between objects, and the effect of lighting, smells and sounds. Similarly, intelligence operations must be calibrated with great care and take into account a number of factors. This includes the security of the operation, including that of the sources deployed, and the impact and sustainability of the operational effect on the target structure or individuals. When you strike gold as I did with Johnson, you don't use it to manufacture cheap jewellery. You use it to create a masterpiece.

Handling Johnson proved a challenging and risky operation. We had to ensure his security to prevent exposing him as a source. Such an exposure would place him at significant risk. Because of his position within the G-Force and the tactical value of his intelligence, he needed to communicate on the fly without pre-arranged schedules. Our telephone communication had to be brief, mainly conducted in code, yet precise enough for us to act upon. He provided information that enabled us to interdict the transfer of weapons or prevent an attack on more than one occasion.

We could only meet with Johnson in pre-vetted facilities, with a support team nearby in case he was followed to our meeting point. Despite all these precautions, we were almost discovered when our meeting location had a plumbing emergency, and the emergency plumber called to the site was a member of the G-Force. Fortunately, we managed to get Johnson out of the building by using an alternative exit while the plumber was busy doing his job in the kitchen. We were committed to providing Johnson the operational, financial, and security environment that ensured a productive long-term relationship, and we invested the resources to achieve this objective.

Although Johnson was a goldmine, he was controversial, and others in the police had different ideas about him. His very position created complexities that most police investigators did not appreciate. They were under pressure after the Staggie murder and understandably wanted immediate results. Our colleagues did not understand the need to build a case over time where the source would not even be involved in providing court testimony. Their modus operandi related to cases dealing with low-level gangsters, small-time drug dealers, and random murderers, and they did not have the patience or sophistication required to manage an investigation into a threat such as Pagad.

We wanted to use Johnson to achieve sustainable results while they tried to get their hands on anyone they could compel to testify. The firearm in his possession, when he was arrested and detained at the Table View police cells, linked him to several shooting incidents. The police wanted to use this to pressurise him into testifying. In the very first days of the Pagad task team, established immediately after Staggie's murder, I had a fallout with Knipe, a sort of demi-god amongst investigators. It was clear that Knipe had an intense dislike for intelligence, possibly a holdover from the days when people like him would be ordered around by junior officers in the Security Branch and could do nothing about it. He also openly displayed a dislike for ANC officers now integrated into the police.

Knipe also had a history with Qibla members going back to the 1985 Lincoln Tavern incident. When his team arrested Johnson, a Qibla member, in 1996, he saw it as an opportunity to get one back on an old organisational adversary. The distrust between ourselves and Knipe's investigation team and his irrational dislike of Johnson informed our approach to conducting the first significant operation involving the source. We ran the operation without involving Knipe's investigative team, knowing they would sabotage it from the word go.

The bombing squad around the Mathey brothers had gained access to a supply of hand grenades from someone at the Denel explosives manufacturing plant in Swartklip, close to Cape Town's False Bay coast. We planned to stop this worrying development and apprehend some of the key G-Force members involved in the scheme. We thought this operation would allow us to make our first breakthrough inside the Qibla core and the nascent but increasingly dangerous bombing squad. We had to do it while protecting the identity and life of a source who possessed the potential to deliver much bigger things.

We had to keep Johnson engaged with the hand grenade connection so we could identify the supplier and arrest the G-Force members who received the explosives. Working with our bomb disposal unit, we doctored one of the grenades we obtained from Johnson, which would later be used in a G-Force operation. The grenade was rigged so it could not cause any damage or injury but still make an explosive bang. Knipe and his investigators were livid once they found out about our 'grenade operation' and pursued an investigation against me and my colleague, Welmar O'Reilly. The Western Cape Director of Public Prosecutions initially decided to prosecute us for defeating the ends of justice but, in the end, withdrew the charges after representations by our attorney. Knipe and company called the operation stupid, even though they failed to arrest anyone for the whole grenade affair or to substitute our excellent source with one of their own.

Johnson's potential to bring down the G-Force was more significant than any source we recruited before or since. Only Adbus Salaam Ebrahim, the Mathey brothers, and Salie Abader equalled his access and stature within the G-Force. He was the type of source that intelligence professionals refer to as 'someone able to deliver the poison.' Yet, once Knipe's team decided that settling old scores and smashing intelligence off its historic perch was more important than exploiting the only real opportunity we had to kill off the G-Force in its infancy, our enterprise came crashing down. The G-Force had two or three cells at this point, had not yet refined its bombing operation, and had very few people experienced in killing or underground operations.

The intention behind Johnson's arrest in early 1997 and his subsequent conviction was to pressure him to testify as a witness in open court, which proved a disaster for our operation and a failure for Knipe and his investigation team. They only convicted someone who had already saved lives in his brief collaboration with us. Johnson was sentenced to ten years imprisonment. My bosses at the CI head office asked that I speak to him and plead that he testify to facilitate what would be a tremendous success for us and prevent a loyal source from going to prison. In mid-1997, I flew to Cape Town and visited him in prison.

When he greeted me with that peculiar, now characteristic smile, I knew that any attempt to convince him to testify was doomed to fail. I, however, made my pitch and went through the motions of explaining the precise implications of the deal – negotiating his release in return for testimony, relocation to the witness protection programme, and creating a new life away from Cape Town. 'Frank,' he used the codename by which he knew me, 'my brother, don't worry about me. It's only ten years, and I'll be out of here in seven.' 'Abu Leila,' I said, 'this is not the old days where you'll serve your sentence on Robben Island alongside comrades. You'll spend your time with the very gangsters you were shooting and bombing just a few months ago. Take the fucking deal and make a life elsewhere.'

Johnson remained steadfast, and I left the prison empty-handed, with a sense of foreboding that the opportunity to recruit someone of his calibre would not come our way anytime soon. Such high-level recruitments in terrorist organisations are fleeting, and we would, in fact, never repeat recruitment at his seniority.

The ease with which the investigators destroyed a valuable intelligence asset also hardened my view about their lack of commitment to solving the Pagad Troubles. I never again trusted Knipe and his cohort of investigators, so I always pushed for their exclusion from sensitive operations. This approach would serve us well in the future as we clawed our way back into the G-Force.

In October 1996, I was transferred to the Crime Intelligence head office in Pretoria to work on the political extremism desk. Crime Intelligence's national head, Nceba Radu, wanted to deploy an ANC person to the desk, which dealt with sensitive political issues and, up to that point, was staffed exclusively by white former Branch members. The composition of the head office was shocking, with three ANC cadres amidst a sea of staff from the Branch and former Bantustan police forces. The place had the aura of a Calvinist society involved in intelligence work. Morning meetings opened with a Christian prayer, and everyone carried their religiosity on their sleeve. While I respect everyone's right to practice their religion, I found the faux morality amongst the Branch people quite irritating and sometimes awkward.

The Intelligence head office was transitioning and reflected the political and cultural dynamics I encountered in the Loop Street office. Pretoria was still much more conservative than my home city and was completely removed from the reality of what was playing out in the streets of Cape Town. One of my fellow team members had a keen interest in Islam in a way that people who have never engaged with the religion in any real way were - as a form of social anthropology, to understand 'them.' The rest were usually well-meaning but too naive to add much value to our efforts to make sense of Pagad and design the means for its defeat. The one person with whom I connected instantly was Willie Els, one of Radu's two deputies, who displayed more interest and curiosity in the Pagad Troubles than any of the staff on the desk responsible for it.

When I departed for my eleven-month stint in Pretoria, the Pagad intelligence team in Cape Town was reduced to Martin of 'and then a small war broke out' fame. Marius Nel, an Afrikaner cop with no intelligence background, later joined him to work on the Pagad task. I got to know Nel well at the covert unit, where he joined Dramat, Martin, and myself towards the end of 1998. Nel had a solid work ethic but was disadvantaged by having lived a sheltered life amongst Afrikaners only.

During my time in Pretoria, the two of them, Martin and Nel, formed the entire provincial intelligence team dedicated to countering Pagad. Their journey was not without its share of challenges and obstacles, a testament to their resilience and dedication. Their efforts continued until Petros was appointed to head the covert unit, bringing Dramat into the Pagad operation.

Knipe's initial Pagad task team was replaced by a second one, this time located under the leadership of Schalk Visagie, who worked in Knipe's Serious Violent Crimes Unit. Visagie, the son-in-law of former South African President PW Botha, was a former Branch officer who worked under Brookbanks at the Intelligence covert office until circa 1997. He brought a few former Branch officers, now investigators, into his task team. He also drew on the expertise of some of the ANC cadres deployed to the Serious Violent Crimes Unit. The replacement was necessitated by the need for fresh perspectives and strategies in the investigation after the first Pagad task team ran out of steam without success. One of his investigators was former Branch officer Captain Bennie Lategan, who a G-Force team would murder after he was marked by Pagad's most notorious and efficient killer, Ebrahim Jenneker.

Jenneker's arrival on the Pagad scene was dramatic. He was arrested at the funeral of a longstanding member of the Hard Livings gang, Moneeb 'Bowtie' Abrahams. Like me, Jenneker would have been very aware of Bowtie's role in the Manenberg gang world, and the accusations that he was involved in Bowtie's killing cannot be dismissed out of hand. That certainly is, in Manenberg, the dominant view of how Bowtie came to his violent end in January 1998. Upon searching Jenneker's car, the cops discovered a small arsenal of assault weapons. He was detained at Kraaifontein police station in Cape Town's northern suburbs.

With the support of the local community, Kraaifontein police station stood out as one of those well-maintained and professionally run stations. It was well equipped and relatively spacious, at least in the square metre per detained occupant sense. So Jenneker was in relatively comfortable surroundings when Dramat and I rocked up at the police station one afternoon. Vearey tipped us off about his presence at the station, and he thought we might have a chance of gaining Jenneker's cooperation, in contrast to the task team investigators, who had failed up to that point.

When we decided to question him, I was struck by a personal connection. I had known his sister very well from our days as youth political activists, which added a layer of complexity to the situation. As soon as I set my eyes on Jenneker, my mind flashed back to Manenberg Avenue in September 1989, when I worked with the Wecsco leadership to coordinate the province-wide Defiance Campaign, which was planned to coincide with the 1989 Apartheid elections.

In Wecsco, we called the student uprising 'the Spring Offensive,' and Manenberg was the site of some of the most violent action on voting day, 6 September 1989. Jenneker was the person who set off the violent protest that started in Manenberg Avenue. He had the persona of a *'kakmaker,'* a shit-stirrer, and one that took the initiative, acted calmly, and with little consideration of risk to himself. Jenneker was a member of the student action committee, which comprised those who weren't inclined to sit in political meetings, discuss politics, and decide on programmes to develop. Instead, they would energetically implement a call for action or take the initiative to make the township ungovernable on protest days. His presence at Kraaifontein police cells proved the adage that old habits die hard and may have, in his case, grown more extreme.

Dramat and I immediately hit it off with Jenneker. He was proud of his achievements, which basically amounted to killing gangsters, and was quite happy to speak of them. Since he was already incarcerated, we sought information about his associates and relationship with the G-Force Security Council. We already knew from other sources that he had a close relationship with Ebrahim and wanted to explore this relationship in greater detail. We thus hoped to secure Jenneker's cooperation in accessing the Security Council. Regular visits to the Kraaifontein police station allowed us to develop an excellent rapport with Jenneker.

The breakthrough came as the Muslim feast of Eid ul Fitr approached, and we realised that he missed his family. Eid is a day where, after fasting through the month of Ramadan, families gather, pray collectively, and eat lavish meals. Even the hardened Jenneker wanted to see his family on this day. We arranged for them to have lunch together at the police station, a gesture that further strengthened our bond. On the Thursday of Eid ul Fitr, 29 January 1998, Jenneker was led from the cells to a spacious room, where he found his family alongside intelligence officers Dramat and myself and a desk decorated with the most delicious food prepared by his wife. The family insisted that we join the lunch, and of course, since such an offer cannot be declined, we spent a few hours further ingratiating ourselves with Jenneker through his family.

The strategy had worked before, and there was no reason to believe we couldn't do it again. We reported our progress to Vearey who, as a courtesy, may have mentioned this to Knipe and one of his senior investigators. It was also possible that Knipe and his task team had bugged our conversations with Jenneker. This meant they had a good sense of the rapport that had developed between us and a subject who continued to refuse any cooperation with them.

When Dramat and I arrived to see Jenneker the following Monday, 2 February, we found that the mood from the previous week had evaporated. He was angry and aggressive. He accused us of being duplicitous, playing the nice guys while our 'friends,' the task team investigators, worked him hard. According to him, they had assaulted him the previous Saturday, and he certainly looked like a man who had been in the wars – all battered and bruised. It turned out that some investigators had visited him that weekend and insisted he speak to them, too. It was a case of 'If you can speak to the spies, you can do the same for us.' Jenneker refused, and this apparently led to him being roughed up.

We were not at all surprised by that sort of behaviour, given the deep cultural connection between the South African police and violence. On top of that, a kind of professional jealousy towards intelligence must have played a role in the police's desperate attempt to compel Jenneker's cooperation so as not to be outdone by ourselves, a bunch of ANC intelligence types. That was the end of any cooperation we had with Jenneker. It also became clear to me that the behaviour of the investigative teams was no aberration but a pattern that boiled down to sabotaging the government's attempts to resolve the Pagad troubles using an intelligence-driven approach.

While we in the different government entities consumed ourselves with internecine conflict and sabotage, the G-Force grew in leaps and bounds, in quantity, effectiveness, and impact. Jenneker played no small part in it, having spurred on the competition to achieve a high number of killings by G-Force cells. While Jenneker and his unit were relatively discriminatory in their targeting, other cells started padding their numbers by killing not only their primary target of drug merchants or gangsters but also families or other bystanders. Our later interrogations of Abubaker Janodien taught us that the indiscriminate approach had become mainstream in G-Force circles after the middle of 1998.

Seizing control of the Pagad infrastructure gave the Qibla core an expanded base to recruit members into the G-Force. By early 1997, they had established active groups across the Cape Flats. We had identified at least twenty-one G-Force cells by the time I returned to the city from Pretoria. This rapid growth was a clear sign of the escalating danger posed by the G-Force. The units were meticulously organised, each with its own stock of weapons, and led by an *amir* who had the approval of the G-Force Security Council. If they planned an operation requiring additional material, cells could request supplies from the Council.

While most attacks involved shootings, the bombing campaign was of greater strategic importance to the G-Force. It created more publicity, spooking foreign governments and local businesses. The constant, palpable threat that the G-Force used to their advantage was the fear of being blown up while shopping or while out to dinner with the family at one of Cape Town's many restaurants. While the gang world came to fear guns, the general population was terrified of bombs. This encouraged the bomb innovation squad to improve their explosive devices and transfer their bomb-making skills to a broader range of G-Force members. They diffused the skill across the organisation and made bomb use more common.

At the apex of the G-Force structure sat the command authority, the Security Council – a body that met weekly after Jumah prayers on Fridays. When the need arose, the Council convened to address urgent matters such as the arrest of key G-Force operatives or the emergence of a unique opportunity to launch an attack. The Council had unfettered authority to authorise all kinds of attacks. The strikes were either general, such as raiding police stations for weapons, or specific, such as the killing of a particular individual. On occasion, authorisation would be issued by senior Qibla leadership from outside the Council, as was the case with the *fatwa* (formal ruling) on my and Dramat's assassination.

The Council usually met in the greater Athlone area, typically at the home of someone who was not publicly involved in Pagad activities. As we ramped up our coverage and surveillance of the G-Force, this created a sense of security amongst members of the SC. It was a false sense of security, given that we had excellent intelligence on where the SC met. At some point, we had tried to exploit this intelligence but failed dismally. G-Force cells had the leverage to operate within the broad guidelines the Council had established, and many did so. Depending on the cell leader, they often approached targeting differently, with some using more discretion in deciding who to assassinate and others less so.

Some were led by mavericks like Jenneker and engaged in operations that the Council could not even dream of until it happened for the first time. The raids on police stations carried out by Jenneker's cell, where they looted armouries for weapons and ammunition, are examples of this boldness. The

Council often deployed individuals from different cells to execute a mission that could not be entrusted to a specific cell. This was the case with Jogger (pseudonym) from the Grassy Park cell, whom they connected to Jenneker's unit to carry out a series of assassinations. They believed that his military training fitted well with Jenneker's modus operandi. This approach of mixing and matching caused significant headaches for us as it diverted from the standard attack patterns we were used to.

Compounding this dilemma was that the Council had control of cells that operated outside of their geographic boundaries. The Jenneker cell quickly outgrew their home base of Manenberg and operated all across the Cape Peninsula. Using the force of his personality and his ability to deliver exceptional results, Jenneker created an entire set of non-rules for himself and his team. The supra-geographic cells were usually bombing units, which by 1998 had shifted from targeting gangsters in the townships to bombing economic, government, religious, and diplomatic targets in the suburbs. In this sense, the G-Force constituted a matrix organisation, with the Council commanding both geographic and mobile cells, some fixed to specific modes of attack and others deploying both bombing and shooting attacks.

By 1998, the most active geographic cells were those in Manenberg, Grassy Park, Mitchells Plain, and several in Athlone. There was also a Lansdowne cell that only came to our attention at the end of July when Dramat and I were called to a bombing scene in Lansdowne. We arrived to find a twin cab van with two dead males, later identified as Faizel Hendricks and Nurulla Allie, both in their early 30s. All evidence indicated that they had blown themselves up while preparing to bomb a target close to the site of the explosion. The covert unit was first to discover that two other members of the cell had survived the explosion, been rushed away from the scene, and were surreptitiously being treated at the Gatesville Medical Centre, which was a few steps from Masjidul Quds, where Pagad held its weekly meetings.

This fortuitous discovery arrived in the form of a phone call from a contact while having my hair cut in Tokai a few days after the 30 July explosion. They simply said, 'There are two guys at the Gatesville Medical Centre who were wounded in the Lansdowne explosion. They are Anwar Francis and Yusuf Salie, although they are registered at the hospital under false names. If you move now, you'll get them before they are transferred to a different facility.' Dramat and I acted immediately but faced the dilemma of a lack of trust between ourselves and the investigators. We needed them to effect the arrests but did not want to risk sabotage similar to the type we had witnessed over the preceding two years.

Dramat called one of the Pagad task team members, Detective-Sergeant Barry Chamberlain, who we regarded as less likely to be compromised than many of his colleagues. He told Chamberlain to meet us at the Athlone police station to follow up on intelligence urgently. We provided no details on the intelligence that required their urgent action. When the investigators arrived at the police station, we asked them to follow us, drove to the Gatesville

Medical Centre, and told them the whole story upon arrival. Indeed, Chamberlain found that the two gentlemen inside the hospital presented physical signs evident of having been involved in an explosion. Francis and Salie were duly arrested. After his release on bail, Francis became a vital member of the SC and, consequently, a significant headache for us.

Francis and Yusuf Williams (who went by the alias Boeta Yu) became the primary conduits for the Council's orders to the G-Force cells. It was clear from source reporting that they commanded authority and respect amongst the entire G-Force, which they used to full effect. They became the core of what grew into a tactical leadership layer – running the day-to-day operations of the G-Force, distributing resources, and connecting individuals and cells. The greater the pressure exerted on leading figures like Ebrahim and Abader, the more the responsibilities fell on the less visible Francis and Williams. At a critical moment, the survival of the G-Force depended on the ability of this intermediate command layer to function. This seemingly insignificant but key dynamic greatly affected our targeting approach in 2000 when we launched what became the culminating operation to neutralise the G-Force.

Two interrelated strands, both common factors in insurgent or terrorist organisations, characterised the evolution of the G-Force structure between 1997 and 2000. The exigencies of survival were one factor, as members were arrested, placed under surveillance pressure, or killed. The G-Force proved to be elastic and resilient. They very comfortably changed structures, modes of operation, and priorities. They sometimes implemented an operational pause to distract and confuse the security agencies, only to activate in often unexpected ways. We see this elasticity in the shifting weight carried by different cells over time so as not to overburden any one cell.

The second factor was the imperative to increase the effect of the damage and propaganda of G-Force operations. The brutality that accompanied assassinations from 1998 onwards, including the increasingly indiscriminate nature of the attacks, certainly had a considerable shock effect. The focus on State and international interests was intended to achieve the same effect. The murder of Lategan and the failed attempt to assassinate Visagie were part of a shift that represented the culmination of its targeting evolution and took Qibla's anti-state project to its logical conclusion.

By 1999, Pagad relinquished all efforts to portray itself as a community organisation, and its rhetoric mirrored its operational initiatives – targeting the State, its supposed Western allies, and Cape Town's Jewish community. The murder of magistrate Piet Theron, the bombing of the Pagad task team office in Bellville, and the attempts to kill myself and Dramat were only some manifestations of this decisive turn. At the political level, Qibla established a new front, Muslims Against Global Oppression (MAGO), to provide political cover and mobilise against Western and Jewish targets. MAGO members all doubled as Pagad members, and some had very intimate links with members of the G-Force, especially the Qibla-linked bombing core.

Moeyn Achmat, a tradesman by day and revolutionary by night, was the leader of MAGO. Achmat loved the limelight provided by his leading role and led protest marches against the USA and Israel. Since the link between MAGO and Qibla was as clear as daylight and diminished the public support they could attract, the issues around which MAGO organised failed to find traction with Capetonians, including the Muslim community. Members obtained explosives from G-Force connections and attempted a few independent attacks. Still, these came to nought, as we managed to frustrate or sabotage all their efforts at building an independent offensive capability. Our success on this front can partly be ascribed to the fact that MAGO members did not possess the drive and singular dedication of G-Force members to carry out terror attacks.

A big concern around MAGO was the high level of foreign intelligence interest in the organisation, especially from the Israeli Mossad. We became aware of several Israeli efforts to infiltrate characters with appealing profiles into MAGO and killed off all of these initiatives before they could take root. The last thing we wanted was the Israelis running around interfering and complicating an already dangerous situation in our backyard. Like ourselves, they must have seen MAGO as an easier target to gain access to the G-Force. They probably sensed that we were onto them and reduced their interference to regular formal requests for information after a while. These appeals most often represented fishing expeditions intended to determine our capabilities more than they sought to gain intelligence on the MAGO target.

At some point, Dramat decided we had had enough of their requests and asked Petros to direct all requests to the Loop Street office.

Of course, the G-Force didn't have a smooth ride as it expanded and became more emboldened. After the Staggie lynching, the police threw an inordinate amount of resources at the organisation. This included the extensive deployment of public order policing units from Cape Town and further afield and support from the army. The idea behind these operations was to place so much pressure on Pagad members that they would basically give up on trying to do anything violent and illegal.

Visible policing units parked outside the houses of G-Force leaders like Ebrahim and followed him everywhere he moved. These efforts were supported by surveillance from various Crime Intelligence units and always created a temporary yet deceptive lull. While the cops celebrated their achievements, the G-Force simply practised patience and outwaited the police. At a place and time of their choosing, they would activate cells that had zero or minimal surveillance pressure, diverting police resources away from some of the key figures. This cycle played itself out over and over again. If the definition of insanity is doing the same thing over and over while expecting different results, South Africa had a police service that had collectively been driven mad by the G-Force.

The most significant investment into policing Pagad was focused on the numerous investigative task teams. These teams, led by Knipe and then Visagie, were dedicated to accumulating and investigating case dockets linked to attacks orchestrated by the organisation. Despite the challenges, they achieved limited success, arresting G-Force members and, if lucky, detaining them without bail, effectively removing them from circulation for some time. Given the sizable pool from which the G-Force recruited, the arrests made by the task teams presented only a minor obstacle. The G-Force easily and rapidly replenished losses in manpower, demonstrating their resilience. It was also rare for G-Force members to be sufficiently deterred by arrest. Once released, most of them seamlessly resumed their operational roles.

We can attribute the failure of the investigative task team to three factors. The first was the quality of the investigators on the job. They, almost without fail, complained about the unfair advantage the democratic constitution provided to Pagad members, whether while under suspicion, when arrested, or after being charged. The fact that suspects had immediate access to their attorneys and could access medical services to ensure they were not assaulted presented a serious obstacle in the minds of many investigators.

The majority of investigators on the task teams came from a culture so heavily weighted in favour of the police that this handicapped their investigative and interrogation toolkit. The democratic constitution inhibited the worst instincts of police investigators and demanded that they act professionally and according to the letter of the constitution. Yet, two or three years into the life of a democratic South Africa and after the demilitarisation of the police, the investigative units had not yet developed a sufficiently critical mass of skilled staff who could operate in a rights-based environment. The culture of *skop, skiet en donder* (kick, shoot and f-up) was still deeply ingrained in the investigative units, and they could not break free from it to confront the Pagad threat.

From the word go, investigations failed because of the nearly complete disconnect and often open conflict between investigators and intelligence. Since the G-Force operated as a covert structure that applied the rules of secrecy, any significant break in this security bubble could result from sustained secret work, security lapses on the part of the G-Force, or pure luck. Luck was, however, in short supply when going up against the G-Force, and the investigators required solid intelligence. In effect, the paradoxical reality of requiring intelligence for investigative success and simultaneously sabotaging intelligence operations resulted in investigative self-sabotage.

The absence of a broad strategy to deal with Pagad was the most significant factor that caused the failure of the task teams and public policing operations. This absence of strategy, initially a result of political decisions, underscored the urgent need for a comprehensive plan. After 1997, the executive was prepared to commit whatever resources were needed to counter Pagad's terror campaign, highlighting the importance of strategy. The security community did not develop strategy and commensurate operational responses until 1998 when the police covert intelligence unit in the

Western Cape stepped into a role well outside of and beyond its mandate.

Petros, Dramat, and I engaged in strategic-level discussions on defeating Pagad with political decision-makers, senior police, and intelligence leadership. In Fraser, we had a reliable ally with the right connections to build inter-agency cohesion and strategic synergy. However, our efforts were constrained by the operational environment in which the covert unit functioned. The covert unit, a part of the provincial CI structure, was tasked with gathering intelligence on criminal activities, including those of Pagad. Unfortunately, it operated in a dysfunctional provincial Crime Intelligence under Du Plessis and, subsequently, Trollip.

At the end of the Millennium, Pagad was ascendant. Their clear strategic focus was on attacking the State and bolstering its support amongst the Muslim population by attacking Western targets. The State, on the other hand, was treading water, and its response was characterised by infighting within the police, the absence of strategic purpose, and a massive failure to keep police management accountable for their multiple failures. The small team around Petros realised early on that we would have to shoulder the more significant part of the burden of digging ourselves out of a hole that was not of our own making. This 'hole' was a complex web of operational, strategic, and leadership challenges that had accumulated over the years.

Together with our close allies in the NIA, we aggressively set to work in close partnership to achieve this. Between the covert unit and Fraser's NIA team, we decided to operate with no daylight between us, fully aligned and mutually reinforcing.

CHAPTER 4

Building Under Fire: The Construction of a Covert Capability

Secret methods are based on common sense and experience. But they must be mastered like an art.
— 'How to Master Secret Work,' SACP pamphlet

The failure of the two Pagad Task Teams by mid-1997 created new opportunities and challenges for Crime Intelligence. For the first time since the death of Staggie, SAPS management acknowledged they floundered in their approach to counter the G-Force threat. Their standard principle was to merge the intelligence and investigation capacities of the SAPS under a unified command, usually led by a detective.

This strategy was based on a simplistic interpretation of the often-repeated call for integrating intelligence, investigation, and prosecution functions to combat Pagad's urban terror campaign. In the process, intelligence work was reduced to a support function for investigations and prosecution. It also reflected the balance of power between detectives and intelligence in the new police service. Intelligence operatives had lost their sense of purpose and pride in their trade due to their experience in the task teams. This model, or rather its crude application, constrained our ability to exercise the creative options that give an intelligence service purpose and make it successful. It also narrowed the range of interventions we could craft, propose to decision-makers, or even deploy ourselves. The task team model, as implemented by the police, was an entirely logical choice for a police service that was still steeped in the old ways of working.

The model was based on the presumption that a problem could simply be solved with the arrest of the key instigators. Even though the strategy had failed on a grand scale in the old police's struggle against the ANC, the law enforcement agency was trapped in this paradigm and could not conceive of other ways to manage terrorism. The idea of a multi-pronged assault on Pagad came more naturally to those of us who had roots in the ANC and were indoctrinated in Strategy and Tactics – the liberation movement's integration of political, military, domestic, and international sites of struggle to achieve our objectives. The question looming then was whether we could apply the lessons learned in the political struggle to our work in state intelligence. The police's admission of failure of the task team concept opened the door to that possibility, and I hoped we would find the appropriate institutional vehicle to make this happen. My view at the time was that this moment presented an opportunity for the intelligence community to step into the leading role that had been left open by the serial failures of the task teams. But first we needed to get our own house in order.

Some significant changes occurred in the Crime Intelligence command structure in the province shortly before the Pagad task team disbanded. Under pressure from the SAPS Head Office, the provincial management had to give some indication that they were moving towards a transformed and more racially representative structure. White former branch officers had dominated the provincial Intelligence structure until that point. In a thinly veiled attempt to conceal their racism, they appointed a few Black officers as commanders of smaller, less significant units. Many of these officers were long-standing members of the old Security Branch with whom the racists felt comfortable because they were less likely than their controversial ANC counterparts to 'rock the boat.' The prevailing situation and pressure from former DIS staff forced Du Plessis to appoint some ANC members to crucial positions.

Petros was appointed commander of the Crime Intelligence covert unit as part of this process. Petros had until then been languishing at the backwater desk dealing with so-called left-wing extremism. We developed a relationship while I was at head office, and during our conversations, he often voiced his concerns about being marginalised by his provincial boss. He was an ambitious officer and did not see himself remaining stuck in the minor post in Du Plessis's office. The covert unit allowed him to escape from under his overseer's thumb and create his own legacy.

The covert unit Petros inherited was diminished and sterile compared to its former self. It is this empty shell that Du Plessis and company were prepared to hand to Petros, with the full expectation that its degeneration into irrelevance would soon see it wither away. Petros was handed a poisoned chalice, and as we discovered not too long after, his superiors acted decisively to bring about its demise. The police Intelligence covert units date back to the 1980s when they constituted the elite of the Branch. These units consisted of the best intelligence collectors and strategic communications operatives. They were entrusted with ultra-sensitive investigations and the handling of strategically placed sources inside the liberation movement.

Due to their high-level access to target structures, the covert units fulfilled functions beyond mere intelligence gathering. These included carrying out calculated communication and influencing operations. The operations entailed using highly placed sources to influence the decision-making and direction of organisations, discredit liberation movement leaders, and trigger internal conflict within those movements. One such example is the infiltration of agents into Winnie Mandela's close circle and the subsequent establishment of the Mandela Football Club. In this case, a Branch informer, Jerry Richardson, became Winnie Mandela's bodyguard and killed a teenage boy who was part of the 'football club.' This murder created an extraordinary amount of internal conflict within the mass democratic movement and between the ANC and its internal political structures.

The scheme also involved establishing alternative structures meant to contest the political hegemony of the liberation movement amongst the Black communities. Infiltrating and handling deep-cover agents as part of the Republican Spy (RS) programme was another function of these units. RS agents were members of the Security Branch whose association with the institution was kept secret, even from fellow branch members. They operated under deep cover, and their assignments typically spanned over several years. Some RS agents were deployed in ANC political and military structures abroad, while others were stationed inside South Africa to infiltrate the mass democratic and trade union movements.

The majority of RS agents who had their cover blown were young white South Africans who had initially infiltrated into progressive white student organisations such as the National Union of South African Students (NUSAS). Having developed credibility within the student movement, the Branch's idea was that they come into contact with the ANC underground and make themselves available for recruitment into its structures. The RS programme was shut down in the early 1990s due to changes in the political atmosphere. After the demise of the post-apartheid regime, many RS agents took up operational staff roles in covert units.

Members of covert units were expected to be particularly adept at intelligence tradecraft. The most talented information gatherers are recruited from overt operational centres such as the one in Loop Street, whilst others are directly taken on from outside Crime Intelligence into the covert units. The latter, so-called 'clean skins,' often operated similarly to deep cover agents or handled sources under false flags. The Branch covert structures and, subsequently, the Crime Intelligence units operated as shallow cover entities without the extensive backstopping that accompanies classical covert teams. Many of its members were known as police officers by at least a handful of people, even if they were recruited when they had just completed their police constable training. This arrangement often applied to Black members such as Martin.

The cover structures fell apart at minimal scrutiny, even during the Apartheid era. One example is the operational front used by Lieutenant Olivia Forsyth (agent RS407), who was captured by ANC intelligence in 1986. Forsyth approached the ANC as a researcher for a Johannesburg-based company engaged in social research in Southern Africa, John Fitzgerald and Associates. Once the ANC developed suspicions about her authenticity and investigated the company, its wafer-thin veneer exposed it as a Branch front organisation.

On the other hand, the Branch's friends in the NIS were more adept at establishing and managing front organisations. In Cape Town, they ran a hugely successful research institute, the Foundation for Contemporary Research (FCR). It attracted authentic international donor funding, employed many senior leaders within the UDF, ANC, and SACP, and survived for several years after the 1994 transition. Many were shocked when they discovered in the late 1990s that the organisation was a front for the NIS. The challenge of operating proper covert intelligence structures is not unique to South Africa. Even the most prominent intelligence agencies are confronted by this dilemma, and only a few have managed to sustainably surmount this problem.

The Soviet intelligence organisations have historically invested significant effort and resources into deep-cover capabilities, establishing Directorate S in the KGB's First Chief Directorate. This directorate was responsible for the famous 'illegals' programme, where KGB officers trained to live and behave like Westerners and were deployed in first-world countries under fictitious identities and established long-term capabilities. The programme continued under KGB's successor organisation in foreign intelligence, the Russian. It burst into the open in June 2010 with the arrest of ten SVR illegals in the United States of America.

Western intelligence services have also used private companies and research institutes as cover institutions. One of the more well-known cases is the 2003 exposure of Valerie Plame by Bush administration officials. She was a Central Intelligence Agency (CIA) official working in deep cover for the front company Brewster Jennings & Associates.

Establishing, managing, and deploying covert intelligence capabilities requires complex infrastructure, and organisational and financial arrangements that are not easily integrated into an enormous state bureaucracy. By its very nature, it is a significantly more expensive form of intelligence structure, as every additional layer of cover adds cost to the institution's budget. Training for the front entities must occur at facilities not associated with the government, and funding for payments to agents and sources should be laundered so that its origin is not easily traceable. Internally, officers working in deep cover are often overlooked for promotion as they lack the networking opportunities that their overt colleagues usually have, where they display and claim the results of their efforts and meet decision-makers outside of intelligence that could influence decisions made by their bosses.

In addition to these generic challenges of secret service structures, Petros faced some unique challenges as he attempted to pivot his covert unit from a peripheral entity to a productive and central intelligence capability. His first order of business was to recruit staff he could rely on, meaning he would have to at least get some DIS officers into the unit. He also needed to resource the unit, enabling it to take on the significant challenges facing the province at the time – particularly in the areas of transport-related violence and Pagad's urban terrorism.

His success depended on being able to select his own team and whether he could make connections beyond the province. Petros's first recruitment had a transformative effect on the unit both during and after his time as its head. Anwa Dramat joined the covert unit from the taxi violence investigation team under the Serious and Violent Crimes unit that Leonard Knipe headed. Dramat had worked with another DIS officer, Yasser Splinters, an old comrade from my days as a student and Communist Party activist in Manenberg.

Dramat was a quiet backroom operator with an exceptional sense of what we call 'operasionele vernuf' in Afrikaans – something akin to operational savvy, but perhaps more aptly, a nose for operational work. He also had a level of perseverance that kept us all in good stead over the next few years. Unlike myself, a complete technology ignoramus, he had a good appreciation of technical matters, an area we were sorely lacking at the time. In addition, Petros brought in my former partner, Martin, and a female operative of substantive skill and initiative, Amber.

Hailing from Cape Town, Amber joined the Branch in the early 1990s and worked in a surveillance unit in the country's far north. She later moved back to Cape Town, where she was deployed at the CI covert unit, then managed by Brookbanks. Amber slotted in well with us ANC newcomers to the police, likely because she had many school friends active in our political circles during the 1980s. Amber was a creative par excellence, and the acting training she received on the side proved highly profitable for our work. Where many officers would think of the most direct route to pitching recruitment to a potential source, she often designed more circuitous approaches that almost always resulted in success.

My integration into the covert unit was a completely unexpected development. At very short notice, I was shifted to the Crime Intelligence head office to help build up the extremism analysis desk at the end of 1996. However, due to the increased threat posed by Pagad and the limited CI operational capability in the Western Cape, I was rapidly deployed back to Cape Town in October of the following year. The entire process of deciding and implementing my move back to Cape Town took no more than seven hours. I switched on my mobile phone one Monday morning, having just returned to Johannesburg from a weekend visit to my family in the Cape. I found a series of missed calls and messages instructing me to head straight to a meeting with Tim Williams, the head of Crime Intelligence. Williams had taken over from Nceba Radu, who had died an untimely death only a few months after I started in the role for which he had recruited me.

Before joining the police, Williams was an ANC commander in Botswana, where South African special forces had failed in an attempt to assassinate him in 1985. Aiming to establish an approach to Pagad that could circumvent the odious and stale provincial police management, I wrote several analyses and operational proposals to Williams covering the Pagad crisis in Cape Town. The fruits of initial discussions around those documents came later when Petros, Dramat, and I were at the covert unit. He started by half apologising when I reported to his office, noting that I had just settled into life in Johannesburg and that my family may also be getting used to the place. He had no idea that my wife, having become fed up with life in Johannesburg, had left for Cape Town, and I was living on my own, hence the frequent weekend trips to Cape Town.

Williams said he needed me to move back to Cape Town to support the operational work against Pagad on the ground. He had already spoken to Vearey, at whose office I would initially be based. The plan was to integrate me into the covert unit, now commanded by Petros, as soon as administratively possible. When I asked when I was expected to move, he told me I should go immediately. 'Just pack a few suitcases, and we'll return your household goods to Cape Town later.' He had a driver waiting to drive me home to collect my bags and take me to an airport in Pretoria, where I'd be flown to Cape Town in the police commissioner's jet. Having just landed in Johannesburg at 8 a.m., I was back on home soil before 2 p.m. the same afternoon. The following day, I reported to Vearey and picked up where I left off at the end of 1996, building human intelligence capability.

Most of my work involved reactivating and expanding my source network. Still, the coordination responsibility Vearey gave me was serving as the CI representative on the interdepartmental intelligence working group on Pagad. I thoroughly enjoyed working with colleagues from Military Intelligence and the NIA in joint analytic production. I benefited from having previously served as the CI headquarters representative on the national interagency working group on extremism. This working group crafted the first national threat assessment of Qibla and Pagad in 1997, and presented it to the cabinet for approval.

While the working group had an analysis mandate, building relationships amongst analysts from different organisations helped strengthen the bonds between our organisations. This cooperation would also be reflected in our operational work within a short time. Human intelligence was the mainstay of my professional life, and in this endeavour, I started working closely with Dramat. We spent the next three years joined at the hip, devising plans, recruiting sources and agents, activating a political project to undermine Pagad's legitimacy, and building a potent intelligence team from scratch.

Dramat and I recruited two more members to build the team's size and capability to match the task we had set ourselves. Danie and Scubadiver were polar opposites, the one an Afrikaner former Branch officer and the other an adrenaline-fuelled character who had spent most of his policing career in the flying squad. Our task was to build a cohesive team from this mixture of relative youth, middle-aged men, and a solitary but exceptional woman, led by a former ANC underground operative.

To ensure operational security, we had to operate more independently and become self-sufficient, and we could not always call on the usual support functions within CI to assist us on particular missions. Even when compelled to request assistance, we were scrupulous about whose assistance we chose, and we strictly applied the need-to-know principle. Although gospel within the intelligence world, this principle was often ignored in the chaos we knew as Western Cape Crime Intelligence.

Senior police commanders, even those uninvolved with intelligence matters, insisted on being informed about every matter, all in the name of openness and accountability. Witnessing the appearance of so many transparency advocates from amongst the circles of the old Branch and detective service was comically heartwarming. Our view from inside the covert unit was that this obsession with continuous reporting was an attempt to control what we were doing while extracting enough information to show that CI was producing something on the Pagad front. The functioning of covert intelligence was generally frowned upon within the CI structures in the Western Cape. Neither Du Plessis nor Trollip supported us, yet they insisted on a continuous stream of reporting. Rare was an occasion where we received feedback on the reports they extracted from us or any guidance on how to proceed.

Both Du Plessis and Trollip went to extreme lengths to undermine the covert nature of the unit. They did this by compelling covert staff to participate in broader police meetings while we tried to create a buffer between the unit and other police capabilities. Petros tried his best to act as our liaison with the outside world, but they often overruled his attempts to shield the covert staff from undue exposure. We had to fight off Trollip's perennial attempts to visit our clandestine facility. In Du Plessis' case, one had the distinct feeling that his attitude toward the covert unit was less malicious and more a result of his poor appreciation of its value. In the end, the effect was the same.

Once appointed commander of the covert unit, Petros faced an aggressive effort to undermine his authority and clip his operational wings. The provincial detective and intelligence management initiated discussions around the closure of the covert unit immediately after he was appointed. The chief architect of this plan was Willem Smit, head of the crime investigation service in the Western Cape, under which Crime Intelligence resided before becoming an independent division. Smit was a notorious security policeman during the 1980s but had become an anti-intelligence proponent as the head of the crime investigation service. The entire crime investigation service management, except Du Plessis, supported Smit's effort to close the covert unit. Given the composition of that management, we were not surprised by this blatant effort to kill off a critical intelligence capability.

We were also not going to take it lying down. To us, the whole effort smelled of old cops (including some old Branch officers) denying the state an intelligence capability it sorely needed. The urgency of their effort was, in no small measure, amplified by the fact that we now had a Black officer heading the covert unit. During meetings with unit members, Du Plessis promised us a fight to the end to ensure the unit survived. We subsequently learned of the rather half-heartedness and ineffectuality of his resistance. Smit and company formally resolved to close the covert unit and transfer its members to other Crime Intelligence units. In the hope of buying his support, they offered Petros a post as Undercover Operations Coordinator. This meant that whenever an undercover operation was required, he could assemble a team, carry out the operation, and then close down shop, twiddling his thumbs until the next operation.

The idea of undercover operations, distinct from sustained covert capabilities, became a popular operational concept in the mid-1990s. This type of operation was typical amongst the specialised detective units, which often had short-term projects and limited target sets. It was a prosecution-driven approach that typically used superficial cover to deploy police officers as agents in organised crime groups. It brings to mind the popular idea of an undercover cop in American films instead of a long-term infiltration and cover approach that we sought to develop.

Our operational concept, which took time to develop, was premised on our judgment that Pagad presented a more complex and expansive threat that required the integration of prosecution, information warfare, internal destabilisation, and political effort. It was not the kind of threat amenable to the short-term undercover operation methodology. Instead, it required meticulous and prolonged infiltration of sources and agents, building and deploying a sophisticated technical capability, and constructing a mobile covert team to respond immediately to rapidly evolving situations and unexpected events.

As its basis, this required a deep understanding of the threat we were dealing with. Such an understanding enabled us to aim toward a culminating point where all these skills and capabilities could be brought to bear to devastating effect. We were not interested in only arresting this or that member of Pagad's G-Force but liquidating its ability to continue functioning as a paramilitary organisation. The reasons offered for the unit's closure ranged from its limited utility to arguing that the closure of covert units was a worldwide trend. We put up a spirited fight to maintain the unit, challenging the motives of those who demanded its closure. The pro-closure lobby argued that the covert unit had, in the preceding two years, proven itself as a relatively useless capacity.

Closure was never even contemplated in all the time that white officers had controlled it. Did Smit and his troupe have things to hide? I still do not know, but it is clear that their motives were less than pure and, at a minimum, that they constituted an attempt to sabotage control of such an essential intelligence capacity run by patriotic Black officers. Despite the formality and supposed finality of the decision to close down the covert unit, we simply decided we wouldn't abide by this decision. In our campaign to ensure the continued existence of the covert unit, we developed a multi-faceted approach.

Our first tactic was to ignore the decision and continue functioning more or less without a budget. Petros found a cost-free apartment where we operated for a few months while we activated the second, most important element of our campaign: securing decision-makers' support at a national level. On this front, we discussed the matter with Williams, who was stunned that such an idea could even be considered and agreed to challenge the decision of the Western Cape police management. Williams was aware that he would require covert capacity, which he could turn to when requiring speedy results in an investigation or when dealing with politically sensitive matters. He had no faith in the ability of the old guard to deliver the intelligence he needed, and a covert unit managed by Petros was his best bet at achieving this.

Williams made his displeasure at the decision very clear and committed to retaining and further developing the covert capacity, especially since its senior staff were former ANC operatives. He instructed us to submit a proposal for our resource requirements including draft lease agreements for covert facilities, and other operational expenses for the next two years.

We submitted the required documentation to Williams via his deputy Els, who appreciated the innovative operational effort, was supportive, and viewed the decision to close the unit as interference in his mandate. As the national head of CI's gathering capability, Els was responsible for the management of all police covert units. We moved into new premises within a few weeks, ready to operate and take on the challenges ahead. The old guard around Smit was caught entirely off guard by the head office instructions authorising the continued existence of the covert unit. For us, it was a victory and an expression of trust from Williams that we intended to pay back with actual results. The task of transforming the covert unit from the personal fiefdom of its commander to a unit of extraordinary achievement would fall on its senior members, all former ANC operatives.

Our first mission was to develop a clear and comprehensive picture of our adversary. Up to that point, intelligence had responded to the terror threat in a reactive manner, with intelligence operatives often tasked to gather intelligence on attacks that had already been carried out instead of engaging in serious sense-making. No serious attempt had been made to comprehensively understand the extremist threat in the province. We decided to produce a threat analysis based on the input of our covert collectors in the field.

A valuable source of information we tapped was our connection with the Muslim community, particularly amongst progressive academics and clergy. We needed to ensure that the entire covert team had an in-depth understanding of Pagad and the broader extremist threat. We started by collating the existing information on the topic from within the intelligence structures of the SAPS. We searched through covert source reports, surveillance notes, and technical intercepts. I was responsible for compiling a threat dossier of the entire extremist spectrum in the Western Cape and its relational links to the rest of the country. This included structures directly involved in carrying out attacks, support structures, ideological forums where extremist ideas were promoted, and even charitable institutions under the control of Qibla militants.

The dossier, the length of a book manuscript, outlined the history of extremism in the province, its modus operandi, organisational expression, and the interactions between the various formations within the extremist fold. It also identified the critical role players in all the structures. Our analysis indicated extensive overlapping of membership and even leadership between the various formations. Despite this, we concluded that the interaction between the different organisations on the extremist spectrum was dynamic and sometimes even conflicting. Personalities played a significant role in the conflicts that became a prominent feature of their interaction.

Given our limited personnel and resources, we had to identify specific key organisational targets. It had to be a node or multiple nodes in the broader

Pagad structure whose elimination or strategic paralysis acted as the lynchpin to defeat urban terror in the province. We were careful not to make fatal mistakes that were common to intelligence failures. In the intelligence trade, it seems standard to investigate structures you know most about or those prevalent in the media. For those of us who wanted to create an impact with strategic and sustained effect, as opposed to the quick grabbing of headlines that faded away after a few weeks or months, this became a concern in the increasingly politicised context of a rampant Pagad terror campaign.

We needed to target the political and paramilitary elements of Pagad's strategy and capability to achieve a sustainable effect. Denuding the organisation of its paramilitary G-Force without a simultaneous and concomitant political and ideological assault would, at best, buy us a year of breathing space. Without delegitimising Pagad's anti-state politics, we were ceding narrative space to them, embedding the political support they still enjoyed, and allowing them to re-calibrate their paramilitary campaign and structures a short way down the line. One of Pagad's defining characteristics, as seen with the visible policing interventions, Operations Good Hope and Saladin, was its ability to wait things out. Police fatigue and Pagad's operational patience meant they retained the ability to appeal to and recruit new members, enabling the inevitable comeback.

Regarding the G-Force, we had to develop an access plan to develop intelligence on their strategy, constantly evolving modus operandi, targeting process, command structure, and geographic dispersion of their cells. Alongside this, we needed to develop a capability that could inform on individuals who showed innovation and boldness within the G-Force. Some, like Jenneker, were active in shooting attacks. He was bold and fanatical in eradicating his enemies, which was quite chilling yet highly effective. How he spoke about murdering gang leaders and anyone who threatened him, in a very calm demeanour, was evidence of that potent combination of extremism, high-risk ruthlessness, and an ability to inspire the same among his subordinates. The same applied to individuals we identified as the bomb innovators, almost all with close links to Qibla, some of those ties going back to the 1980s.

The need to identify and subsequently neutralise the imaginative and daring category of individuals arose from the outsized effect of their activities on Pagad's operational tempo. Their actions set forth an informal competition amongst the cells, where they tried to outdo each other in the number of victims they killed. This was one of the key reasons why murders became more indiscriminate around 1998.

The case of the bomb innovators was both perplexing but also a fascinating challenge for us. They were the individuals who first introduced explosive devices into the Pagad arsenal, starting with the rudimentary pipe bombs detonated by a striker firecracker. They were responsible for obtaining hand grenades from a government arms facility and, over time, introducing several different trigger mechanisms to their bombs. They moved from strikers to various timing devices and, ultimately, cellphone-activated explosives. Their experiments were intended to create distance between themselves and the bombs at the point of detonation, and they managed to inflict a more significant number of casualties. In terms of the bombs themselves, our one saving grace, simply by the stroke of luck, was that even though they graduated from the gunpowder-only devices and introduced ammonium nitrate into their bombs, they never entirely managed to get the formula right, which significantly reduced the lethality of their devices.

Explosives had a more profound psychological and political effect, even though many more people were killed in G-Force shooting attacks than during bombings, which might explain why the individuals involved in the bombing campaign were more ideologically aligned with Qibla. The fact that bomb attacks expressly earmarked political targets over time is also reflective of the character of this grouping. The bomb innovators started amongst a small group of old Qibla cadres, many of whom had operated as comrades-in-arms since the mid-1980s. By 1998, the bomb innovators had more or less fully constituted their team, and they would not easily let in any further outsiders. Their ideological training, commitment, and high level of security distinguished this group from general G-Force members.

In 1996, Abrahams and his Qibla comrades recruited a novice from Heideveld township on the Cape Flats into the bomb innovator's circle. They struck gold, as they found he was an ideologically committed, sharp-thinking, and wily character who operated under the radar but could not escape the increasingly extensive network the covert unit had begun establishing. He appeared everywhere the covert unit looked, but always fleetingly and never long enough to pin him down. Dramat and I missed him by seconds during an operation in 1998 while he was transporting explosives they would use in an operation. After an extensive and long-running surveillance operation, our paths crossed again, and we found him in a personally compromising situation. Whereas this would often be sufficient to sway someone to become more cooperative, our Heideveld man was made of much sterner stuff. He scoffed at our approach, went on his way, and remained a free agent, bombing his way across Cape Town.

The bomb innovators presented a much harder nut to crack than the shooting cells, which were typically composed of a mix of reformed gangsters, recovering drug addicts, and former neighbourhood watch members. However, the rupture in their armour came through two operatives who straddled the bombing-shooting division of labour, creating a security breach that allowed us access to their plotting. Dramat and I spent our days thinking through approaches to crack the Pagad nut. I had always believed in approaching planning like I have writing: think, think, and think again, clarify thoughts, explore options, and only then start writing down plans. Too often, intelligence officers felt compelled and were sometimes pressured to get plans down on paper prematurely.

We spent time in our office planning, sketching the G-Force's changing structure and personnel, our access and support network, and the likelihood that any particular approach might succeed or fail. We thought and exchanged ideas when travelling to meet colleagues, sources, or political figures. The time we spent eating meals together was, more often than not, consumed with thinking and strategising. Every day brought new insights and new ideas. I also spent much time with my team members, Martin and Amber, exploring the same issues. In the end, we decided to investigate the terror attacks as a criminal conspiracy, thereby targeting those giving instructions and providing training as well as resources, instead of merely arresting the ordinary foot soldiers carrying out attacks. I started the initial discussions on more systematically attacking Pagad when I worked at the CI head office and had to write a paper on the subject for the Minister of Safety and Security.

We wrestled with two interrelated issues – one relating to prosecuting people not directly engaging in violence and the other with the classical dilemma of gathering evidence instead of intelligence. The first dilemma arose from the need to neutralise the G-Force infrastructure at all levels. The second related to the problem with recruiting witnesses who could be deployed proactively into Pagad to gather evidence that could be presented in court during a prosecution. We thought that an investigation under charges of sedition enabled us to entangle a broad range of conspirators, from bombers to members of the command structure and even those providing political guidance to the organisation's terror infrastructure. There was no shortage of irony in the fact that the Branch's Willie Els and the ANC's David Africa were now jointly looking at how to use a piece of Apartheid-era sedition legislation to address the first sustained terrorist campaign against the ANC government.

Ultimately, we did not have the means to gather the evidence for that kind of prosecution. It was an unfortunate case of our aim by far exceeding our means. This misalignment had to be solved by discreetly building a combination of evidentiary and intelligence capabilities.

Three years later, Els worked from the covert unit when that potential, which had, in the meantime, ripened, was about to mature and deliver the fruits we could only dream of back at head office. Those head-office conversations and the Pagad brief we compiled for the then minister of Safety and Security, Mufamadi planted the seed of an approach that integrated intelligence and evidence-gathering. This approach also sought to prosecute a collection of conspirators. It had built mutual respect between Els and me, which served us well when the covert unit launched its audacious assault on Pagad. Once Petros was firmly embedded in his position, Dramat and I got things going on the operational front. Together with the initial members of our covert Pagad team, we set to expand our collection footprint, building on a small but already trusted source base. We were nowhere near where we wanted to be but had the best platform to launch our effort.

The reasons for this limitation in our source capability were manifold, and some have been explored already. The one major obstacle impacting our ability to recruit and deploy suitable sources was the paranoia and naivety around sources becoming involved in violence, an almost guaranteed outcome for anyone engaged in G-Force activity. The Crime Intelligence management in the province was terrified of the consequences of such an eventuality and put paid to any efforts to recruit the kind of sources that could become entangled in violent actions. This disqualified nearly every valuable source we could recruit inside the G-Force.

Even if we attempted infiltration into the G-Force from outside by a 'clean skin,' he would be expected to prove his commitment to the organisation and his loyalty to his brethren by directly engaging in violence by planting a bomb or shooting someone. The controversial hand grenade saga was still fresh in everyone's mind, and although the Director of Public Prosecutions (DPP) withdrew all charges. A marker was laid down and was clearly intended to intimidate and whip CI into line when recruiting high-risk sources. It had the additional and intentional effect that once our sources found themselves trapped in that dilemma, they became vulnerable to being pressured to testify as state witnesses, thereby losing the anonymity we guaranteed them upon recruitment.

It was a roundabout way of clipping our wings and simultaneously transforming sources into witnesses. We would not play this game, but Du Plessis was a different kettle of fish. The Johnson saga affected his confidence and shaped how he wanted us to treat the decision-making around such sources. Despite his best efforts, we decided to find ways to circumvent these self-imposed limitations, and so we did.

In 1997, the DPP issued guidelines for entrapment operations carried out by the police, including its intelligence structures. The guidelines were meant to interpret Section 252(A) of the Criminal Procedure Act and provide operational clarity to investigative and intelligence units. In legal terms, it dealt with the admissibility of evidence obtained through entrapment or undercover operations. These guidelines profoundly affected intelligence work, specifically our ability to infiltrate and neutralise terror cells. In essence, it denied an intelligence officer the opportunity to recruit a member of a terror group if such a person could become engaged in any form of criminality. What made matters worse was that the CI management interpreted the guidelines so broadly that almost any recruitment became problematic.

One of our key sources, a member of a G-Force cell involved in carrying out bombings, had his services terminated due to becoming increasingly involved in the activities of the cell. This happened at a time when Cape Town experienced a spate of bombings. Du Plessis was insistent that we could not allow this source to work for us, and with the stroke of a pen, we lost valuable direct access to one of the most active G-Force cells. Of course, this did not stop the cell from carrying out attacks. On the contrary, this would be the very cell later tasked with killing Dramat and myself. In general, both the DPP and provincial CI management displayed an acute lack of understanding of the modus operandi of the G-Force. They failed to appreciate that, to gain credibility, cell members had to participate in criminal activity at some stage and that sources would not always have prior warning leading up to an attack into which they were drawn.

It had happened at times that two or three cell members planned an attack and then made their way to the home of an unwitting cell member, picked him up, and proceeded to carry out the attack. The last member to join the operation would be briefed on the plans and their specific role on the way to the target location. Despite this, the DPP still insisted on a prior written application before he authorised a source's involvement in criminal activity. Even then, any participation in a violent offence was out of bounds.

The one exception to this attitude was Percy Sonn, who had a history as an anti-apartheid lawyer and was a close associate of then Minister of Justice Dullah Omar. He had a low tolerance for the Apartheid-era prosecutors still making the rules in the prosecution service and always tried to find ways to make things happen operationally, as opposed to the default of preventing them from happening. He later rose to the position of head of the Investigating Directorate on Organised Crime (IDOC) and its successor organisation, the Directorate of Special Operations, commonly known as the Scorpions. Dramat and I went to see Sonn to seek guidance on managing the challenge of building an intelligence network in the face of the recently issued Section 252 (A) guidelines. He advised us not to hold back and deal with the challenges as they presented themselves. He also informed us that he would be taking over the IDOC and that our intelligence work fell squarely within his area of authority at IDOC. We would work things out between ourselves, and he had no intention of blunting our efforts.

Sonn remained true to his word, and when the need arose to call on his support with sources who were expected to or had already engaged in criminal activity, he assessed each case on its merits. He then authorised operations if the intelligence or prosecutorial return was sufficient. But Sonn was not yet the IDOC Director, and even after his appointment, our colleagues in Crime Intelligence and the detective service were too conservative in how they wanted us to deal with high-risk sources. Our view was that we could not paralyse ourselves pre-emptively in anticipation of a source's involvement in terrorist attacks. The restrictions imposed by the DPP guidelines became an excuse for inaction and incompetence by those who had taken on the task of combating Pagad half-heartedly. We refused to walk this path, hiding behind what we regarded as an ill-considered approach to the management of sources.

No target structures and individuals were out of bounds for us. This was our motto and proved to be our recipe for success. It was also the basis for a stormy relationship between ourselves, the DPP, and his deputies, who were responsible for implementing the guidelines. Since we were recruiting covert sources and not witnesses, we could not agree to such conditions unless the sources volunteered to do this. Even then, we retained a veto on such a request. Sources were scarce, and the effort required to recruit them was extraordinary. Hence, recruiting them simply to quickly place them onto a conveyor belt in an open court did not make operational sense.

When we started the concerted effort to expand our G-Force source network, the organisation had already morphed into a more covert cell-based structure. By then, they only recruited people who were introduced to their circles by a trusted existing member. The G-Force held fewer general meetings and implemented a greater degree of compartmentalisation. The Security Council did not represent all the cells but consisted of a small and trusted group of individuals. The Council sometimes invited individual cell commanders to its regular Friday meetings to provide a report or receive specific instructions. However, for security reasons, the standard operating procedure was for one member of the Council to communicate with a cell commander.

Despite the poor state of our source capacity at the time, our technical intelligence capacity was even worse. Almost all the equipment in use was antiquated leftovers from the old regime. Most of it was obsolete, and the few workable items functioned properly only on rare occasions. Much praying and finger-crossing was needed to get a CI bug to work. On one occasion, we managed to gain access to a house used to plan assassinations and bombings. This breakthrough resulted from cultivating a months-long association with the occupants of the house. I was obviously quite excited at the opportunity to listen to the planning of these conspirators, fully confident we could use this information operationally, or even in court, to convict senior G-Force leaders of direct involvement in attacks.

After a lengthy struggle to obtain a listening device small enough not to be noticed by anyone walking around in the house, we duly installed the device right in the room where the targets met to discuss their usual business: murder and mayhem. The technical team provided a receiver and informed us it could monitor conversations at a distance of 1.5 kilometres. To be safe, we obtained a monitoring facility approximately four hundred meters away. This was a massive breakthrough as the monitoring facility was in a hostile area frequented by members of the G-Force. Many lived close to the house we intended to use as a monitoring facility. Once inside the facility, we duly switched on our receiver but heard... absolutely nothing. Dramat instructed, 'Let's drive towards the target house with the receiver in our vehicle and see at which point we start picking up the signal.' That was eminently sensible, so off we went, from four hundred metres to three hundred, two hundred, one hundred, and still nothing.

We finally picked up a signal right in front of the target house. We were disappointed in the equipment but decided to push ahead nonetheless. Dramat, who thought only of solutions and not excuses, urged us not to throw in the towel in light of the operation's significant possibilities. It was a simple case of shifting our monitoring facility from 1.5 km to 400, and ultimately to 20 metres in the most hostile territory imaginable. We found ourselves not quite precisely inside the belly of the beast but close enough to hear it breathe. After a taxing effort and working the connections in our network, we managed to get a house right next to the target house. Our receiver worked, and we picked up discussions clearly from there.

The next problem was that we could not move in and out right next to our targets every day. We solved this problem by relaying the signal to our covert facility. Again, our technical 'experts' guaranteed that the relay would work. Against our better judgment, we trusted them and put the necessary arrangements into place. However, fate was against us as the relay did not work, and we couldn't make head from toe of the discussions in the house. This must have constituted the most significant lost opportunity of the years we worked against Pagad. Sabotaged by a refusal to invest in modern technology, it was a transformative opportunity that would have shortened our operation by at least a year. Such situations repeated themselves time after time. They were to be our fate as long as we relied on the technical capabilities of the provincial technical support team.

Whilst we did not have the required source capacity, we had a few valuable sources that had not been optimally managed and utilised in the two years preceding. One of our most important and immediate tasks was to optimise the use of existing sources. With better management and more careful directing, they could produce much greater intelligence yield in quantity and quality. Before Pagad's open turn to violence, I recruited a young *alim* (an Islamic scholar) who was respected in the community. This gentleman, to whom I will refer as Scholar, was recruited employing the classical intelligence technique known as the false flag, where an intelligence officer presents himself as a representative of an entity other than his actual service. That is to say, I come carrying one flag, whereas I really represent another.

One winter morning in early 1996, I met him at the upmarket Vineyard hotel in Cape Town's leafy Newlands suburb, with me ostensibly having just arrived from Johannesburg. An associate of Martin, who knew the potential recruit well, introduced me as the representative of a consortium of Black businessmen from Johannesburg who were particularly concerned about the developing situation in Cape Town and its potential for violence. If the violence and disruption became entrenched, it would not bode well for our investments in the province.

We required reliable people to brief us regularly on developments in the province, specifically regarding Pagad's evolving strategies and its turn to violence. Naturally, we were prepared to generously reward such persons as a measure of our gratitude. After lengthy discussions regarding working procedures, we signed a contract outlining the responsibilities of the 'researcher.'

As an afterthought, I mentioned that we prefer to keep these contracts and our relationship confidential. Should our arrangement become public knowledge, our very risk-averse investors might end it and terminate the project's funding. That was the last thing our new researcher wanted, and he committed to maintaining all the secrecy required to keep things moving smoothly. In intelligence parlance, this type of recruitment is known as an infiltration. We sent someone who was not a member to join the target structure and infiltrate the right places. Our new recruit was particularly resourceful and ingenious. Before long, he became a trusted member of Pagad and was respected by members of the G-Force.

Scholar was bedded in when the covert unit initiated our campaign to penetrate the G-Force. He was well-placed to identify potential recruits and monitor the general mood within G-Force circles. He could tell us whether and when they were particularly incensed by a certain gangster or upset about a particular political matter. This enabled us to issue general warnings to potential targets, be it gang leaders or embassies of foreign countries. I extensively used him to conduct talent spotting of potential sources.

Talent spotting is the art of identifying persons who could be recruited and are ripe for an approach. To do this, the talent spotter needs to be so close to the recruitment target that he must be able to observe and report on the person's mood and emotional well-being. He must also be able to assess the target's ideological commitment and identify any pressures that might sway, or internal conflict that the target is experiencing. These could be financial pressures, an illicit affair, or theft from their workplace. In short, anything whose exposure would be so detrimental to the target that they would commit the ultimate betrayal and work with us rather than have it exposed in public. The approach was not necessarily abrupt and direct. Where necessary, we had to be sympathetic to the situation of the potential recruits, especially those with financial or marital problems.

Fortunately, Scholar was a likeable and caring young man who just crept into people's hearts. They entrusted their dearest secrets to him, and he, in turn, transmitted them to us. He worked with dedication and at a pace that far exceeded the monetary gain he obtained from our collaboration. At some point, we became concerned for his mental well-being, as the strain of the work, as usual, started to show, even though he refused to mention this to us. We then got into the habit of setting aside a week or so every year and arranging a holiday for him and his wife or one of the number of lovers he had on the side. Whatever made Scholar happy made us happy.

In the 1998 to 1999 period, we carried out several recruitment attempts. Some were successful, and others were not. That is the nature of a business where one takes a step in approaching someone you've typically never met or, if so, only fleetingly, and asks them to set aside their beliefs and work against people who are often dear to them. We only had source reports, intercepts, and an evaluation of the target's susceptibility to recruitment. In the end, the outcome of a recruitment pitch happens in a specific place and a concentrated time. The outcome of our efforts was often determined by small details such as the mood of the target at that given moment, which might be different from the general mood you have been observing and upon which you're making your pitch. It might be the place you are meeting that makes the target feel unsettled. Is it too busy, or too eerily quiet? Or it could be the recruiter's face, voice, or attitude. We've all had first encounters with people and immediately taken a liking or dislike to them. The same applies to source recruitment.

Many factors need to be calibrated with the utmost sensitivity and precision. Since things can change during the conversation, the recruiter needs to think on their feet, make amendments in minor or significant ways, and adjust the pace at which things develop, sometimes speeding it up and sometimes slowing down. A good recruiter works like a jazz musician, not a classical one. They improvise, create, and develop unscripted synergies in the moment, unlike the classical musician who mainly interprets the music. Whilst trying to develop an intelligence capacity, we operated in a hostile environment within the police. Daggers were still out for us after we outmanoeuvred the old guard over their attempt to close down the covert unit.

Our boss at the time, Du Plessis, had shown no interest in understanding the threat or finding innovative ways to combat it. His involvement was limited to giving his officers a hard time if they tried out methods he found objectionable. Inevitably, other people and teams, with no mandate to collect intelligence, would initiate operations. We would then be instructed to slot in with these operations. Since these were mostly publicity exercises, they had no concrete strategy and defined role for intelligence.

We did our best to avoid these and concentrated on developing the capacity to achieve our objectives. We were fortunate to be able to work directly with Tim Williams at the head office.

At a national level, a consensus emerged that urban terror had to be fought at the level of intelligence infiltration and penetration of G-Force cells. The intelligence chiefs agreed that joint operations between the SAPS, NIA, and Defence Force must be intensified. We were excited at this opportunity since it increased our independence from the provincial CI management. It also meant that we could utilise the impressive technical and surveillance capabilities of the NIA and SANDF. At this point, Arthur Fraser, who had just been appointed as the provincial manager of the NIA, entered the scene. He would significantly alter the landscape of counter-terrorism operations in the province. Fraser had just completed his term at the Truth and Reconciliation Commission, where he was involved in the investigation of human rights abuses by the former Apartheid security and intelligence services. He came from a prominent political family, had a sister as a cabinet minister, and was a unit commander in the ANC's Operation Vula in the late 1980s. Through Operation Vula the ANC secretly infiltrated some of its most senior and experienced leaders inside the country to provide leadership to its underground structures and the mass democratic movement. Fraser worked with Charles Nqakula, who commanded Vula operations in the Western Cape.

While I was at the Crime Intelligence head office, the two of us investigated an old apartheid-regime intelligence network that had infiltrated the ANC and Communist Party during the 1980s. Since we worked together very well, Fraser then tried to poach me from Crime Intelligence into the NIA, but I enjoyed working with our small team in CI too much to make any significant career moves at that point. Fraser's aggressive but considered operational attitude would sync well with our approach to Pagad and became a strong pillar of support for our cause. I arranged a meeting between my boss, Petros, and Fraser so that they could coordinate the integration of our respective approaches and capabilities. Petros, who had been operating in a hostile environment in SAPS, was very relieved to meet Fraser, a comrade with whom he could work without fearing being marginalised and undermined. It was the start of a partnership that would shape the contours of our joint effort against Pagad.

The cooperation between the different agencies resulted in numerous successes for the unit. One of the most successful operations concerned the penetration of the Grassy Park G-Force cell. Jogger, a NIA agent, infiltrated the cell over two years. When he joined Pagad, he was a Christian. To gain the confidence of the G-Force leadership in Grassy Park, the cell amir instructed him to convert to Islam. The amir, Moegsien Barendse told him that only Muslims could be trusted to carry out the jihad against gangsters and what he called the illegitimate ANC government. Jogger was lectured on the principles of

Islam by Moegsien Barendse, the *amir* of the Grassy Park cell and an Imam at a local mosque.

During 1998, Jogger started participating in pipe bomb attacks. The cell was also extensively involved in the theft of motor vehicles. Initially, stealing cars was meant to supply vehicles to G-Force cells for attack use. These would be used either as getaway vehicles or as 'car bombs.' Later, realising the ease with which cars were obtainable, members of the cell started stealing cars for personal financial gain. They would steal and sell the whole vehicle or strip it and sell the parts on the black market.

The theft of vehicles became so rife that the police issued a public alert to vehicle owners whose cars were stolen. They were asked to report such vehicle thefts immediately so that police could be on the lookout for specific vehicles. Later, G-Force members started stealing licence plates and substituting these for those on stolen cars. This tactic was very successful, as most people never reported the theft of their licence plates. They tended to assume that it was some mischief from naughty kids in the neighbourhood. Jogger's position within the cell became untenable as he inevitably became involved in more dangerous actions. On several occasions, he disarmed bombs he was supposed to use against targets identified by his G-Force commanders. Sensing that he was becoming involved in a dangerous and irreversible scenario, he requested to terminate his involvement. The only alternative was to start killing innocent people.

The difficulty with his request to be withdrawn was that the G-Force would not accept an abrupt and unexplained withdrawal from activities. For obvious reasons, they felt more secure when members remained actively involved in terrorist activity. This situation placed unbearable pressure on Jogger, who was participating in activities that, morally, he could no longer justify. The G-Force was so impressed with him that they wanted him to join a unit involved in assassinating businessmen. Soon, he would be expected to kill someone to prove his loyalty and abilities as a 'soldier.' He was not prepared to continue under such circumstances and decided to come out in the open and testify against fellow G-Force members as a state witness. By then, the inter-agency arrangement included the newly established Directorate of Special Operations, popularly known as the Scorpions. Conceived as a South African version of the FBI, the directorate placed intelligence, investigation, and prosecutorial expertise under the same roof. Experts from the respective disciplines would work in project teams dealing with specific crimes and targets.

A multi-agency team was appointed to debrief Jogger and carry out a takedown operation on the Grassy Park cell. The chief prosecutor at the debriefing was Willie Viljoen, the same person who handled the inquest into the Staggie murder early in 1998. Viljoen, an apartheid-era prosecutor, was not known for his fondness of ANC members. In the 1980s, he prosecuted several members of the liberation movement, including some who were now involved in anti-terror intelligence operations. He was closely associated with old-guard SAPS members and had a cynical view of intelligence.

On this occasion, he subjected Jogger to a particularly hostile interrogation. He had no appreciation that the man was a source who risked his life and that of his family to infiltrate the G-Force. Jogger, rather stubborn himself, would not entertain the likes of Viljoen and refused to cooperate with him. The debriefing was then taken over by Dawood Adam, a competent advocate who joined the Scorpions from private practice. Adams' skills as a defence advocate came in handy when interrogating potential state witnesses. Whilst building a case against his targets, he would visualise in his mind's eye all the possible responses a defence team could develop from what a witness is saying. This was of great help to the investigators involved in Pagad-related cases.

After several days of debriefing, the SAPS Special Task Force swooped on houses of the Grassy Park G-Force cell. Barendse, Riedewaan Hendricks, and Faried Mohammed were arrested on charges ranging from theft of a motor vehicle to carrying out attacks against gangsters and drug merchants. They were also charged with the 1998 bombing of a synagogue in Wynberg. The arrest of the cell, one of the most active at the time, was a severe blow to the G-Force. The loss of Barendse was particularly damaging to the G-Force and Pagad more broadly. He gave the organisation and its activities religious legitimacy since he was an Imam. He also played an important role in the G-Force SC.

Initially, the group did not believe Jogger was the source of their arrest. They could not believe such a trusted person had betrayed them to the intelligence services. Barendse, who regarded himself as Jogger's mentor and the one who brought him into the fold of Islam, was particularly depressed. Reports from prison suggested he did not cope very well with Jogger's exposure as an intelligence source.

My gratitude to Jogger extends far beyond the ordinary services he provided as an agent. On more than one occasion, he saved my life and that of another colleague. The successes of the covert unit did not go unnoticed, at least not within G-Force circles. Through several operations, some of our identities became known to G-Force members. This situation was not helped by the insistence of Viljoen that Martin and I testify at the 1998 inquest into the death of Rashaad Staggie. Viljoen's insistence, supported by Knipe and the Pagad investigators, meant we were compelled to testify in open court. This meant exposing not only ourselves but also sensitive methods of work. I testified in a court packed with Pagad supporters and G-Force members.

The trouble started immediately. One day, after testifying, I was on my way to a meeting close to the court building when I bumped into a G-Force member, Nadthmie Barodien. He walked past me and promptly alerted a group of about twenty G-Force members near the court. They gave chase, and I had to evade them by running through the city's eastern outskirts, ultimately ducking into a nearby building. This incident was only a taste of things to come and an effect of the irresponsible attitude of some prosecutors and investigators. Their hatred of the ANC cadres now deployed in intelligence knew few limits, and exposing us to potentially fatal consequences was not one of these.

By mid-1998, Qibla and the G-Force had extensive deliberations and issued a *fatwa* that Dramat and I had to be assassinated. Somehow, they had obtained our residential addresses and started planning their mission. The Grassy Park cell was given the responsibility of carrying out the attacks. At that stage, I lived in Wynberg, a suburb seven minutes from Grassy Park. The cell instructed one of its members, known as Imtiaaz, to visit my home, shoot me and my family and bomb the house.

As it happened, that particular fellow was related to a family friend. They assumed he could easily access the house, and I would not display the necessary vigilance if he visited my home. Fortunately for me, he could not muster the resolve to carry out the mission alone. The cell then planned to accompany him on the mission, with him doing the shooting and the rest throwing a pipe bomb and grenade into the house. Jogger and Riedewaan Hendricks conducted a reconnaissance of my home on at least two occasions.

As events were unfolding, Jogger kept his NIA handlers informed. They regularly briefed Dramat and me on the plans against us. As our boss, Petros raised the matter with Du Plessis and requested the implementation of security measures at our houses or our temporary relocation. Du Plessis' concern was that nothing had happened to us yet, and he was not eager to spend money combating threats that had not yet materialised. The confirmation he required was an actual attack on one or both of us. At the same time, members of the Pagad Investigation Unit were guarded by the elite Special Task Force. Once again, we had to rely on the support of the CI head office. We discussed the matter with Williams, who instructed Du Plessis that security measures should be implemented to protect ourselves and our families.

Whilst the exact security measures were being discussed, the Grassy Park G-Force cell had come under pressure from the Security Council for their delay in carrying out their assigned mission of murdering me. They sped up planning and were finally ready to execute the attack late one evening in 1998. This was the point where the relationship between ourselves and NIA paid off in direct personal terms. I received a telephone call from Fraser. 'David, please move quickly. G-Force members from Grassy Park are on their way to your house to kill you!' 'When are they leaving Grassy Park?' I wanted to know. Fraser replied, 'They left a few minutes ago and are travelling in a minibus. From what I know, they are armed with firearms, at least one hand grenade, and possibly a pipe bomb.' He told me that Jogger, who was travelling with the cell, had made contact with him, warning of the impending attack. They were traveling from the neighbouring Grassy Park suburb, which gave me about three or four minutes to act.

Not knowing where the assailants were at that point and unsure whether others might not already be in the vicinity, I decided that it was too risky for the family to leave the house. I woke my pregnant wife and nine-year-old daughter, herded them to a back room furthest away from the street, and covered them with mattresses, the only protection available against possible bomb fragments. At the time, we were issued special police radios with an orange 'officer in distress' button that activated a general alert. The police being the police, my faith in this magical button having any effect was close to zero, but desperate times called for desperate measures, and there was I, pressing a button that would magically conjure up an army of cops right at my doorstep.

Meanwhile, I had taken up a position outside the house, waiting for the attackers. I knew Jogger had been briefed to provide me with backup should the situation explode, and that we could manage the situation ourselves. We, of course, held the advantage of foreknowledge and the element of surprise. I knew the cell was on its way, had a good sense of their weapons and numbers, and had one amongst them who was on our side. It was an extraordinary advantage, and in the seconds after Fraser's phone call, I tried calculating how best we could neutralise the imminent attack and, if possible, arrest the perpetrators.

But lo and behold, the orange button actually worked! To my astonishment, the police responded incredibly fast and made themselves known at my front door within three minutes of me pressing the now-proven magic button. I appealed to the cops to conceal themselves and switch off their flashing lights so they could arrest the G-Force members who would imminently be at my house. They replied that it was protocol for them to make their presence known. I'm not sure who created this protocol, but according to Jogger's later report to his NIA handlers, the G-Force cell, noticing the intense police movement in the area, aborted their operation. We lost our opportunity to catch the entire Grassy Park cell red-handed. At the same time, former DIS operatives, including some who had integrated with me into Crime Intelligence, heard the alert on their radios and came to the house to offer assistance. These included Peter Jacobs, Joseph Makhura, a former MK operative, my old Communist Party comrade, Splinters, and Whitey, another Manenberg comrade who, like Makhura, was a trained sharpshooter. Jacobs and some of the other DIS operatives took my wife and daughter to a friend's house, where they stayed until it became safe for them to return home.

This incident and the threat that continued for some years thereafter put a lot of stress on my family. The fact that my wife was pregnant at the time made the matter much more stressful for everyone involved. My daughter was severely affected and her schooling suffered for it. Until today the long-term effects of this traumatic event have not been properly processed and I sometimes wonder how it continues to affect them. For the next week, until Williams instructed the special task force to provide security to Dramat and me, my residence was secured by a hastily convened and informal task force consisting of former DIS members who volunteered their time to assist a brother comrade.

The morning after the aborted attack, I discovered that Fraser's deputy had called Petros as soon as the

NIA received Jogger's intelligence of the impending attack the previous evening, to pass on the warning to me. Petros's phone was switched off, and the NIA deputy's emergency call went to his voicemail. The following day, when I briefed Petros on the previous night's events, he played the voicemail for the first time, where we could listen to the NIA deputy, in his usual slow but authoritative tone, saying, 'Petros, please tell Africa that Pagad is on their way to kill him.' Thank goodness for redundancies, in this case, Fraser, who just decided to make a direct call to me anyway.

While engaging in operations like the one in Grassy Park, our primary mission remained to expand our human source network. By the middle of 1998, the situation on the ground had become critical, with regular assassinations of Muslim businessmen, attacks on their businesses and residences, and attacks on Muslim clergy and academics who were critical of Pagad. A comprehensive information network was more necessary than ever. Despite the arrest of some G-Force members, no successes had been achieved in linking any senior Pagad figures to the violence plaguing the province. New cells easily and quickly replaced those that were neutralised. The G-Force leadership had a vast pool of members to call upon. They had also implemented a tactic of staggering the deployment of cells. This tactic involved intensively using one or two cells while 'resting' the others.

The strategy had several advantages. Firstly, it made their control over the activities of the G-Force much easier, as there were fewer cells and individuals to control at any given time. The simultaneous utilisation of all the cells had previously caused problems for the leadership. It also meant that the operations were more secure as the leadership and the cell commander could more thoroughly screen members for specific operations. Using a particular cell or two over time also created difficulties for us. As soon as we came to grips with the modus operandi of a specific unit and identified its members, they would go quiet. Cells were usually active for a few months at a time, giving us just sufficient time to identify the chief protagonists and possible sources for recruitment. Once we had achieved this, another cell would be activated.

Another complicating factor was the operational methods of the various cells, whose profiles were widely different. Mastering an understanding of one cell did not help much in preparing us for the dynamics associated with the next cell that would be activated. The only constant factor was the leadership of the G-Force. We increasingly realised that this was where we had to get in to achieve our objective of paralysing the organisation. Despite all our efforts, we had limited success in directly accessing the G-Force leadership. Our approach then became to create an information net around them and gradually move into the inner circle. It required recruiting sources with physical access to the target individuals, their meeting places and vehicles. This potential source pool included family members, domestic workers, gardeners, friends, and neighbours.

The idea was that this access would help in profiling our targets. Such people might also know of compromising activities in which our targets engage. We always welcomed such information. At the same time, they could provide information on the general movement of our targets and the identities of persons or vehicles who regularly visited them. This enabled us to link targets to events if only based on suspicion. The thorough follow-up of such information led to many successes. Over time, we were successful in establishing this capacity. It delivered results beyond our expectations, as many sources provided detailed movement reports and even documentation from target figures. Physical access to targets' homes, businesses, or vehicles also facilitated our ability to conduct technical monitoring of these targets.

After approximately one year of groundwork, we had achieved considerable success in developing a source network. Our understanding of urban terror had advanced significantly compared to the limited foundation with which we started. In the collective security community in the province and nationally, the covert unit became highly regarded for our knowledge of the threat. I continued my involvement in the interagency working group, and Petros, Dramat, and I frequently briefed senior national security leadership in Cape Town and Pretoria. Paradoxically, our provincial management did not recognise our contribution. Though we were not obsessed with validation, we were proud of the achievements we had already accumulated and the direction in which we were now inexorably moving.

By now, we had the feeling of working from a solid foundation, had coalesced as a team, and had momentum on our side. It was now a matter of when, not if, we'd be able to make the crack in the Pagad edifice that would make it collapse. The junior non-commissioned officers in our team felt the appreciation that we, as their unit leadership, had for them and could also sense the prestige now attached to the unit. It made them feel special, which was one of the main factors in keeping pace with the relentless intensity demanded of them by Dramat and myself, without any of them ever complaining.

The level of responsibility I gave my team reflected the unit leadership and staff's growing self-confidence. The team were not mere followers of commands, and I insisted that they participate in planning. Each was given personal responsibility for intelligence on specific cells or individuals, cultivation, and recruitment plans related to these cells. I spent many late night and early morning hours with my team, assessing the day's developments and planning for the day ahead. Covert was becoming special, operating as a cohesive unit and poised for success.

CHAPTER 5

A Barely Perceptible but Decisive Shift of the Tectonic Plates

A right strategic decision is the prime condition for winning victory. Once we have taken the right decision, the decisive question is to organise the realisation of this decision in a way suited to the practical situation.
—**General võ Nguyen Giap**

Green Point Main Road was its usual bustling self on Christmas Eve of 1999, with cafes and restaurants packed with locals and tourists enjoying the suburb's good weather and eclectic mix of eateries. Some, searching for Mediterranean cuisine, headed to the popular Mano's Cafe, conveniently situated on the Main Road and within walking distance of the famous V&A Waterfront. A loud bang brought an end to many people's night out and wreaked devastation on the police officers sent out to investigate the warning of a possible explosive device at the restaurant. Seven police officers were wounded, two of them critically.

The ambush of police officers outside Mano's Restaurant set the stage for the next crucial phase in the battle against urban terror. The bombing, taking place at the height of the festive season and on the eve of millennium celebrations, was daring and devastating. The blast brought the message from the terrorists home to the powers that be – they could strike any target at any time. Even the police were no longer safe. The minister for safety and security, Steve Tshwete, and the national DPP, Bulelani Ncguka, visited the scene of the bombing and the injured officers in the hospital.

Tshwete, known to not mince his words, stated to the media that the intelligence services knew who was responsible for the attack and that they were not looking beyond Pagad. Although we agreed with him, this was a conclusion based on intelligence. It was not the evidence that could stand legal scrutiny in court. While the modus operandi of the attack certainly made Pagad a prime candidate for responsibility, we had no specific intelligence, let alone evidence, pointing to Pagad members having carried out the attack. I was summoned to a meeting in central Cape Town early on Christmas morning to discuss the previous night's ambush. Across the road from parliament, at the offices of the Scorpions on Plein Street, I met and greeted colleagues from various security agencies, including several colleagues from the police head office.

Petros, Dramat, and I accompanied the national police commissioner Jackie Selebi to the meeting. Fraser and his deputy represented the NIA. Attending from the Scorpions were Sonn and some of his prosecutors. Bulelani Ngcuka and his usual coterie of advisors were also at the meeting. The odd person in the room was Sakumzi (Saki) Macozoma, a former political activist who was present in his capacity as Chair of the MTN mobile phone company. Macozoma appeared to have been on Christmas holiday in Cape Town at the time of the ambush and was called in to discuss what support the mobile phone networks could provide to track the movement of suspects and to assist with investigating the bombs that were now commonly triggered via mobile phone.

There would be no Christmas celebration for anyone in attendance, although someone did rock up at the meeting with a bottle of Glenfiddich whiskey and a large platter of snacks. While some of the senior officials present had no issue with alternating between whiskey and counter-terrorism, those of us managing minute-by-minute intelligence operations in the field concurrent to our meeting refrained from doing so. Between the covert unit and Fraser's NIA team, we were running down leads, tasking sources, and monitoring technical intelligence to see if we could pick up anything concrete about the previous night's attack.

Opening with an update on the latest information gathered from the crime scene, Ngcuka chaired the meeting. He also reported on the medical condition of the police officers who were injured in the attack. It was clear that everyone was under pressure to deliver immediate results, if not on the specific attack, then at least on other outstanding Pagad-related matters occupying the public mind. Ngcuka indicated that the president had given clear instructions. He expected the arrest of those responsible for the Manos and other G-Force attacks, and he required this within days. Frustrated by the evident lack of urgency in prosecuting G-Force members, his patience had run out.

The president had good insight into the intelligence produced by the collective intelligence community. He obtained this through departmental channels or the regular briefings the community delivered in person to his national security advisor, Vusi Mavimbela – who later took up the role of director-general of the NIA. We began by discussing the modus operandi and the type of explosive device used in the attack. The nature of the detonating mechanism used to trigger the explosive was of particular interest. The fact that the device was remotely detonated already gave us a good indication of who might have been involved in building the bomb. The skills to manufacture such a detonating mechanism were limited to a few G-Force members.

Whilst many G-Force members knew how to construct a simple 'striker' pipe bomb, this device required more technical expertise and experience. A 'striker' bomb was simply a metal canister filled with gunpowder and nails, detonated by lighting a striker firecracker sealed into the canister. The person using the bomb lit the firecracker, threw or placed the device, and then literally ran for his life, aiming to get as far from the explosive as possible before it exploded six to nine seconds later. The device used in this attack consisted of a similar canister but was detonated using a cellular phone embedded inside it. In such cases, the bomber can place the device, move a safe distance away, and from any place with a cellular phone signal, detonate by calling the number registered to the phone inside the bomb.

This method, which would become the G-Force's preferred method of detonation, posed a far greater danger as the bomber or a secondary watcher could observe the device from a distance and only detonate it when it was likely to cause the highest number or most impactful casualties. Popular with terrorists worldwide, this tactic enabled the assailant to set off the device when police arrived at a scene, either after an initial bombing or in response to a bomb threat. The Christmas Eve bomb was an example of the latter. While we had a general idea of who might have manufactured the explosive device, we still needed to figure out the identity of the actual bombers. I presented the meeting with background on the evolution of the bomb innovators circle, including the pre-Pagad history of some of its members, the skill set of the circle, and the gradual improvement in their explosive trigger mechanisms.

The Mathey brothers were, at this point, singled out as persons of interest, as they had the requisite skill level to construct that sort of device. There was no evidence of their direct involvement, but we had to explore various hypotheses in the search for potential suspects. Throughout the day, we slipped out of the meeting to call sources or meet with them somewhere and headed back to the meeting to report progress. We began to form a picture of who might have been involved in the attack by triangulating our understanding of the G-Force modus operandi, the targeting focus of the bombers' circle, and source reporting on rumours within the G-Force. Though the information we gathered was insufficient to achieve an immediate breakthrough in the case, we were expected to do something or be seen doing so. And it had to happen soon. The team was working on a deadline set by a principal who was in no mood for excuses or delays.

Our next step was to assess the current organisation of the G-Force, with a specific focus on the particular cells and individuals that could manufacture the type of device used on 24 December. Save for an unexpected break in the case, we realised that we were unlikely to develop sufficient evidence to arrest individuals specifically for the Mano's bombing. We decided to delve into Pagad-related cases from the previous three years and establish whether there were grounds to arrest and prosecute some figures we suspected of involvement in the attack. It made no difference whether we arrested them for their role in the Manos attack or previous transgressions. They simply had to be arrested.

The point was to deal a decisive, if temporary, blow to their bombing campaign while at the same time responding to the president's rapidly approaching deadline. The logic was that these arrests, coupled with increased and aggressive surveillance, would cause at least a short-term imbalance within G-Force ranks and ensure a smooth festive period and millennium transition for the rest of the city. Since we had no sources with immediate and direct access to the bomb innovators' circle, we usually had to wait a week or two before a clearer picture of a specific bombing emerged. G-Force members observed strict secrecy in the immediate aftermath of an attack. However, after a week or two, someone would somehow speak or let something uncanny slip. In many instances, it was simply to satisfy the egos of the attackers. Some were unsatisfied with the quiet knowledge of what they achieved for their cause and organisation but needed affirmation from others. As usual, our sources were only too eager to listen in while stroking their egos.

Two cases only tangentially related to the Mano's bombing held immediate potential for success. One was the 1996 Staggie murder case, and the other was a case where an M-26 hand grenade and pipe bomb were discovered at the residence of Shahied Mathey in December 1996. The decision to use these two cases as launchpads for our intended arrests opened an unexpected can of worms. It exposed the rot in the investigation and prosecution teams who had spent much of their time and capital investigating, criticising or attempting to neuter intelligence in the previous three years. When Ngcuka requested the relevant case dockets, we struggled to obtain them from the Pagad investigation unit. Hostile as usual, the investigators refused to hand the dockets to the Scorpions. After some telephone calls from Ngcuka and Selebi, they were delivered to Viljoen, the prosecutor assigned to these cases. He was asked to brief us on the progress in the cases and the evidence obtained thus far.

Viljoen was responsible for case management, preparing the dockets for court in case of a trial, and providing direction to the investigators on gathering evidence. The idea behind the formation of the Scorpions was the active involvement of the prosecutors in their cases. Instead of being mere recipients of completed case dockets from police investigators, they were as much a part of the investigation as the detectives investigating the case.

Dockets in hand and with an eager audience waiting to hear how we could use the existing evidence to arrest suspects, Viljoen was clearly uncomfortable with reporting on the cases under consideration. He mumbled a few remarks about the cases and the difficulties the investigators experienced in concluding them, none of which anyone had been alerted to until then. A cursory glance at the dockets indicated they were dealt with unsatisfactorily. The case of the explosives found in Mathey's house was alarming. It appeared that over the preceding three years, no actual investigation had taken, as the investigation diary, where investigative steps are logged, did not even cover half a page. Only half a page for a case concerning explosive devices found literally inside a key G-Force commander's residence!

Whilst this reflected negligence on the part of the investigators, Viljoen, to whom they reported, clearly made no effort to remedy this situation. He had given no leadership in the case concerning a vital member of the G-Force and a lynchpin in its bombing campaign. Everyone in the meeting was furious. Whilst we had been pointing out these types of cases, it was the first time that Ngcuka was exposed to the incompetence prevalent in investigating urban terror cases. Viljoen received a thorough dressing down and was instructed to immediately rectify matters. He would spend the next few days trying to redress three years of delays and mismanagement. Viljoen found little sympathy in this instance. It felt like a case of threat management by willpower – if we willed Pagad and its terrorist activities away, we wouldn't need to do anything practical to ensure their demise.

The Staggie murder case presented challenges of its own. In many respects, we thought it would be a much easier case to prosecute if we could access the evidence that we knew existed and had been displayed in public. By then, it was common knowledge in investigative circles that evidence existed linking Ebrahim to the scene of the events resulting in Staggie's death. The problem was the refusal of the media present on the scene of that fateful night to testify and make available their material as evidence against Pagad members. Without their testimony, our chance of a successful conviction was slim.

The same difficulties had previously confronted Viljoen when he led the inquest into the killing of Staggie. Then Minister of Justice Omar negotiated an agreement with the media, excusing them from testifying. The subpoenaed journalists, who were present at the scene of the murder, also threatened to take the matter to the constitutional court. We faced a tough decision in this particular case. Not only were some journalists old comrades of mine from the 1980s, like Benni Gool, but they also had a legitimate argument that the state could not expect journalists to suffer the consequences of police incompetence and inaction. Journalists are not an extension of the police or intelligence services, and if the cops had followed the intelligence provided ahead of Staggie's murder, they could have ensured the presence of the police video and photography unit to record the scene.

What confronted us, however, was an increasingly desperate situation, and the time had come to decide on the matter. The options were either to let the case be and simply conclude the inquest, thereby stepping away from prosecuting anyone, or to proceed with charging those Pagad members against whom some evidence of criminal action, even if not murder, had been gathered. Nevertheless, we could only do this if we subpoenaed the journalists concerned and coerced them into testifying. Ngcuka made the call and decided on the latter course of action. The journalists would be compelled to testify, and if they refused, would face the consequences – arrest and imprisonment.

The millennium hype offered terrorists all the publicity they could have hoped for. With Cape Town packed with tourists, we were racing against time. We were acutely aware of the need for a breakthrough on the bombings, as the situation was becoming increasingly desperate. We had to make a breakthrough or get ourselves into shape to confidently pursue the Staggie and Mathey cases. Ultimately, our weak hand compelled us to pursue the latter option. Following the 1996 cases, a decision was made to arrest Ebrahim and the Mathey brothers.

The planning and execution of such an operation is a complex task, including the integrated and seamless deployment of various services and forces. As intelligence officers, we had to ensure that our information network was in place to predict possible responses to the arrests. A key factor was the safety of the arrest teams. Dramat and I briefed our team and engaged sources with greater intensity in the few heated days between Christmas and the day of the arrests. To some people, the presence of the news media was an essential element of the operation, with Ngcuka leading the argument that we facilitate their presence during the arrests. The Scorpions were keen on this high-drama kind of action, as was Tshwete, who had to show the public that the police were getting somewhere in the fight against urban terror.

The intelligence agencies were more concerned with effecting smooth and violence-free arrests than with staging a media show. In this, we had the unequivocal support of Selebi, who found the whole idea quite bizarre and forcefully expressed his view in one of the planning meetings. The last of these were attended by more than thirty representatives of the collective security community. A large SAPS detective delegation was present, to my surprise, headed by Knipe. These same people refused to cooperate with the Scorpions, delaying the delivery of the case dockets. Ultimately, they were shown up for delivering essentially empty dockets when they could no longer avoid doing so.

One of the issues we discussed included obtaining arrest warrants for all the targets. This was no easy task as the magistrate was correctly concerned that people were to be arrested for crimes committed three years earlier. However, after lengthy explanations and the skilful organisation of the Scorpions' Advocate Dawood Adam, who played a crucial role in presenting our case and addressing the magistrate's concerns, we obtained all the required warrants. The covert unit had to provide profiles of targets to the arrest teams. While Ebrahim was a popular Pagad figure and well-known to the police and Scorpions, the Mathey brothers were well-known to the small community of intelligence operatives and otherwise largely unknown outside of that circle. The profiles were essential for those affecting the arrests to inform them of whether they might encounter an aggressive person, what the possibilities of crowds gathering at their house during the arrest were, and whether there were any chances they would attempt to flee.

The fiasco surrounding the search of Shahied Mathey's house in December 1996 was a valuable lesson for us. In that instance, an unprepared arrest team without sufficient protection were quickly surrounded by several hundred Pagad supporters and assaulted. The team had to promptly vacate the house, leaving valuable evidence behind. However, we were committed to learning from this mistake and ensuring it would not be repeated in the impending operation. The covert unit's meticulous planning extended to the identification of items to be seized from the targets' houses. This was not a random selection, but a decision based on our understanding of the potential intelligence value of certain items. We focused on materials that, while not immediately useful to an investigator, could hold significant intelligence value if properly studied and analysed.

Political literature provides clues to the target's political perspectives and the specific issues he is engaged in. From my activist days, I recalled that the literature we read at any given time concerned the armed struggle or usually related concretely to the problems we were organising around. For example, from 1988 to 1990, there was a proliferation of banned literature on the theory and praxis of insurrection. Prompted by an influential school of thought within the liberation movement, the literature promoted an insurrectionary seizure of state power. As student activists, we would mobilise along those lines, enhancing this particular perspective on struggle. The same applied to Pagad, and we expected this material to be used even more by the targets we intended to arrest, who were not ordinary G-Force foot soldiers but established members of Qibla with a high level of political consciousness and ideological commitment.

The meticulously planned operation commenced at 04:00 on 29 December 1999. Intelligence operatives, detectives, police reaction units, and army units gathered at Bishop Lavis police station for a final briefing. The arrest teams were dispatched to the Ebrahim and Mathey residences. The high-risk police special task force was responsible for Ebrahim's arrest. As the teams arrived at the target houses, the Pagad leadership began calling members to mobilise support and assemble at the affected houses. However, unlike on previous occasions, they could not even enter his street. The army had established a secure corridor around the house, which allowed the SAPS detectives to search and seize whatever material they could. Ebrahim was surprised to hear that he was arrested for Staggie's murder three years earlier. He had been involved in so many incidents since then that he probably expected to be arrested for anything but a case that had been lying dormant for years.

The real surprise developed during the raid on the Mathey residence. Apart from arresting Shahied and Nazier Mathey for the illegal possession of explosives relating to the find in their garage in December 1996, police found some interesting material in their house. These included a copy of the 'Anarchist Cookbook', an internet guide to making bombs, and several cellular phones in various stages of disassembly. In light of the recent use of cell phone-detonated pipe bombs, this was an interesting discovery. Given Mathey's technical background, it seemed plausible he could have modified the cellular phones for detonating mechanisms.

The arrests of Ebrahim and the Mathey brothers created quite a stir at the SAPS head office. Williams summoned Petros and me to Pretoria for consultations on the most recent arrests. At the same time, he instructed Ray Lalla, the KwaZulu-Natal head of Crime Intelligence, to join us at the meeting. In the weeks preceding our briefing to Williams, who would be joined by Selebi, extensive consultations occurred between our covert unit and Lalla.

Lalla was a veteran intelligence operative and commander of Umkhonto we Sizwe. In the 1980s, he headed the movement's intelligence function on the Regional Politico-Military Committee in Swaziland, from where he operated into KwaZulu-Natal. Lalla brought a wealth of experience and was eager to share it with us. He was not bothered by minor issues, had a very relaxed persona and engaged with us as equal comrades, even though we were working together in a bureaucratic environment where he was, by some measure, our senior. He advocated exploiting the close and covert cooperation between our unit and his structures to launch a grander-scale operation to bring down the G-Force. The camaraderie between Lalla and ourselves developed from sporadic interaction in the early days when we integrated into a substantial partnership as the Pagad threat intensified. Lalla had valuable insights from his handling of the long-running political violence in KwaZulu-Natal and thought it might be of particular value to us in Cape Town.

When we met Selebi and Williams, they wanted us to update them on the arrests. They were interested in how the recent arrests would play out within the G-Force and how they might respond. I expressed the view that the arrests had bought us some time to come to terms with the introduction of the new bomb trigger mechanisms and some relief from political pressure. Selebi, who was present at the Christmas meeting following the Mano's bombing, was impressed with our contributions in those conversations and specifically that our unit had become the go-to place for the Scorpions when they required intelligence on G-Force suspects.

Selebi's assessment regarding the Scorpions was accurate. The fact that the Scorpions relied almost entirely on us and Fraser's NIA team for information presented a paradoxical situation. This is because when it was established, the directorate almost exclusively recruited former Branch members who had left to work as investigators in Knipe's Serious and Violent Crimes unit. They actively ignored the capable ANC intelligence people that we recommended to them. This brush-off became one of the many feuding points between ourselves and the Scorpions.

Despite the potential we saw in the present situation, I weighed in with my experience of having walked the Pagad path since day zero. I cautioned people at the head office that our effort to bring about Pagad's downfall was only beginning. The response to the Mano's bombing had brought about a new dynamic that presented a favourable environment for the work we were attempting to do. The certainty that investigators and prosecutors had lost credibility was the most significant output of the post-Mano's situation. Their exposure diminished their ability to target the intelligence capabilities arrayed against Pagad. Their limited view on tackling our adversary and the straightjacket they perennially sought to impose upon intelligence were constant sources of irritation for us. Seeing that they were now on the back foot would buy us significant freedom of manoeuvre. Unfortunately, between us and the investigators, matters had come down to a zero-sum game we simply had to win.

The other critical factor emerging from the post-Mano's situation was the realisation that Viljoen had overstayed his welcome in the effort against Pagad. If we were to have any hope of securing convictions against important G-Force members, it was clear that he needed to be replaced by someone more capable. Advocate Adams was a former human rights lawyer well-known in ANC circles. A problem solver who appreciated the big picture and strategy, he would not allow minor issues to prevent us from making decisions of considerable strategic effect. We saw proof of this in superb effect when we went to him with our most significant request and probably his biggest prosecutorial decision, the Riverside (pseudonym) case.

Adams was always impeccably dressed, with an equally impressive mind, yet a casual and engaging approach. Unlike the many bureaucrats who engaged with others in point form as if they were completing a multiple-choice examination, he was a conversationalist. Having just joined the Scorpions from private practice, Adams held exceptional insight into the defence strategies the accused might deploy should we get to prosecuting key G-Force figures. He became a central player in the emerging and increasingly cohesive alliance consisting of our covert unit, the NIA team, and the Scorpions. After Viljoen's spectacular and embarrassing exposure, Adams brought in two prosecutors. Eunice Grey and Faiek Davids would prove themselves eminently suitable for defeating Pagad.

Our meetings with Selebi, Williams, Lalla, and others in Pretoria continued at a frenetic pace. Our primary proposal was to conduct a medium to long-term undercover operation to infiltrate the G-Force, using sources across the intelligence spectrum. Our covert unit would operate with selected officers from Crime Intelligence in KwaZulu-Natal. Williams and Selebi were fully supportive, particularly in acquiring technical equipment. Their support was a welcome change after the disappointing display of the technical equipment we had installed in a G-Force planning facility earlier. We were relieved to meet and start working with some capable officers at the head office, who had access to equipment their colleagues in the Western Cape could only dream of and were far more innovative. This collaborative support was a significant boost to our operation.

These technical officers inquired about our targets, whether they stayed in one place or moved around, how they manoeuvred, and whether we had sources with access to target facilities or vehicles. All of this was to explore the options available in exploiting or creating access to targets for technical coverage. We handled a few sources with the level of access we were now discussing, and the conversation played a role in all of us being more alert to how we could utilise sources beyond the information-provision realm. Our head office technical intelligence team identified one mid-level officer in Cape Town who could act as their man on the ground supporting our operation. Once formally briefed on the project, he could do the technical work on our behalf.

Following our discussions, Williams tasked me with drafting a comprehensive project proposal by the next working day. This proposal was crucial as it needed to outline the threat, identify key targets, allocate personnel, present an operational plan, and propose a budget. As the unit's planning specialist, I drafted the project proposal in line with Williams' instructions. Understanding his preference for concise documents, I ensured the proposal was comprehensive yet succinct. After a thorough briefing on the plan, he approved it and provided the necessary instructions for budget allocation and personnel deployment.

Williams deputised Els to oversee the operation from head office. He also co-opted a technical and financial manager to assist us with our requirements. At his discretion, Williams selected individual operational and support staff from head office to join our team. He instructed their respective commanders to detach them to work with Els without disclosing any details about the nature or target of the operation. The 'old boy's network' in the police extended far and wide, and we had to maintain the secrecy of the operation to ensure its success. Informing the national managers of these individuals would have led to the leakage of the operation to our Western Cape management, whom we unanimously agreed should be held at arm's length from the operation.

Now that Williams had secured us the head office support team, we would head back south and practise a deception and denial operation against our troublesome management, principally Trollip, denying him any but the most generic access to the operation. Also excluded from the exercise was the National Undercover Operations Unit. Having independently realised their obvious unsuitability for the Pagad project, Williams supported our position on the national undercover office, which was supposed to manage the police's covert intelligence capabilities. Their task included guiding covert units, developing policy, and initiating national undercover operations. Most of its senior members were detectives from the old Narcotics, Murder and

Robbery, or Organised Crime units, and they struggled to grasp their role within a more political National Security intelligence environment. They ran the undercover operations unit like a glorified detective unit, similar to how they would have run short, quick-bust drug purchasing operations.

Headed by a Colonel Barnard, the officer working on Pagad issues was a maverick named Ken. Ken was, for some reason, always flanked by the unit's psychologist, who had responsibility for ensuring the mental well-being of Crime Intelligence officers working in deep cover within criminal organisations, as well as high-level sources who faced severe psychological challenges. They were both incredibly energetic and well-meaning, but I found them unsuited for the needs of an operation of the sort we were constructing. They did well with the standard organised crime undercover operation and employed a strictly prosecutorial angle.

Members of the few provincial Crime Intelligence covert units, who typically had their origin either in the Branch or the DIS, were more comfortable with long-term operations and were not impressed by the modus operandi or composition of the national undercover operations unit. Having been to Cape Town several times on attempts to initiate ill-conceived and poorly planned operations to infiltrate Pagad, the national unit had not succeeded in these efforts. This was mainly because they had involved everyone in these operations except the covert unit, which contained specialist knowledge of the Pagad threat. Instead, they operated within their old buddy system and worked closely with the head of the overt CI office in Cape Town.

Williams instructed that we report directly to Els and brief him and Selebi regularly. He specifically instructed us to exclude anyone from the Western Cape CI structures unless he gave prior consent. This included our own provincial management, to which we ordinarily accounted. By then, undercover investigations in the SAPS remained undercover in name only. The process of approving a formal undercover operation included so many people that the secrecy of the operation was usually compromised early on. As part of undercover operational administration, units were burdened with information and other bureaucratic reports that had no material effect on the success of operations.

This bureaucratic overload diminished the willingness of covert units to launch formally-approved undercover operations. Many shied away from it and went ahead with the undercover operation without the official green light. More practical intelligence work could be done this way, meaning less time spent compiling pro forma reports. On the flip side, the drawback was resource limitation and the potential for conflict with the DPP if things were to go awry with a source engaged in criminal activity.

Another prerequisite of police undercover investigations was the compulsory inclusion of an investigator in the project team. Usually acting as the head of the operation, such an investigator would be appointed by the provincial detective service. Given the mistrust and open antagonism between ourselves and the detectives, we avoided such an appointment. Instead, we appointed Roger Sampson, one of our own unit members. He was a former Branch investigator who had worked in Namibia during the South African occupation, and we found him much more efficient than the so-called specialists in the police's Pagad investigation teams. Like most Black investigators in the security branch, he held the relatively low rank of inspector after almost twenty years of service. Despite his meticulous manner and the detail with which he investigated cases, he was never regarded as competent enough by the old guard to head an investigation of this complexity or importance.

During the 1980s, the Branch used the model we were now trying to implement, where intelligence and investigators were co-located and their work led by the intelligence component. Branch investigators were indoctrinated in intelligence and had greater awareness of the threats they investigated because of their proximity to their intelligence colleagues. They also appreciated the sensitivity regarding the utilisation and protection of sources. This made for much better integration and utilisation of sources and ensured a seamless transition from intelligence to evidence. The arrangement also meant that intelligence officers could be continuously guided on using sources to identify or gather material that held potential evidentiary value. The dominant model within the SAPS at the time was the temporary detachment of investigators and intelligence operatives to a task team targeting specific individuals or entities. The culture clash was too significant to enable a productive relationship.

My August 1996 clash with Knipe in the first task team was a case in point. He prioritised evidence above all else, even at the expense of source protection, while I valued constructing and sustaining an intelligence network. Neither of us was wrong per se, but it simply made no sense for us to work together in the task team format as applied within the police. With Sampson as our investigator, there was no us and them, only us. He sat in on our operational planning sessions, knew a lot about our sources, and saw the material we obtained from them. Notably, he also knew how we struggled to develop our capability and appreciated the need to sustain it instead of utilising it for quick wins at the risk of its collapse.

Petros was appointed provincial commander of the operation, while I was responsible for the intelligence gathering section, working under Dramat's general direction. Having just been appointed as the commander of the covert unit, Dramat also had other responsibilities, including a very demanding operational situation aggravated by the explosion of transport-related violence in Cape Town. Fortunately, as with my counter-terrorism team, he had a capable team under the leadership of another DIS officer, Mbu, who brought colossal credit and prestige to the unit with an unprecedented breakthrough in the transport violence environment. Dramat's intelligence management in multiple and complex crises was an early indicator of his leadership competency. This aptitude ultimately catapulted him to the position of founding head of the Directorate for Priority Crime Investigation, colloquially known as the Hawks.

Petros and I briefed Dramat on developments arising from our short visit to Pretoria when we returned to Cape Town. Although I coordinated the specific intelligence-gathering section in the operation, its implementation would require the covert unit's resources and infrastructure. When needed, we could also call on other operatives at the unit to assist with specific tasks. Dramat managed this process exceptionally well, providing all the necessary assistance without prescribing how to do our work. He also acted as a buffer to external roleplayers, giving us the breathing space needed to work undisturbed.

Next, I briefed my team on the operation. I outlined the mission in concrete terms – infiltrate the G-Force, including its Security Council, gather intelligence that can be converted into evidence and exploited for use in prosecutions and maintain a close watch on the political dynamics between Pagad and its political adversaries within the Muslim community. We would broadly recruit persons directly involved in G-Force cells and with direct knowledge of attacks. We would use mobile surveillance to observe targets, particularly those we previously identified as manufacturers of explosive devices and the new trigger mechanisms. We would also employ extensive technical coverage and monitoring of G-Force members involved in the planning and executing of attacks.

We spent a few days discussing specific ideas for carrying out our plan. Our first step would be to conduct a thorough study of each G-Force cell – identifying and profiling members, modus operandi, and activities of the cell, possible weapons storage and training facilities, their modes of communication, support structures to the cell, and relations with other G-Force cells. We would then identify the weakest link in the structure: a current cell member, an outsider with a good chance of being accepted into the unit, or a friend or family close to a member. We found interesting facts about some important G-Force members when we identified possible sources and their personality weaknesses. Despite their pious appearance in public and amongst Pagad members, we established that many engaged in activities that contrasted entirely with this image. Some senior members were involved in extra-marital affairs, sometimes with the wives of fellow G-Force members.

One member of the bombers' innovation circle was of particular concern to us. He disappeared from home regularly for three to four hours late at night. Like his wife, we suspected he might be conducting some covert G-Force business and tracked him for a few nights, only to discover that he was meeting his lover, a fellow Pagad member. When we found the two in a very compromising position on a beach road in the upmarket suburb of Camps Bay, we were surprised by the relative innocence of his nightly escapades. For at least a few hours every week, our bomber was a disciple of the slogan 'Make love not war', which opened up an avenue for us to approach him or his partner in crime. We decided to go at him in this instance, but he remained steadfast and rejected our approaches. With hindsight, approaching his lady friend would have had a better chance of success.

We had to craft the actual approaches once our source target analysis was complete. No recruitment is guaranteed, especially in a target structure where religion is a decisive motivating factor and exercises cohesive and disciplinary functions. The additional and obvious fact that exposure as a source automatically resulted in a *fatwa* authorising your murder, was a decisive push factor. Ebrahim Gallie, a member of the G-Force cell in Manenberg and state witness in cases against fellow cell members, was assassinated on 14 May 2000. The same fate befell some of the other G-Force members who became state witnesses or were suspected of being intelligence sources.

There was an intense fear amongst G-Force members about whether they should cooperate with us. Many feared for their lives and those of their families. Some of them had been involved in actions against state witnesses and sources, and therefore they knew the consequences of being exposed. A number of those we approached refused to cooperate, either out of fear of the inevitable retribution if uncovered or an unyielding commitment to their cause. We had a soft spot for the latter type, as some of us were involved in the anti-Apartheid struggle, and appreciated a measure of ideological resilience.

Walid (pseudonym) was one of our operation's early and significant recruitments within the G-Force. We did not pursue him as a covert source but as a state witness in cases against G-Force members. The operation to recruit Walid was one of the few examples of cooperation between intelligence operatives and detectives working in the Pagad Investigation Unit. Walid was a member of a G-Force cell operating in the Salt River area that was involved in the use of pipe bombs. He first came to our attention after his arrest on Cape Town's N1 highway, together with two other cell members. Members of a police reaction unit found the group, allegedly en route to an attack, in possession of an illegal pipe bomb.

He was again arrested by the Pagad Investigation Unit in May 2000, this time for his role in the murder of two gangsters in the Brooklyn area. Before his arrest, we developed a keen interest in Walid and one of his close associates. The Pagad Investigation Unit approached Walid and offered him immunity from prosecution if he testified against other G-Force members involved in acts of terrorism. Although he considered the proposal, his initial inclination to refuse was influenced by his convictions. According to him, testifying against fellow G-Force members breached his religious obligations as a Muslim. Like others, Walid was brought to believe that any action against his brethren would turn him into a *munafiq*, a hypocrite and a traitor not only against Pagad but Islam itself. The fact that many innocent women and children were killed in the course of Pagad's so-called jihad failed to occupy the minds of ideologues or adherents like him.

To secure Walid's cooperation, we went to the target profile we had previously developed, looking for an issue or trigger we could use to sway him to our side. After much debate, we concluded that the road to gaining his cooperation was through his wife. Like so many people who are casually involved in killing, he somehow managed to maintain a very affectionate and gentle relationship with his wife, Mymoena. Both in their early twenties, we felt they may be swayed by the realisation of a permanent or long-term separation imposed by imprisonment. Yet, Mymoena would have to be the one to express her horror at this likelihood. We learned that she received almost no material support from Pagad to sustain herself and her family, which included a newborn baby. With her husband in prison, she had no alternative means of subsistence and relied on Pagad to provide her with money and food. Yet, the organisation had so many families of incarcerated G-Force members to feed at that time that the task became impossible.

We identified this opportunity and rushed to seize it. Amber, our star operative, approached Mymoena using a charity organisation that provides food relief to the families of prisoners as a cover. Over weeks, she supplied the family with food and money for electricity, phone calls, and diapers for the baby. During these interactions, Amber planted the idea of persuading her husband to testify within Mymoena's mind. Initially resistant to the idea herself, the combination of material desperation and the persuasive powers of Amber turned her into an advocate of the concept.

She started having this conversation with her husband during her frequent prison visits, but only in the most general terms. It was not yet an offer but an incipient operation taking shape. In this scheme, you discreetly and incrementally shift the target mentally from point A to B without them noticing that such a switch is taking place. It is the application of incipient warfare at the micro, personal level. When she assessed the situation and found the time right, Amber exposed her true colours and intent. She reintroduced herself as an intelligence officer keen on gaining Walid's cooperation as a state witness. In the end, Mymoena spoke to him and informed him of their neglect while he was in prison. The wife highlighted the subsequent support she received from the lovely lady from intelligence, without whom she and his newborn baby would have been left destitute. This was now a case of what the Japanese call *jukushishugi*. In the book, '*An Impeccable Spy*', Owen Matthews translates this to 'waiting for the persimmon fruit to ripen and fall into your lap.'

In subsequent conversations with Walid, he recounted the anguish of making the decision. He had shared a prison cell with fellow G-Force members, which was not the most conducive place to contemplate betrayal. He was indoctrinated and welcomed into a small band of brothers, developed close personal relationships with some of them, and conducted dangerous work alongside them. He now faced the dilemma of choosing between his family on the one hand and his brothers and what he still believed to be a good cause on the other. It was a stark and binary choice that Pagad had created with the neglect of his family. Like all people who turn in this manner, he had to rationalise the betrayal of his fellow conspirators.

Dramat and I spent a few days with Walid, debriefing him to develop our understanding of the G-Force and some of the individuals central to its operations. By this time, he was eager and resourceful, providing insights into some areas of G-Force operations where we had hitherto only had a slight peek. After coordinating with the investigator handling his case, we removed him from Pollsmoor prison, where he was held with fellow Pagad inmates. He was taken to a magistrate, where he confessed to the murders with which he was charged and indicated his willingness to testify against his co-accused. Simultaneously, his family was removed from their home in Salt River and taken to a safe house before being admitted into the witness protection programme.

In late 2001, Walid started testifying in several cases involving G-Force members. When asked why he had chosen to testify, he told the court the story of the support provided to his family by the intelligence services. Why were we successful in turning Walid where the investigators had failed? The first and primary reason was the covert team's creativity in deciding how to approach him. Whereas the investigators would naturally approach him directly, we had intelligence on him and his relationship with his wife, which allowed us to exploit a weakness in his armour.

The second reason was patience, the hallmark of all good intelligence officers – of which we had a significant reservoir. We rarely felt compelled to rush into an approach and had no issue cultivating someone gradually over time if we assessed that this was worth its weight in intelligence. This is the combination that Amber's effort and creativity brought together and which the rest of us supported. It was a sizable fish of significant intelligence and prosecutorial value that we, together the prosecutors, had caught. By no means would Walid be the last.

Our operation coincided with a dramatic increase in the frequency of explosions. The expectation to conduct a long-term operation while delivering intelligence of immediate tactical value placed much pressure on us. Shortly after our return to Cape Town, while the Mathey brothers were appearing at the Wynberg Magistrates Court, a pipe bomb exploded outside the court. On 22 May 2000, a homeless person discovered a pipe bomb outside the New York Bagel restaurant in Sea Point. He alerted the police after unsuccessfully trying to deactivate the bomb by knocking it against the pavement, and they deactivated the device. Less than a month later, on 10 June, a similar bomb exploded in a car parked outside the same restaurant.

Our provincial management also imposed demands on us. Trollip was appointed the provincial head of Crime Intelligence at this point. Having previously headed one of the Pagad task teams, he was keenly interested in Pagad affairs, unlike his predecessor, Du Plessis.

Trollip fell victim to 'responsiveness syndrome,' launching a new initiative every time something newsworthy on Pagad emerged. This became a weekly occurrence. Like many in police management, he was driven by the belief that something must be seen to be done, no matter how poorly considered it might be. Trollip had somehow found out that we were involved in a covert operation under the direction of Williams, and made every attempt to insert himself into the operation and frustrate our efforts. Despite knowing our reporting procedure directly to the CI head office, he persistently demanded to be briefed by Petros. Initially, Petros refused to brief him, referring him to his national boss, Williams. We later offered him briefings comprising less sensitive information to get him off our backs.

Trollip, nonetheless, was relentless. His next play was to insist on a briefing at our covert facility. Though he had no reason to visit the place, which constituted a security breach, he was insistent. After holding him off for months, we relented and agreed on a date and time for the meeting. He was brought to the facility, and after the customary tea and small talk, we moved to the conference room, which doubled up as a war room. This was the place where we schemed, analysed and tracked our targets. It was the room where we decided the fate of G-Force members – to make a pitch and recruit them or go all out to neutralise them.

The war room was approximately eight by four metres and had a conference table at the centre. The one long wall was covered with area maps, G-Force network maps, and target photos. The other had a whiteboard running across the length of the wall and was where we took notes during meetings or planning sessions. Chairs were arranged on the long sides of the table, and one each at the head or foot of the table. Ordinarily, protocol required that a senior visitor like Trollip was seated at the head of the table.

A couple of minutes before the start of the meeting, I went into the conference room to clear the whiteboard. As I started wiping the board, I noticed that someone had written *'Attie Trollip is varkkoppig'* (Attie Trollip is pigheaded) on the board. To make matters worse, the perpetrator had written with a permanent instead of erasable whiteboard marker. In the couple of minutes I had, I could not erase it. So there we were, minutes away from starting a meeting in that very room, with a potentially serious incident that could blow up in our faces. I removed the chairs at the head and foot of the table and whispered into Dramat's ear. We carefully shepherded Trollip into the room, ensuring that he sat on the whiteboard side of the room, where the two of us flanked him. Trollip was short in stature, and the inscription 'Attie Trollip is pigheaded' was above his head, clearly visible to everyone seated on the opposite side of the table. Everyone maintained their composure, and Trollip left none the wiser, again carefully manoeuvred out of the room and into a waiting car.

My team's dedication was unwavering. We worked tirelessly, often around the clock. Our typical day started when we reported to our office at 6:30 a.m. We spent the first hour reading the latest newspapers and updating ourselves on information reported during the night and into the early morning hours by sources. We also used this time for daily planning. The morning often presented us with new developments that complicated a current operation or opened up new opportunities, and I ensured that we spent this time working through these. After this, we wrote reports to various provincial and national clients. Depending on the volume of information we gathered in the previous twenty-four hours, the exercise could take up the rest of the morning. Then, we set out to conduct field-based operational work, where the most exciting part of our job began. In addition to meetings with sources at safe houses, surveillance, monitoring, and transcription of technical intercepts, the work included collecting profile information such as travel records, educational background, and family details on targets. This also entailed rendezvous with our surveillance support team, the NIA, and military intelligence staff working on the Pagad case.

We usually met at the office at 5 p.m., reported on the day's developments, and planned operations for the evening. A large part of this included the monitoring of Pagad and G-Force meetings. We would be home by 10 p.m. on a good day. However, we were living in extraordinary times, and our schedule was frequently interrupted by shootings and explosions. Such inevitable events meant working through the night, sometimes for days.

I also spent time compiling analytic pieces, primarily for our own internal use, our principals' consumption at head office, and our interagency collaboration. I continued participating in the interagency analysis working group and still contributed to its work while benefiting immensely from the relationships I had developed there.

Despite the demanding nature of our work, we tried to maintain a balance between our professional and personal lives. This work situation negatively affected the personal lives of operatives. Apart from the increasing personal security risk, most of us were in long-term relationships. We also had children we needed to see and spend time with. My son was born in 1999, during a hectic operational period. Dramat dropped me at the hospital an hour or so before my wife gave birth so I could be present at that important event. Our kids only saw us intermittently. When I arrived home from work, mine were asleep, only waking after I'd left for work the following day. As he often woke during the night, I could spend some time with my newborn son. I would then talk, sing, and walk around the house with him.

We tried, as best we could, to give operatives time off to spend with their families, but this would often be interrupted by an incident that required our immediate attention. The explosion on 10 June 2000 outside the New York Bagel restaurant occurred while I was having a rare dinner with my wife at our favourite restaurant in Constantia village. After the explosion, I had to organise my team and get the latest reports from the crime scene. We had to make urgent contact with sources to determine the location and movement of possible suspects. Purely coincidentally, and almost exactly two months later, a bomb exploded outside the very restaurant where I had dinner with my wife on the day of the New York

Bagel restaurant bombing. We all experienced disrupted dinners, parties and other important events; and Pagad obviously had no intention of letting up and providing us with a reprieve from the frenetic pace of work.

By the middle of 2000, Cape Town was gripped by a state of panic due to the pipe bombs that detonated every week. Indicating an attempt to raise the impact of bombings to a qualitatively different level and causing mass casualties, this round of attacks had some disturbing features which were absent in previous attacks. G-Force members were now using ammonium nitrate, commonly found in fertiliser, as a component of their explosives. The correct mixture of fertiliser and gunpowder can exponentially amplify the effect of an explosion. This was the recipe used in Oklahoma on 19 April 1995 by the American terrorist Timothy McVeigh when he bombed a federal building and killed more than 160 people.

Our sources had previously reported that Pagad members were experimenting with the use of fertiliser but that they had not been successful in finding the right mixture and detonating mechanism. Even on the occasions when they had used fertiliser in bombs, it did not significantly enhance the effect of the explosive device. However, the intention was clear – to create an atmosphere of terror and helplessness among the population through producing mass casualty events. Their tactic was further enhanced by how they selected targets and the timing of attacks. During 2000, there was a significant move towards targets frequented by large crowds. Venues such as the V&A Waterfront or upmarket shopping malls that attracted tourists became more frequent targets.

The period between May and September 2000 was the most hectic of my involvement in anti-Pagad operations. The intensity and audacity of the bombings stunned everyone, including those of us in the covert unit. Despite the progress in developing our intelligence network, we failed to proactively pinpoint any of the attacks. This was a source of incredible frustration within the unit. It seemed that all the effort we had put into the investigation in the preceding three years was too slow to bear fruit and that our adversary remained a step ahead of us. It was even more unfortunate that our arch-nemeses, the bomber's circle, introduced a new and potentially devastating type of explosive device. There were more frequent, though fleeting, moments of doubt about the possibility of success. We needed a significant breakthrough to energise and motivate the team.

This was a time when the G-Force operated with a sense of impunity, and the community lost almost complete faith in the ability of the state to guarantee its security. Indeed, by September 2000, the state could not credibly issue such assurances. Once again, the entire security community went into overdrive. Additional personnel were brought into Cape Town, and new initiatives, all labelled strategies, were discussed and adopted, only to be aborted swiftly after another bomb blast. The call for cooperation and the sharing of intelligence rang out once more. Ministers, senior police, intelligence and military officials were dispatched to the city to assist and guide operations. None of it worked. It was simply an attempt to show the public we were serious about dealing with urban terror. It was all a broad-stroke effort which may have, with some luck, produced some positive results.

At the same time, many in the security community were waiting for the breakthrough that everyone assumed would arrive at the opportune time. This hope was premised on the bombers making a mistake or one of them confessing to their crimes and betraying their fellow *mujahideen*. None of the many security teams flooding into Cape Town worked towards infiltrating the bombing cells and destroying them from the inside. None that is, except the covert unit and our comrades from the NIA and Lalla's team in KwaZulu-Natal. As luck would have it, Els provided an unwitting opportunity for a gathering of minds between our KZN friends and me. This paved the way for precisely that kind of breakthrough we had been waiting for.

CHAPTER 6

Lancer: Building a Weapon to Pierce Pagad's Armour

Give me a lever long enough and a fulcrum on which to place it, and I shall move the world.
—**Archimedes**

In August 2000, Dramat and I were appointed by Willie Els to a team tasked with designing a standardised profile for an Crime Intelligence source handler. We had to explore the skill set, personality and aptitude required of a successful handler. Els initiated the project, which was intended to craft a tool we could use to determine the recruitment, training, and deployment of officers within Crime Intelligence. Instead of working from the inherited and contaminated Branch material or merely adopting similar profiles designed by foreign intelligence services, this was an effort to develop a set of characteristics that suited our country's contextual dynamics and operational conditions. He brought together what he considered the best intelligence officers in the country, most of whom came from the covert units.

Deena Moodley was the KZN officer participating in the project, a protege of our comrade, Lalla. Not only was Moodley a capable operative, but he was also not afraid to think outside the box and had a creative approach to wicked intelligence problems.

During the mid-1990s, he headed the intelligence task team into the violence that plagued the town of Richmond, KwaZulu-Natal. When presented with the thankless mission of ending years of political violence, Moodley jumped at the task, relishing the prospect of bringing some of his ideas to fruition in the province's challenging environment.

He soon established a covert intelligence team consisting of young and energetic operatives mentored by Lalla, whose approach was to let them roam free, falter, learn, and succeed on their own terms. They developed an impressive information network, gathering the intelligence required to impact the situation. In a short time, they had identified and neutralised the perpetrators of the violence. They destroyed a sophisticated network of violence that had been operational for more than a decade. The impact of their work was extensive and sustained, which was precisely what we intended to achieve in Cape Town.

The profiling team spent a few days in Pretoria with a team of psychologists and talent specialists from one of the big consulting firms. Having participated in developing the personality-skill matrix, Dramat returned to Cape Town. He did not want to leave the unit without its two most senior members while the high operational tempo persisted. The rest of us then decamped to a remote training base in the Limpopo Province, about a three-hour drive from Pretoria. The Maleoskop facility was where we spent a week profiling, interviewing, and recruiting fresh blood for Crime Intelligence. The camp at the time served as the tactical training centre of the police special task force.

The recruiting pool consisted of newly graduated police officers from the police college in Pretoria. Selebi informed Williams, who wanted to expand the division, that the 300 recruits were at our disposal, and we were free to choose any or all of them for CI. We liked the idea, especially those of us from the covert units who thought we could use 'cleanskins' who were not yet contaminated by the experience of being police officers or might otherwise not be generally known to be police officers.

Maleoskop was not just a remote training base, but a perfect location to let our minds roam free, think, and engage in meaningful conversations. It was here that Moodley and I clicked immediately, spending many hours in dialogue. He was keen to understand the challenges we were experiencing in Cape Town, and I was eager to gain detailed insight into their Richmond success. Like Lalla, Moodley saw it as their responsibility to assist comrades like ourselves in Cape Town. The more successes former DIS officers could achieve, the stronger our collective influence over the division would become, and the more secure we could be in transforming CI into a modern post-Apartheid intelligence structure.

I was convinced the methods of Moodley's Richmond intelligence task team could be utilised effectively in the Cape Town context. The first method related to the need for centralised control in the intelligence domain, with no secondary or competing capabilities within Crime Intelligence. The second, which we already started to implement, was the proper integration of investigative capacity co-located with the covert intelligence team. The third was the most sensitive and risky, the deployment of CI officers in deep cover within the G-Force. The last of these was the most sensitive type of operation carried out by Crime Intelligence. It would be a very complex and challenging exercise in the context of the G-Force, an organisation operating with high levels of security, drawing from a specific and limited pool of Muslims. Yet, in the Maleoskop bush, one could dream, plot, and plan. If we could get at least two of these to work, we would be well set to make a sustained breakthrough.

Between interviewing and assessing the 300 recruits, Moodley and I developed an idea we thought deserved to be pitched to Lalla, Petros, and Dramat. I was sure that Lalla and Dramat would naturally take to the idea, as both were attracted to bold and decisive operational approaches. Petros was slightly more conservative but could most likely be convinced with a well-presented and articulated proposition.

Whilst we were discussing ways to resolve the Pagad dilemma in the safety of rural Limpopo, another bomb exploded outside the United States Consulate in central Cape Town. The explosive device, placed inside a vehicle, also contained fertiliser and would have caused extensive casualties had it functioned properly. Once again, there were no concrete clues about the bombers' identity. Even when we trawled through hour upon hour of footage from the city's extensive close-circuit surveillance camera network, we failed to identify the bombers or even find anything that would link us to a specific person. It was like a spectre had entered the city, activated the bomb and disappeared into thin air.

The bombing contributed to a growing sense of helplessness on the part of Cape Town's citizens. Business, political and religious leaders called for stern action against the perpetrators of these attacks. Given the latest target, the pressure from the US administration and other diplomatic missions intensified. The situation also risked South Africa becoming entangled in the American obsession with 'Islamic fundamentalism,' something we were desperate to avoid and which I thought would exacerbate our problem and diminish our ability to defeat Pagad. Our adversary, though, was upping the ante, now brazenly targeting foreign diplomatic and economic interests, as well as synagogues. Pagad wanted us to respond in ways that would lead us into the trap Western countries presented as an embrace. This would have given credence to their claim that the South African government was part of a broader anti-Muslim project driven by Western interests. They would fail.

During my time in Limpopo, I maintained constant communication with Petros and Dramat, keeping them updated on the discussions between Moodley and myself. Upon my return to Cape Town, I briefed them on the proposed operational concept. Petros initially had concerns, fearing that the new concept would render our existing operation obsolete. I reassured him that the two concepts were complementary and that the lessons from Moodley's operation would only enhance our existing efforts.

I also had a distinct feeling that Petros was concerned that Lalla would overshadow him if he became more centrally involved in our operation instead of just offering hands-off support and advice as he was then doing. Lalla, however, was a quintessentially laid-back character and not the sort to obsess over power, and I could not see such a risk at all. We would need more time to settle my boss' concerns, and the best option was for Lalla and Moodley to come to Cape Town so we could sit down like comrades, speak frankly, and thrash things out.

Meanwhile, Moodley was back in KZN, briefing Lalla on our discussions and proposal. Having been engaged in conversations with us previously, Lalla grasped the urgency of what had become a desperate situation, and the need for immediate action. He flew to Cape Town with Moodley for consultations with Petros, Dramat, and myself. Contrary to police protocol, he never met Trollip, his Western Cape CI counterpart. We housed Lalla and Moodley at one of our safe houses in an upmarket Cape Town suburb and spent three days discussing and refining our idea.

The first order of business was to allay Petros' concerns. I briefed Lalla on these in advance and in his typically casual but disarming manner, he was prepared to support the new initiative as and when we needed it. Lalla emphasised the importance of locating command and control at the site of the battle, that is, in Cape Town. The logical consequence was that Petros would retain control, but this time with a more expansive mandate. Petros was relieved, and we agreed on the details.

Several meetings occurred at this juncture that radically affected our endeavour to implement a slightly adjusted and renewed effort to combat urban terror. Having taken the day off one September morning, I received a call from Williams. He instructed me to immediately go to Trollip's office and accompany him to a meeting with Selebi. I informed Williams that I was not suitably dressed for a meeting with the national police commissioner. I was walking around with sandals, old jeans, and a t-shirt, to which he simply replied, 'Africa, just get there immediately!' Trollip was less relaxed about my state of dress when I got to his office, but I reiterated Williams' emphasis on 'immediate!' and off we went to meet Selebi. Trollip was in a suit, and I was in torn jeans and sandals, and we were on our way to see the national commissioner for what must have been something urgent. Williams had advised that Selebi wanted to have time alone with me to prepare for the official meeting. When I asked how we would make it happen, given that I would be heading there with Trollip, he replied, 'Don't worry. The chief will engineer it.'

The meeting took place at Selebi's office on the 7th floor of the parliamentary building that housed ministers and directors-general of national government departments. When we arrived, Trollip and I were met by senior officers from head office. This included the loud, forceful, yet intelligent Andre Pruis, Selebi's deputy national commissioner. When Selebi arrived, he informed everyone present that he needed to urgently go to the Foreign Affairs office in the same building and, turning to me, said, 'Chief, I don't know this building well. Please show me where the foreign affairs offices are.' This must have sounded odd to those who knew that before he was appointed police commissioner, Selebi was the director-general of Foreign Affairs. Who was I to ask questions, though? Selebi obviously knew exactly where to go, and took me to his old foreign affairs office, which I then learned was on the 17th floor. We had a 15-minute meeting. He informed me that Williams was the one who had advised that we have a quick meeting before engaging the senior managers who were waiting for us on the 7th floor.

Selebi had two questions and asked that I be frank when responding. His first question was to the point. 'Can you guys solve this Pagad problem in the next six months?' My reply was slightly less direct. 'Yes, we can, chief, but we must be allowed to operate unhindered by the rest of the organisation. Our primary challenge is the dilution of our efforts through unnecessary taskings and competition by other offices that are actively instigated by our provincial management.'

'I understand,' Selebi said. 'What resources do you need from me to ensure success within our six-month time frame?' Having been through endless discussions and planning sessions with Dramat and Petros and, more recently, with Lalla and Moodley, I had the answer to this question at the tip of my tongue. 'Sir, the primary prerequisite for success is the previously raised issue: freedom of operational movement and centralised control of all Pagad operations in our unit. We have tried this before, but your explicit authority as an instruction would be of great help.'

Selebi said that he had assumed that his previous guidance to the provincial management was sufficient. He realised that he had to be more forceful in communicating this. When he asked what practical support we required, I told him that we needed the surveillance team detached to us or to at least be at our disposal whenever we needed them. I told him that the surveillance team had raised some resource requirements and that providing those resources would go a long way in boosting their capabilities. Additionally, I outlined some organisational and resource needs for the covert unit, suggesting that Els be placed within the covert unit for a short time to facilitate the transfer of resources and get things going. Selebi was now ready to present his subordinate managers with a *fait accompli*. Our 15 minutes were up, and we returned to the senior police management who had gathered on the 7th floor. Williams had been right about Selebi's ability to engineer things.

Selebi opened the meeting by saying that, due to the police's failure to come to grips with the situation in Cape Town, he felt that his position as national commissioner was at risk. He went on to inform those gathered about an important development the previous day. 'The president called me to a meeting yesterday and asked me a very odd question. He wanted to know whether South Africa had a police commissioner. "Yes, Mr President. I am the police commissioner". The president then said that he assumed the country was without a commissioner, given the freedom with which Pagad continued to bomb, murder, and destroy. He said that he was nonetheless relieved to hear that we do actually have a commissioner and that I am the incumbent.' Those unfamiliar with Selebi's rhetorical style tried to figure out what was happening, but it all became crystal clear in his last statement regarding the meeting. 'The president then told me that failure to resolve the Pagad problem within six months would mean that the country will, in fact, be without a national commissioner.' Selebi's job was on the line, and he needed to act decisively to retain it. Without saying so, he indicated to those present that they might face the same fate if we failed within the timeframe that the president had clearly defined.

Selebi went on to say that he had recently given much thought to the Pagad problem and how we should tackle it. He had, for obvious reasons, been focused on it since his meeting with the president. He had made some decisions and wanted to inform those present how we'd proceed. The chief had not gathered us to discuss what to do but to inform us of what would be done. He then outlined his plan, which was essentially what I had briefed him on during our short meeting on the 17th floor.

Selebi proceeded to give a detailed analysis of the situation in Cape Town, even identifying the key perpetrators involved in the manufacture of explosive devices at the time. Those present were surprised at the national commissioner's acute grasp of the situation in Cape Town and the specificity of his decisions. They must have come away from the meeting convinced that he must indeed have recently been doing much thinking on the subject.

The meeting was brief and productive. Selebi supported the covert unit's efforts and instructed that we were not to be burdened with unnecessary responsibilities unrelated to Pagad operations. He stressed that we should be free to operate with the focus required to end Pagad's campaign of terror and advised that his decisions have the force of a national instruction. To clarify his instructions and provide details of how they would be implemented, the commissioner would send a team of senior managers to Cape Town to brief the local role-players.

Selebi's plan was officially launched as Operation Lancer. This undertaking was not just a top-down directive, but a collaborative effort that had evolved through a series of conversations. Lancer was conceived from discussions Dramat and I had on the road, pitched to Petros, then to Williams, took shape in the Maleoskop bush, was polished over Lalla's cooking at our safe house, and was about to take off after Selebi's perfectly engineered intervention. Now, with the force of national instruction, Operation Lancer granted the covert unit absolute freedom of movement and operational autonomy.

After the meeting, Selebi asked me to remain behind as he wanted me to join him in briefing Tshwete, which started mid-morning and was a fascinating encounter. I remember the details of the event clearly for two reasons. The first was an extensive argument on the relationship between Pagad and Qibla. Tshwete started by saying that he knew 'these Qibla chaps well. I spent time with them on the Island.' His position was that the Qibla leadership should be our main target, as they have complete control over Pagad anyway, and targeting them would collapse Pagad and the G-Force. Tshwete stated this position as gospel truth, with the conviction that only a politician can.

I disagreed with him and highlighted that the relationship between Pagad and Qibla was more dynamic than a simple one-way hierarchy of the organisation's early days. Though Qibla was behind the formation of Pagad and its members retained the key decision-making positions within the G-Force, the Qibla members within Pagad had developed an identity of their own and identified much more with Pagad than Qibla. One of the reasons for the emergence of this dynamic was simply the personal power that positions in Pagad had granted Qibla members. While Qibla remained a small organisation that operated in the shadows, Pagad publicly commanded the support of thousands. People like Ebrahim, a loyal and staunch Qibla member, had amassed the power of life or death over his G-Force subordinates and increasingly over the organisation's ever-expanding list of enemies. He enjoyed and was obsessed with his newfound power, displayed it for all to see, and wanted to be recognised by Qibla for this, too. These factors gave rise to tensions between Qibla members in Pagad and those like Achmat Cassiem and Yusuf Patel, who remained outside of Pagad.

Our success hinged on an accurate understanding of the Qibla-Pagad dynamic. This appreciation directly shaped our strategy, resource allocation, and deployment of effort. We had come far in moving the police and the collective intelligence community to focus on Pagad and the G-Force as the primary targets. Refocusing on Qibla as Qibla ran the risk of setting us back, perhaps permanently. Tshwete maintained his position but moved on, asking, 'What plans do you chaps have for dealing with this situation in Cape Town?'

Tshwete was the minister of sport before his appointment to the safety and security portfolio. Before Selebi and I could brief him on the commissioner's latest decision, he told us to wait a minute. There was an important cricket match on television, and he wanted to see how it was going. We were then all compelled to sit there watching the game, with the minister analysing this or that player's performance, run rates, and bowling performances and shouting instructions to the players through the television. Our meeting resumed in earnest when the cricketers broke for lunch, and we got back to discussing the decision Selebi had taken at our previous meeting. Tshwete supported the initiative and was forceful in reminding Selebi of the six-month timeframe and the need to be decisive in ensuring his orders were followed. The whole day was a performance par excellence, from Selebi's engineering to Tshwete's cricket pause.

In Pretoria, Selebi summoned his senior management, including Williams, and announced the decision to launch Operation Lancer. Unlike the previous police operations targeting Pagad that sought to temporarily limit the organisation's freedom of movement, Lancer was to be a covert operation that would eliminate the Pagad threat. Immediately after he decided to launch Operation Lancer, Selebi dispatched a delegation to the Western Cape consisting of Willie Els, André Pruis, and Martin Naude, a senior head office investigator.

Pruis, who was probably the key strategist in the police, assumed the role of no-nonsense policeman, contrary to the diplomatic Els. He convened a meeting at the police college in Bishop Lavis. The provincial police commissioner and his management were in attendance. Trollip led a CI provincial delegation, including Petros, Dramat, and myself. Pruis commanded respect amongst old guard cops because he was a thinker, unlike most of them. More importantly, he was himself an old Apartheid-era securocrat, which provided him credibility in their eyes. He often spoke roughly and forcefully and that helped in persuading others to toe the line.

From the very beginning of the meeting, Pruis made his mission in the province abundantly clear to all concerned. In contrast to previous delegations, his team was not there to consult with the provincial police management but only to relay and ensure compliance with the instructions from the national commissioner and the president. Pruis's determination to ensure compliance was palpable. He stated that he was aware of the sensitivities amongst some sectors of the SAPS management in the province concerning Operation Lancer and that Selebi was in no mood for compromise. He expected his instructions to be carried out to the letter. He told the assembled management, 'For those here who think of defying the commissioner's instruction, I am here as an informant – Selebi's informant.'

Operation Lancer was distinguished from previous police operations by several unique elements. First, we implemented the concept of a single, integrated command of all the police's anti-terror intelligence teams. This meant that all intelligence staff engaged in the Pagad operation would be concentrated in one facility, in this instance the covert unit's facility. The investigative element of the operation also changed in that investigators would now be available to the covert unit to complement the work done by the covert unit's investigator, Roger Sampson (pseudonym). Soon, we would have an opportunity to test this mode of cooperation, and it worked exceptionally well.

Our relationship with the Scorpions under Adams had solidified by then, and the new prosecutors he brought on board after the Viljoen fiasco reinforced our confidence in his ability to manage the prosecutorial side of the operation. The fact that Adams had surrounded himself with competent prosecutors he could trust played a significant role in this.

I always thought mobile surveillance would be a critical element of Operation Lancer, second only to human intelligence collection. We needed to equip the surveillance team with the required tools, and once we had done so we'd be entitled to work them hard. Dramat and I had an excellent relationship with Joe (pseudonym), the surveillance team leader with whom we worked. He was an agile officer and very responsive to our requirements. We met regularly, usually on the road, as we all seemed to be in perpetual motion. When we had a chance, we'd sit down, exchange notes, and discuss how to improve their work and what they needed from us to enhance their surveillance work. Joe and his team worked under the tired Len Nel, the technical intelligence equivalent of our own hapless Du Plessis. They, however, produced excellent results even with the limitations of the size of their team and resources.

Lancer defined the improvement in our interception and monitoring capability, and the covert unit took bold operational initiatives to optimise using this capability. Dramat, who had an affinity for this work, sat with the team to work through scenarios under which we could access target communications, meetings, and vehicles. The days of dysfunctional equipment from our earlier days were now a thing of the past. Wherever the G-Force conducted their affairs, literally and figuratively, they could be sure that we'd be making aggressive attempts to hear, watch, and track them. A member of the G-Force could not be sure whether the supplier of his telephone was on our side, if the guy installing his satellite dish was a spy, or whether the Internet cafe where he discreetly carried out his communications was safe. The deployment of the new technology brought us one of our most significant successes not long after the commencement of the operation. Apart from the Keg & Swan operation, where technology provided a breakthrough, the other successful technical operations due to the ingenuity of the covert unit are best left unmentioned. Lancer showcased a spectacular integration of covert human intelligence, technical collection, analysis, and rapid exploitation of the intelligence produced.

Whilst all this conceptualisation took place, pressure to refine and concretise the operational plan for Operation Lancer mounted. Petros, Dramat and I had a clear idea of how we wanted the operation to unfold. Most importantly we had to make critical decisions on prioritising targets, sequencing, and expanding our collection team.

Intelligence is a precise craft, and targeting requires the commander to understand the intelligence consumer's requirements and arrange their capabilities accordingly. It affects everything from the type of resources we deploy, the specific taskings given to sources, or what we would try to extract from arrested G-Force members during interrogations. In Operation Lancer, we had multiple consumers, starting with the tactical units, such as the special task force that required exact intelligence to arrest or interdict G-Force members en route to or in the act of executing an attack.

The Scorpions required a different kind of intelligence for prosecutorial purposes, even if they could not use such intelligence directly in court. In investigating a conspiracy, they required intelligence on the Pagad and G-Force network, decision-making in this network, and role allocation. Our political bosses required strategic intelligence to determine policy, make informed public statements, and initiate relationships that had the potential to further blunt Pagad's political influence in the Muslim community.

The totality of these actions aimed to bring the G-Force tumbling down and leave Pagad politically neutralised. For this purpose, Dramat and I cultivated an extensive and impressive political and ideological network. We ran this influence operation in close association with Fraser at the NIA. What was left was sharpening our targeting on the tactical response and prosecutorial angles. Petros was inclined to adopt a broad front assault on the G-Force, and in our initial targeting meeting, proposed we target the totality of its Security Council command structure and all its subordinate cells.

I approached the problem from a different, net-centric perspective, developing a targeting approach that targets the G-Force as a network rather than a set of structures. In reality, it functioned much more dynamically and as a fluid network, which had significant advantages for them. This meant the leadership could retain some distance from high-risk operational activity, rapidly reorganise, and build redundancies into the organisation's system. Dynamic networks can scale up or down, hibernate and resurge, and retain an inherent resilience buffer to survive an assault. Pagad had, until Lancer, masterfully achieved this by immunising the SC from cells, engaging cell commanders individually, often by deploying an intermediate layer of operational commanders. Boeta Yu was this intermediate layer's most active and influential member. They carried instructions from the Council and provided funds and logistical support. In the case of bombings, where the cell did not have its own bomb-making capability, they arranged for the delivery of explosive devices.

This intricate web made intelligence collection more difficult, as it was not a case of simply following an instruction from A to B. For bureaucrats indoctrinated in top-down, neatly drawn organisational blocks, appreciating this kind of dynamic network did not come naturally. We had to identify its centre of gravity and focus our efforts there to bring down the G-Force's net-centric system. This approach differed from the two most commonly used police approaches, which either target the so-called high flyers or adopt a broad swathe against everyone involved in the target structure.

In his classic book on strategy, *On War,* German strategist Carl von Clausewitz described most accurately what we needed to do: 'Out of the dominant characteristics of both belligerents, a certain centre of gravity develops, the hub of all power and movement, on which everything depends. That is the point against which all our energies should be directed.' The net-centric approach to defeating a criminal network is premised on the fact that its commanders, in this case the SC, had to maintain communication, even if they worked through intermediaries. This situation provided a buffer between them and G-Force cells and, simultaneously, a vulnerability we intended to exploit. We agreed that our approach should focus on identifying our adversary's centre of gravity and the points from which we could breach, disrupt and destroy it.

What was the G-Force's centre of gravity, von Clausewitz's *point against which all our energies should be directed?* In our context, it was the strategic focal point of the G-Force, the target whose neutralisation would significantly weaken the organization. We identified two prime targets whose centrality derived from very different calculations. First, we targeted the bomber's circle because they had been the most dedicated implementer of Pagad's shift to a broader anti-Western bombing campaign. The attacks against the US consulate, as well as the Planet Hollywood and New York Bagel restaurant, were the start of a bombing campaign that evolved to include synagogues. By exploiting good human source reporting, we had already thwarted two attacks against synagogues in Cape Town. Yet, a failure to neutralise this group led to the inevitable lapse in which they would succeed in their attempts. The political effect of a successful attack on a synagogue or a deadlier attack against a Western diplomatic or economic target would be politically and economically devastating.

The second target was the intermediate operational layer of senior G-Force members who facilitated the SC's decisions. Their implosion would leave the Council severely compromised. Not only would they have to engage more directly with G-Force cells and risk increased exposure and arrest, but they would also have to build the same level of trust that had developed between the intermediate layer of commanders and the cells. Critical players in this cadre, like Boeta Yu and Frances, had built deep trust with the G-Force's geographic and specialist cells. They accompanied cells during attacks, provided them with guidance and material, and were central in supporting them and their families in the event of arrest. Replacing this level of mutual respect and trust would be no easy feat. This small group of individuals operated at an impressive, fast-paced tempo and compelled us to follow suit.

Having completed the broader structure target selection, we moved on to individual target selection, which took place jointly with the investigators. As the intelligence team, we conducted a comprehensive threat analysis, identifying and prioritising the various layers of targets. The inclusion of each target on our list was motivated by the details of their involvement in the G-Force, their position in the structure, and their known involvement in acts of terrorism. On the other hand, the detectives simply handed in a list of names without any background or motivation. How they identified these people as urban terror suspects remains a mystery. Despite their lack of substance in motivating their target selection, the investigators insisted on keeping their targets on the target list.

As a tactical move, we agreed to include their names on the target list. At this point, we thought that unnecessary battles over a name list would not do us any good. When we briefed our team, Dramat and I omitted names we regarded as inconsequential. From the start, we focused on real targets instead of phantoms. Our approach to targeting differed from the 'catch-all' target selection that often characterises police operations. This emphasised looking at the G-Force as a system constituted by interrelationships and mini-networks. It required us to understand the level of institutional cohesion within the G-Force, identify the layers, nodes and relationships that made its terror infrastructure effective, and determine what constituted the critical capabilities without which it would not be able to operate with the impressive level of success it had achieved.

We did things this way without explicitly informing Petros of this deviation. He was heavily invested in a targeting approach that was too broad to realistically achieve with our limited resources and time. We needed to concentrate our efforts on a smaller and more precise target group. The boss had a long list of people he wanted to send to prison, while ours was a very short list of targets we tried to neutralise to collapse the G-Force. We worked with our list without upsetting anyone, maintaining the farce that 'everyone must go to prison' when needed.

If we succeeded, targeting the G-Force in this manner would produce a spectacular coup for the covert unit, and we certainly hoped it would. We needed to execute an almost perfectly sequenced operation in which the politics were tightly choreographed, and the shock effect was profound and irreversible. Though we believed in the maxim that those who prepare their work well make their own luck, we would need more than a small measure of luck.

The stars were aligning in our favour, and the previous six years' work was now reaching a culmination point. Dramat also felt and displayed this confidence and communicated it to our team and the newcomers who would shortly join us. We could also see it in the faces of the NIA team with whom we worked daily. Something had changed; forces were now arrayed not against Pagad or even the G-Force as a whole but a small group of G-Force members whose fate lay in our hands. Our efforts were no longer dispersed, and as the G-Force would feel soon enough, once the state's considerable and focused capabilities were arrayed against a small group, it became very uncomfortable very quickly. Covert and our partners in the NIA and Scorpions would be the lance that pierced their hitherto impenetrable armour.

With the covert unit playing a role whose significance was entirely out of proportion to its place in the bureaucracy or its size, we fought for Operation Lancer to concentrate an impressive array of resources and forces. Having won that battle, we had to coordinate all these resources across the tactical and strategic spectrum. In such a complex environment, coordinating such an intricate range of institutional relationships without, at some point, dropping the ball is very difficult. Human error, technical hitches, miscommunication and plain exhaustion could all come into play and mess up our carefully crafted plans.

We had to design two sets of liaison and coordination mechanisms. On the one level, we required coordination of the overall operation between intelligence, investigations, and the various tactical response capabilities. Concerning the latter, we were granted privileged access to the police's special task force and the army's special forces. Lancer required the ability to rapidly and seamlessly exploit tactical intelligence on planned or ongoing attacks and access to these structures would exponentially enhance our ability to do so. Having the country's best reconnaissance teams at our disposal meant a new level of surveillance capability. At the same time, the world-renowned police task force was unrivalled when it came to rapid and effective responses to high-risk situations.

At another level, we had the responsibility of liaising with our sister intelligence services, the National Intelligence Agency and Military Intelligence. Legislation enforced our obligation to liaise with these agencies through the National Intelligence Coordinating Committee (NICOC) and its provincial representative.

Due to his background the PICOC coordinator, Brookbanks, could not win the confidence of either the provincial NIA leadership or the CI covert unit, which he previously headed. This inevitably meant we had to find creative ways of sharing operational information with our colleagues at the NIA without using the formal PICOC structures, a mission made easier by the strength of our relationship since Fraser's 1998 arrival in the province. The relationship between our unit and NIA in the province had developed into very close operational integration. We ran joint operations, followed up leads together, and shared responsibility according to which entity was most suited to a specific task. The trust between us was absolute.

We poached Peter Jacobs, from the Border Policing unit after informing Williams that he would play an indispensable role in the operation's intelligence work. Unlike many of us from the ANC who integrated into police intelligence, Jacobs was a cop's cop. A stickler for detail, Jacobs was a straight shooter with an obsessive attachment to protocol. He was the skilled information manager and strict taskmaster we thought eminently suitable for establishing a competent analytical and information management capacity. Jacobs also acted as a buffer between us and the often burdensome police managers who wanted reports simply for the sake of it, or because they felt their ranks entitled them to such. Jacobs was just the type of person we needed to keep Trollip and the rest of SAPS provincial management at a sufficient distance so they could not impact our work negatively.

By the second week in October 2000, we had worked out detailed plans and had established the mechanisms for command, control, and coordination. We still lacked the required collection capacity and needed a much larger HUMINT capacity and around-the-clock surveillance. We intended to select operatives from the Western Cape, KZN, and Gauteng to join the existing capacity of the covert unit. During earlier discussions, Lalla had agreed to make one of his surveillance teams available to supplement our existing capacity. Afrika Khumalo, an old ANC comrade at the helm of CI in Gauteng province, also detached a surveillance team to the operation.

Operation Lancer would be the first counter-terrorism operation in post-Apartheid South Africa conceived in its entirety and almost entirely commanded by officers from the former ANC intelligence and military structures. It would test the skills we acquired in the ANC underground and what we had learned inside the police since 1995.

At this point, I had to go to Pretoria to brief Selebi on the progress of the planning phase of the operation and to appraise him of the response of local police actors to his instructions. It was meant to be a quick fly-in, which would see me back in Cape Town that same evening. Sitting on the plane to Johannesburg, I felt what had by then become a regular and familiar pain in my lower back. The pain was caused by lower back muscle spasms that could go on for days and be quite debilitating. Nothing helped mitigate the suffering; it would disappear after two or three days. I took a torturous taxi ride to police headquarters and headed to the national commissioner's office.

Selebi could see that I was in pain when I arrived and asked what the matter was. When I explained the whole back pain issue to him and that it was painful to sit up and brief him even then, he said, 'That is not a problem. There's no reason why you can't lie down on the floor and brief me. After the briefing, I'll arrange for you to see my physician and ensure my staff gets you to a hotel so you can stay overnight and rest.' So, lying on my back on the police commissioner's office floor I spoke of the team we had put together, Jacobs' entry into the operation, and the support we had been receiving from Els. I informed him that we were busy with a few source cultivations and that even if only some of them materialised, we would be well set to make a breakthrough against the G-Force. He was keen to know how the old police establishment in the province had reacted to his instructions regarding the concentration of authority under Petros. 'So far, so good, commissioner', I responded. 'Let's see how long they can maintain their discipline and withstand their instinctive need to interfere in our work.'

After the hour-long meeting, and true to his word, Selebi asked his staff officer to arrange a doctor's visit and a hotel stay in Hatfield, just outside the city centre. The doctor gave me an intramuscular injection, and I fell asleep promptly after a quick meal at the hotel. Still sore but more mobile, I flew to Cape Town the following day to rejoin the team.

Unity of command in the collection domain was an absolute prerequisite for Lancer's success. The police had a number of teams working on Pagad, often acting at cross purposes and rarely in a synchronised fashion. A decision was made that the entire intelligence gathering capacity on urban terrorism should be placed within the covert unit. At the time, I thought we should work with the small team we had and retain the prerogative to select which individuals we wanted to integrate into Lancer. But that was not to be, and we were compelled to bring on board staff from the CI overt offices across the Western Cape. While we were happy with the additional personnel, this approach had shortcomings. Chief amongst these was our inability to select our own team. We probably would have chosen most people who eventually joined the operation, but we were unhappy with others. Many of these operatives were not pleased to work with or be commanded by us either. This would be sorted out at the first briefing for intelligence personnel seconded to the operation.

The gathering was held in the Northern Suburbs of Cape Town and attended by all intelligence personnel seconded to the operation. The intelligence commander Petros was present, while Els and Naude represented the police head office. Trollip also participated as the CI head in the province. Els and Naude started the meeting by introducing Operation Lancer and the imperative of its success. They also emphasised that we were working under time pressure and were expected to produce a favourable outcome soon. In their calculation, we had three to six months to make a significant breakthrough. They explained the Lancer command structures and the necessity of respecting them.

The new structures and orders issued by Selebi and Williams superseded all existing line-functional command structures for the duration of the operation. Els's emphasis on this point did not please Trollip at all. He intervened a few times, emphasising that he was still the CI commander in the province and that Petros remained accountable to him. The more he emphasised this, the more Els disabused him of this view, and emphasised the opposite: Petros accounted to the Lancer command structure at the head office and not the CI provincial management. His only responsibility to the SAPS in the Western Cape was to brief the provincial commissioner on the operation's progress. In discussions afterwards, it was clear that Els was, to put it diplomatically, highly displeased with Trollip's antics during the meeting. He felt that Trollip was openly undermining his authority and, by implication, that of Selebi.

Jacobs and Petros outlined their plans concerning their respective responsibilities in the operation - information management, and overall intelligence command. Petros emphasised that he only wanted people on the team who were committed to the mission. He informed all present that, although they were already seconded to the operation, he would give them the rest of the day to consider whether they wanted to be part of it. If not, they were free to inform him and be relieved of their secondment to the operation. Apart from being a positive management instrument, this also played straight into our hands. We knew some individuals we did not want as part of the operation would voluntarily excuse themselves rather than work under our command. By the end of the day, a few individuals had chosen to leave, though the vast majority opted to stay. We were generally happy with the selection and felt we could succeed with those who chose to stay and join the small team already in place at the covert unit.

The newcomers outnumbered my small team two to one, and though they were welcome, the experience and insight of the team already in situ had to form the basis of the expanded team. I did not want to make the mistake of expansion equating to diluting quality, effort and capability, as it often does in the police. The next crucial battle was the centralisation of human sources under the command of Petros. Crime intelligence had an extensive source capacity in the urban terrorism terrain. Although much could be said of the quality of these sources, we felt it imperative to transfer all human sources to the covert unit for the duration of Operation Lancer. Unfortunately, many people in CI regarded sources as personal property rather than state assets.

Despite the closeness that develops between handlers and sources in the face of demanding and sometimes life-threatening circumstances, the source and the handler must understand that sources work for the institution, not the individual. The custom in CI was for handlers to move sources around, sometimes trying to handle them from far-away places. When we issued instructions that all urban terror sources from the various CI offices in the province be transferred immediately, we encountered opposition from numerous quarters. We, however, remained firm and insisted on implementing the directive, which we communicated as a national instruction. After a few days, all the required sources were transferred to Operation Lancer, now handled by the expanded team at the covert office.

The success of Lancer depended ultimately on the intelligence-gathering capacity of the operation. The expanded team would consist of a few members of the covert unit, but mostly of members from the various overt offices. Our interaction over the preceding four years had not been pleasant and, at times, openly hostile. We realised that the operatives joining us were only instruments in a larger battle, used by their managers, mostly former Branch officers. As we worked together, we found many of them to be competent, committed, and eager to contribute to the operation's success.

Meanwhile, Lalla and Khumalo dispatched well-resourced surveillance teams to bolster the limited capability in Cape Town. This support was helpful because our comrades sent operatives who could blend into the Cape Flats demographic that constituted Pagad's operational environment. A sizable percentage of the Cape Town surveillance unit were white officers who simply could not fit into the townships and suburbs of the Cape Flats.

An undervalued but significant factor in Operation Lancer's success was the increased productivity of the surveillance team after their integration into the operation. Operation Lancer provided them focused target guidance based on our centre-of-gravity analysis and a constant stream of tactical intelligence from our human sources. For the first time, they knew who we intended to take down and focused their efforts on this small group of G-Force members. Based on our source intelligence, they could also recalibrate their surveillance efforts against the G-Force.

As with most police units, we were under-resourced under normal circumstances. Our staff capacity suddenly expanded by ten more people, which posed a significant challenge. We found the assistance of an old cop like Els, with all his contacts, particularly useful in our quest for resources to kickstart the operation. This was no easy task, and the bureaucrats at the police Head Office refused to make it easier. Having Selebi and Tim Williams on our side was always helpful, and with Els on-site, we could problem-solve easily and speedily.

Within a week, we had a fully resourced unit with furnished offices, vehicles, and communications, and a budget to match the mission. Els enjoyed the opportunity to engage in fieldwork again. He had the beaming face of an old hand that missed the dynamism of working on the ground. He advised and opened doors for us, but he also got involved in the minutiae of equipping the office. When we added space to our office, he was one of those who took to the brick wall between the two spaces with a sledgehammer and opened a makeshift door between the spaces. He told me in so many words that he felt liberated to work with officers who knew what they were doing and did it with the energy we displayed. Notably, he never questioned our ability or judgement.

Apart from the administrative and logistical nightmare of setting up the new capacity, we still had the job of conducting intelligence operations against Pagad. We began with the integration of the additional staff into our operation. Like all recruits before them, they were indoctrinated into the functioning of a covert unit – something entirely alien to them. They could no longer act as cops, walking around with guns exposed or driving police vehicles. Working undercover requires different rules, but more importantly, a different posture and approach to work. Members from the overt units had to be familiarised with the cover stories we used and develop backstopping in cases where they risked exposure. They had to create a cover story that could withstand curiosity from our targets or even innocent parties, such as the very friendly and curious neighbours in the office complex where our facility was located.

Next, we had to familiarise everyone with the target terrain. It was essential to develop a common perception of our target. All of us, former covert and overt operatives, had to have the same targets, know their weaknesses and understand our plan to bring them down. We had to march like an army in unison, unlike the disorganised and incoherent bunch that CI in the province had come to represent. Between Dramat, me and the older hands at the covert unit, we delivered briefings on Pagad and the G-Force, their modus operandi, individual targets and the opportunities available to access them. In briefing the new arrivals, the soft-spoken Dramat emphasised that our mission was a maximalist one, which he concisely and accurately summed up as 'fucking up the G-Force.' Formal documents reflected it as 'developing and exploiting intelligence to destroy the G-Force as a cohesive entity.'

Part of this exercise included conducting a human source audit and an analysis of our source requirements. Despite the number of sources brought into the operation by our new colleagues, we assessed the majority as poorly deployed, and under-exploited. We redirected several sources to areas where they could provide greater utility. Still, in the end, the collective source capability fell short of what was required: in-place sources that could provide forewarning of attacks, identify weapon storage facilities, and identify vehicles used in attacks.

The advent of Operation Lancer initiated the twenty-four-hour working day at the covert unit.

When we started the operation, Dramat and I called all the operatives to the war room, briefing them on our objectives. We also told them we wanted to achieve our objectives well before the six-month timeline. Our mission was more ambitious than that of the national commissioner. Whereas he merely required a halt to the bombing within a six-month time frame, we intended to decimate the G-Force's cohesion and command capabilities and halt the bombing in a much shorter time frame.

I'm sure some of the operatives, and likely our commanders, thought we had lost our minds. *Pagad has been a thorn in our flesh for almost six years, and now the nutcases Dramat and Africa are proposing we dismantle them in half a year!* However, given our newfound freedom of manoeuvre and resource base, we were confident we could achieve these objectives in the allotted time. We also felt that if we could not do it at that stage, we would never be able to do it. We felt October 2000 was the proper conjuncture for commencing this operation, and we were at our most positive and motivated in years.

We informed our operatives that beginning that same day, all of us would be living at the office, alternating our time between working and sleeping, with a ratio heavily weighted towards working. If conditions permitted, we could see our families for a few hours daily. This rule applied to all of us, Dramat and myself included, and we would only rescind it once we achieved a serious breakthrough. Surprisingly, no one objected, which was a sure sign of commitment amongst the team. Everyone went home to collect clothes and sleeping bags while the ever-resourceful Els found money for the air mattresses we would use to take short naps in the office. Once everyone had returned, the concrete planning of our first recruitments started. The first breakthrough, which was huge and beyond anyone's expectation, came soon enough.

CHAPTER 7

Covert Unchained: Turning a Snow Flurry Into an Avalanche

Bold and intelligent daring should always characterise the commander and all his subordinates. Reproach is deserved not by the one who, in his zeal to destroy the enemy, does not reach his goal, but rather by the one who, fearing responsibility, remains inactive and does not employ at the proper moment all of his forces and means for winning victory.
—WWII Red Army field manual

After prostitution, espionage is reputed to be the second oldest profession in the world. It is no wonder that our first significant recruitment in Operation Lancer came from a combination of these two age-old trades. In October 2000, before the launch of Operation Lancer, Amber had started profiling a senior G-Force member and assessed him as vulnerable for recruitment on the grounds of sexual compromise. I will call this middle-aged businessman, centrally involved in planning and directing attacks by G-Force cells, Irfaan (pseudonym). We established that he was involved in several extra-marital affairs, none of which his loyal and very religious family was aware of. Subsequently, we found a young, attractive woman to befriend him. She was a professional sex worker and worked for us under a false flag, believing that I was a private detective setting up a sting operation on a man whose wife had initiated divorce proceedings. The process turned very nasty, and his wife wanted to use evidence of his infidelity to extract a more significant portion of his wealth as a settlement. Through a series of events, we stage-managed the first innocuous and entirely 'accidental' meeting between our lady friend and target, which went very well. After the first meeting, she maintained daily telephone contact with Irfaan.

Initially, the conversations were entirely innocent, revolving around family and friends, news, and the weather. When Irfaan mentioned that he was a Pagad 'welfare committee member, she showed little interest, preferring to discuss less serious matters. After a week or so, and to the lady's supposed surprise, his conversation became rather overtly sexual. He wanted them to meet one evening and pursue their relationship at a different level. Our lady, who presented herself as a young middle-class woman of considerable means, offered to organise a hotel room for the two of them. He could not come to her house as she still lived with her parents, who would not be particularly impressed with him spending the night in their daughter's bedroom. For obvious reasons, they could not meet at his house either. The lady made a particular suggestion, though. 'Why not meet next Friday around noon?' Irfaan didn't think twice about the significance of the proposed day and time and agreed to her proposal.

The operation to recruit Irfaan was kept a close secret, even within the confines of the covert unit. If we succeeded, Irfaan would be our most highly placed source since Johnson. Given the context of the recruitment, he'd be about as valuable as they come. We did not want to risk his exposure before or after the recruitment. Despite the secrecy, we had to assemble a substantial team to execute what would be a complex and high-risk recruitment operation. In such a case, there is always the possibility that a target is aware of your scheme and is playing you. If so, his objective could be two-fold.

He may play along until we make our approach, thereby exposing the personnel involved in the recruitment pitch. More dangerous would be going with the flow in coordination with other G-Force members. In such a case, they may have set up an ambush for those making the recruitment pitch. For this purpose, our team consisted of a defensive component, a technical and surveillance unit, and a team that would make the recruitment approach. The show's star would be our lady, eager to get one back in favour of a woman desperate to divorce her unfaithful husband. I would conduct the actual recruitment conversation, which is much like a sales pitch, except that the ability of the other party to reject your product is limited.

Irfaan set off to meet his newfound lover the following Friday shortly before noon. I still do not know the story he gave his wife, but he arrived at an up-market Cape Town hotel with a bag of clothes and toiletries. Our surveillance team monitored him from when he left home to ensure he was alone and not bringing any uninvited guests to the party. It was clear upon arrival that he was alone and just out to enjoy a day of passion with his lover. While he didn't bring along any friends, our lady had the company of our technical team, who monitored all the activities in her room from just a few metres away. We had decided to record the entire afternoon's events to add weight to the recruitment approach. Visuals and sound can be two of the most powerful tools for persuasion in our trade.

Irfaan was all smiles and excited as he walked down the hotel passage to the room where he would meet his lover. He knocked on the door, and after greeting her, however, his demeanour changed. His tone became more serious. In the monitoring room, we were shocked by the words that came out of his mouth as he stood on the threshold, looking straight into our lady friend's eyes. 'Are you working for the NIA or any other intelligence service?' he asked. Looking somewhat puzzled and honestly believing the question nonsensical, our lady simply responded, 'No, what are you talking about?' Having better things in mind, our hardened G-Force commander left the matter there, literally and figuratively crossed the threshold, and started chatting with his new girlfriend. One thing led to another, and Irfaan had fallen right into our lap before long.

After we gathered sufficient compromising video material, some of my team members burst into the room, presenting themselves as local 'vice squad' cops. They claimed to be investigating allegations of prostitution made against the lady in the room. They found Irfaan and the prostitute in the most compromising position possible. He assured the cops that his lady friend was no prostitute and they were merely spending a day together as consenting adults.

The lady, however, immediately confessed to being a sex worker and took out a large wad of bills she claimed he paid her to have sex with him. When they searched the room, the cops found tablets that looked similar to Mandrax. They informed Irfaan and his lady friend that, unless they could provide a satisfactory explanation, they would both be arrested for offences relating to the illegal possession of drugs and prostitution.

The 'vice squad' cops asked both Irfaan and his lover for identification and called their details through a so-called central police 'information centre.' This was nothing more than our monitoring facility next door. After a few minutes, the 'information centre' gave the cops instructions to take the lady away but to detain our G-Force man with an armed escort in the room until someone from intelligence arrived. On the video link in the monitoring room, I could see the panic in Irfaan's eyes when he heard that intelligence officers were on the way to see him. The expression on his face was of someone whose entire life had just imploded. He looked shocked and confused by the events unfolding before him and from which he could not extricate himself. More so, he was not allowed to get dressed until said intelligence officers arrived. So he sat in a corner, waiting for two men who would change his life forever.

When we arrived, we introduced ourselves as intelligence officers from Pretoria who had been deployed to Cape Town. The police in the province had become so discredited that we resorted, as standard practice, to introducing ourselves as head office personnel. Some people were also more prepared to work with strangers from afar rather than people in their backyard who they might bump into at any time. Before we got into the meat of our conversation I barked some expletives at the cops keeping watch over him for forcing the poor man to sit there, stark naked. I told Irfaan that he could get dressed, take a seat, and have something to drink. Once he was settled, my first statement to him was, 'Irfaan, what are you doing here? Are you not supposed to be in the mosque with your G-Force brothers for Jum'ah prayers?' Jum'ah is the communal prayer performed by Muslims in a mosque on a Friday at around noon, the exact time our married friend and pious G-Force member decided to meet a sex worker.

Timing can change a relatively minor infraction into a complete disgrace, and that was the situation in which Irfaan found himself. I outlined the gravity of his situation and compounded matters further by telling him that the vice cops claimed to have a video recording of the entire afternoon's festivities. Further, I informed him that I was aware of his position within the G-Force and that we could come to some accommodation to extricate him from his present predicament. He surely did not want his family and the community to be aware of his indiscretions. One never knew what the cops would do with the videotape of his few minutes of unbridled passion. It might have to be used in court, or some irresponsible cop might slip it to a contact in the media or an anti-Pagad organisation within the community. In such a case, not only would he be affected, but his organisation would also be discredited. 'Think about it for a moment, Irfaan. What would the G-Force do to someone who dishonours the organisation in such a manner?' The long sigh that followed his silence confirmed how ready he was to be turned.

Trying to win some space, Irfaan requested that he be allowed to consider our proposal and get back to us with an answer in a few days. From experience, I knew that providing someone under pressure with such a reprieve often backfired. When given an opportunity to think about what they perceive as a betrayal, not just of individuals but a cause they hold dear, most people would rather confess to a lesser crime such as infidelity than work for the enemy. The shock of what he was experiencing would wear off, and he could consider his situation more carefully. We could not allow this and had to press our advantage. He had no cards to play and would not be let off the hook.

I refused him the opportunity to consider the proposal over a few days and demanded an immediate response, failing which he would have to face the devastating consequences of his actions. Before he could answer, I received a call from the surveillance team informing me that he had arrived at the hotel in a stolen car and that they had found an unlicensed gun inside. I added these to the list of factors he needed to consider when responding to our more-than-generous offer.

Realising he had no viable alternatives, he agreed to act as a covert source for us. We got him to complete the necessary documents and immediately debriefed him. Over several hours, we extracted sufficiently compromising and actionable intelligence from him. It was adequately valuable and exploitable but also damning and pointed right at him. This was a solid basis for the initial phase of Irfaan's forced marriage to the covert unit. At the end of that Friday, we all felt proud of an immaculately executed operation. For the first time since Johnson, we had high-grade G-Force 'poison' at our fingertips.

At last, we caught the big fish we had been angling for the past three years. We bid goodbye to our new source and told him to go home and wait for our next call. I advised him to forget about how we made our acquaintance and focus on building a mutually beneficial future relationship. His secret was safe with us as long as we profited from his access to the G-Force. Irfaan left the hotel, got into this stolen car sans illegal gun, and sat there staring blankly ahead for about thirty minutes. It must have felt like a lifetime. Then he left to go home and meet his G-Force brothers, now with the focus on trapping them.

Although we appreciated the general value of the source we had just recruited, it was only later that we realised the full extent of his involvement in G-Force killings. Our first post-recruitment meeting took place under even more secure conditions. We knew that a source recruited in this coercive manner could resort to extreme actions to retaliate against us, both as a form of revenge and as a means of regaining the confidence of his betrayed comrades. In fact, on previous occasions, G-Force members suspected of being informers were instructed to kill other suspected informers or intelligence officers to prove their loyalty to the organisation.

Alongside Amber, who did the groundwork that gently guided Irfaan into our trap, I was his handler. We made our meeting as relaxed as possible in the hope of gaining the confidence of our new asset and putting him at ease. Although he had no option but to work with us, we knew that a cooperative source always produced more reliable and valuable information than one working exclusively based on compulsion. If we could win his confidence, we would avoid having to constantly filter bullshit from reality. Sources have kept handlers occupied for months by manufacturing just enough fiction to satiate them.

The full extent of the G-Force's current activity became clear during the debriefing. It became apparent that we had recruited a source that could, on his own, satisfy a sizable chunk of the information required to make Operation Lancer a success. There were, until then, many activities that were not linked to the G-Force. These included murder, robbery and extortion which were just reported as normal crimes. Irfaan could make the connection between these incidents and the G-Force. He recounted these events in such detail that we concluded he must have been involved in many of them.

Within a few days, we were able to present Petros with a detailed picture of the current structures of the G-Force, a list of inactive, dissolved and new cells, attributes of operational cells, as well as the identity of all persons serving on the Security Council. Where we often had general information, we could now report details of the G-Force's previous operations, adding dates, places, weapons, and vehicles used. Whereas we previously understood that G-Force operations were financed through extortion and robbery, our new source provided our first detailed intelligence on this aspect of the organisation's operations. Some G-Force members extorted money from businessmen yet never handed it to the organisation instead using it for personal enrichment.

Irfaan's information on the bombings was less detailed than the rest of his reporting. He only had suspicions of who could be involved in the manufacture and use of explosive devices. Since this was our key priority, we tasked him to develop a closer relationship with those he suspected of involvement in the bombings. We hoped that he could get close enough to them to alert us to possible bombings before they were executed. He was unaware we had received intelligence from another source on two of the suspected bombers he mentioned. We had begun to envelop them, focusing surveillance on them and tasking other sources in their orbit to gather more specific information about planned bombings.

While we were excited by the wealth of information we obtained from this source, it also posed a serious predicament. This was the age-old dilemma of a source too well-placed not to be involved in attacks. Since he was now under our control, Irfaan could no longer randomly participate in planning and executing attacks. We had to discuss this issue with our superiors at the highest level and obtain their support in handling this valuable yet risky asset. As part of his Lancer responsibilities, Petros briefed Selebi and Williams weekly. On this occasion, he and Dramat went to Pretoria to discuss the matter with the two principals and the complexities of handling such a source.

Many people in SAPS had knives out for us and would marvel at the opportunity to link us to so-called 'third force' activities on the urban terror terrain. The previous decision to charge me for the dud hand-grenade operation and Du Plessis forcing us to cut one of our G-Force sources loose were still fresh in our minds. We had to be careful in how we approached handling Irfaan. At the same time, we could not keep a source with that level of active involvement in attacks a secret forever. The information he provided was of such a nature that we needed to inform other role players to prevent attacks. Any other approach would be reckless.

One such occasion occurred on a night we debriefed him at a city hotel. He received a call from a senior G-Force commander instructing him to attend an emergency meeting. The problem with these meetings was that you never knew what they were about until you arrived. It could be a meeting arranged simply to discuss a security breach in the organisation, ideas about fundraising, or an instruction to kill someone. It could even be a ruse to get someone to a meeting with the intent of killing them. We instructed Irfaan to call us at the earliest possible opportunity and report on their deliberations. Early the following day, he called to relay that after some general talk on the state of the G-Force, the discussion pivoted to information on an ongoing surveillance operation against a G-Force member.

The cell had noticed a surveillance officer who was seen monitoring the house of a G-Force member. They had gathered details on the surveillance officer's vehicle, observation position and routine, all of which Irfaan now recited to us. He was called to the meeting as he would form part of the team that had to kill our surveillance colleague. We checked the details he provided with our surveillance unit and confirmed that one of their operatives occupied the exact spot identified by the G-Force. He was rushed out of there faster than you could say 'G-Force.'

This was also a valuable lesson to our surveillance team, who had, until then, regarded themselves as relatively immune to threats from their targets. Watching people from a distance sometimes creates a false sense of security. No one thought that the targets would also be on the lookout. Indeed, this unjustified confidence did not exist after this episode. Apart from its intrinsic value in saving the life of a fellow intelligence officer, we were pleased that Irfaan's information was confirmed by an independent source. Despite the volumes of information we obtained from him, it was always difficult to evaluate its reliability. As a rule, very few people had access to the type of information he reported, and making inquiries at other agencies would expose him.

Selebi and Williams were impressed with our progress, which we achieved less than three weeks after the commencement of the operation. They reiterated their support for our efforts and initiatives, including Irfaan's recruitment. The launch of Operation Lancer had been such a morale booster amongst our operatives that almost any objective seemed entirely feasible. Unlike the restrictive conditions imposed on them at the various overt offices, the newcomers to our team now worked in an environment where we supported their initiative and creativity, and laboured alongside them. Dramat and I worked at least as many hours as our team members, slept on the same crappy air mattresses, and took the very same security risks we expected them to.

In some cases, instead of recruiting a source close to the key target, we enlisted the key target themselves after discovering helpful recruitment pitching information. While our new spy gadgets were impressive, we consistently emphasised the importance of human source access, without which we would be navigating blind. Even the most advanced technology cannot give the same insight that humans can – the adversary's intentions and morale, the organisational cohesion and internal conflicts, the thinking and mentality of individual targets, and their likes and dislikes. Human intelligence was our bread and butter, and it reigned supreme.

While our old sources continued to slave away, they must have been motivated by the newfound excitement of their handlers, as they all started producing more valuable and accurate tactical information. Scholar, our longstanding and loyal source, provided us with unprecedented and exceptional information on one of the cells involved in the spate of bombings in 2000. He had obtained information on which bombings they were responsible for and even gathered information on who manufactured these explosive devices. Several sources confirmed his information this time, and our spy tech provided similar information. We were now firmly on the track of the bombers.

In late 2000, we established that a G-Force cell operating in the Athlone area had carried out most of the bomb attacks during that year. The members of this cell were well known to us, and several of them had previously been arrested on terror-related charges. The information was of such high quality that it left no doubt about their responsibility for the attacks. What was left was developing intelligence that would enable us to arrest them in the act, while executing an attack. This task took up a considerable amount of our twenty-four-hour working day. We spun a web around our targets, covering their movements and activities at all hours of the day without them knowing. Although there might be an occasional lapse in monitoring, we were confident that we had a firm grip on the targets. Their sense of bravado and impunity, developed over the preceding four years of operating without much risk, greatly assisted us. These characters had committed terror with such regularity that they felt they would never be caught. Their guard was lowered, and this was the opportunity we were waiting for.

For some reason, Thursday, 2 November 2000, was unusually quiet and didn't start with any expectation of something spectacular about to happen. Most of the team had left the office early on that day. A source contacted Amber at around 11 that morning to inform her that he would be using a car that G-Force members Faizel Waggie, Shahied Davids, and the latter's brother, Naziem, had previously used to carry out attacks. The source had to visit G-Force members in prison, and there was a 3-hour window in which we could have the car. To say we were very interested in this car is a gross understatement. Waggie and Shahied Davids were the two G-Force members who were suspected of being involved in several bombings that year. Amber instructed the source to bring the vehicle to us, and we provided him with an alternative car for the day.

We then met with our technical team, who installed a tracking device and several bugs in the vehicle. We could now see where Davids and Waggie went and listen to their conversations inside the car. While our technical team was busy with the target car, most of my team had taken the afternoon and evening off to spend with their families. The story of the bugged car, however, took such a series of twists and turns that everyone had to be recalled to the office and deployed for what would turn out to be about fifteen hours of non-stop drama.

We returned the car to our source when he returned from his prison visit, just in time for him to deliver it to Waggie's house at around six that evening. It looked just as it did when he handed it to us, with dust, smears, and dirt in the exact places we found them. Dramat, Amber, and I returned to our office and set up the monitoring equipment to confirm it worked. Though we had tested it at the technical team's workshop, we now had to do so from the actual premises where the monitoring would occur. Our previous experience sobered us to the reality that these magical devices sometimes simply refused to cooperate.

Technical intelligence is unlike human source intelligence. Once installed, the mechanism cannot be redirected, nor can it be instructed to ask probing questions or follow up on leads. It is stationary and delivers when it does, not a minute before or after. However, because of the potential benefit in that it produced intelligence that was more or less indisputable, we learned to exercise patience. Hitherto, we had spent thousands of hours listening to devices planted in target houses, shops, or offices, yet had never obtained direct forewarning of an attack. However, luck comes to those who are prepared, and a truckload of luck arrived early that Thursday evening.

Dramat switched on the twin monitoring platforms we used on the target car. According to the tracker, the source had just arrived at Waggie's house in Bridgetown. The bugs worked well and activated as Waggie and Davids entered the car. After the customary greeting *salaam wa alaykum* between the three G-Force members, one of our targets got right down to business. 'It's good that you brought the car back in time. We need it for an operation tomorrow morning.' Our source, who had an intimate relationship of trust with our two targets, asked what they were plotting. 'We're planting something in Durban Road. The one in Durbanville, not Mowbray.' This was of great help as there are two Durban roads in the Cape Peninsula. The other target then provides further detail, mentioning that they intend to plant a bomb in a flower pot. That is where the conversation ended. They then drove our source back to his house and returned to theirs.

Dramat, Amber and I looked at each other in astonishment. 'What did we just hear?' one of us asked. 'Yes, that's it. We all heard the same thing,' Amber jumped in. Tomorrow morning it is!' Not only was what we caught unmistakable, but it also presented the sort of tactical intelligence we had been dreaming of. While we previously succeeded in preventing attacks, on this occasion we had intelligence that would allow us to arrest two of the most capable and active G-Force targets en route or at the site where they intended to detonate a bomb. We now had the rare combination of precise intelligence, technical tools, surveillance capability, and a tactical response team to make an impressive success of the opportunity. But we still had to coordinate all these capabilities in real-time and strike at the right moment, all without alerting our targets that the net was rapidly and decisively closing in around them.

Dramat contacted Petros and asked him to come to the office immediately as we had something urgent to brief him on. He also arranged a meeting with Joe, our surveillance team coordinator. We called the rest of the team, summoning them back to the office. 'Come now, we'll provide details once you are here.' No one complained or requested to either be excused or come in later. Just a unanimous 'I'm on my way!' By seven that evening, our team had gathered in the war room and were being briefed. We updated them on the afternoon's developments and the intelligence derived from the monitoring equipment in the target car.

Petros informed us that the surveillance team had stood down earlier in the evening and no longer had eyes on Waggie or Davids. Like us, they were overworked beyond exhaustion, and Joe felt that his team needed a break before picking up their targets again the following morning. Whereas my team was meant to follow up with sources and monitor technical intelligence and were not trained as surveillance officers, they now had to stand in for the pros who had withdrawn for the night. They additionally had to run down leads from sources and monitor the devices inside the target car.

In the month following the launch of Lancer, the surveillance team significantly improved the quality of their intelligence. The one reason for the leap in quality was the support we had facilitated for them through our engagements with our comrades Lalla and Khumalo. The second, more significant factor that increased the surveillance team's productivity was their integration into Operation Lancer. This gave them strategic target guidance and a constant stream of tactical intelligence.

While we fitted our target vehicle with spy technology earlier in the day, the surveillance team were on Boeta Yu, whom they were tasked to monitor. During this process, they noticed Waggie and Davids arriving at Boeta Yu's house. A sudden rush of movement to and from the house, initiated by our two targets' arrival, indicated something uncanny. At this point, the surveillance unit did not have the benefit of the breakthrough intelligence we only gained later that day. When Daniel (pseudonym), the surveillance team leader, noticed the scurry of activity, he immediately shifted his team's deployment from Boeta Yu to the two bomber targets.

His decision, which appeared risky and even irresponsible to some, resulted from years of working the G-Force target, exploiting the most recent intelligence his team received from us and that essential quality of a good intelligence commander, the ability to smell when someone is up to no good. It is what von Clausewitz calls the *coup d'œil*, 'the rapid discovery of a truth which to the ordinary mind is either not visible at all or only becomes so after long examination and reflection.' And what a coup it turned out to be! As Waggie and Davids left Boeta Yu's house, the Operation Lancer net swarmed around them in the form of Daniel's surveillance team. Despite their best efforts to conduct a surveillance check, they had no idea that dozens of eyes were trained on them.

Daniel and his team pursued the targets discreetly, following them first to a mosque in Grassy Park, where they stayed for nearly an hour. Despite his self-confidence, he wondered whether he had made a potentially catastrophic mistake in letting his team shift targets based on what most people would call a mere hunch. As he was processing this contradiction and trying to figure out whether to go back to Boeta Yu, the duo came out of the mosque. There was a marked difference in their demeanour compared to when they first entered. The targets immediately adopted an operational posture, indicating they were about to execute a risky action.

Waggie and Davids were now engaged in active counter-surveillance, trying to shake off whoever they assumed might be following them. While Davids was driving, Waggie was facing backwards in the car, pointing at random vehicles behind them and warning them off. They hoped that surveillance, if any, would be spooked by this and withdraw from the pursuit. However, they had no idea who they were dealing with. They were being pursued by a team that fitted right into the local demographic, led by an officer with an intimate knowledge of the terrain and a calm mind, and would not let the duo shake them.

Daniel's team followed our targets to Blue Route Mall, a stone's throw from Pollsmoor prison, where some of our ANC comrades, including Dramat, Vearey, and Jacobs, spent time under Apartheid and the place which many G-Force members also called home. The surveillance officer was right behind them when they paid for their goods and noticed the duo purchasing a 1.5 kg bag of fertiliser. They then returned to Grassy Park and purchased twenty litres of diesel. These were the vital ingredients in the most recent bombs utilised by the G-Force. Davids and Waggie then went into a garage at a house in Grassy Park, hitherto unknown to us, where they remained for about three hours. The team could hear the sound of a grinder on metal from the garage, which made them believe the duo was busy constructing a bomb at that very moment.

Through the masterful reading of a situation and the exercise of initiative, surveillance uncovered a G-Force bomb manufacturing facility. By the evening of 2 November, we had Waggie and Davids linked to a bomb and knew of their plans to execute an attack the following day. It felt like a situation approximating Mao Zedong's statement: 'There is great chaos under the heavens. The conditions are excellent!'

If we could shape the situation to our wishes, we would add one final piece to the puzzle and one tool to react when the G-Force cell activated its operation the following morning. The final piece in the puzzle would be the exact location where they intended to attack, and the reaction tool would be to have the special task force arrange a welcoming party for them when they arrive to place the bomb. Our ability to effectively achieve the second relied partially on our ability to complete the remaining part of the operational puzzle -exactly where will they place the bomb? But we only partially relied on having all the pieces to the puzzle. With what we had in hand, and especially our ability to track them, the special task force could surely intercept and arrest the cell in possession of the bomb, about to, or having planted it.

Dramat and I set off to Durban Road at about ten that evening to find the intended bombing site. Surely it couldn't be that difficult to locate a flower pot on Durban Road, could it? During the eighteen-minute drive from our covert facility to Durban Road, we were both excited by the operational prospects and terrified that the smallest mistakes could mess up all the effort and the apparent breakthrough we had achieved. We wanted everything to be prepared to perfection and rolled out like a well-choreographed and rehearsed performance. Did we deploy our team in the right places tonight? Will the bugs and trackers still work tomorrow morning? Might our targets decide to use a different vehicle at the last minute? By the time we reached Durban Road, we felt that we had done what we could and simply needed to find the exact target of the next morning's planned bomb attack. Well, that was easier said than done.

The Durbanville section of Durban Road is approximately 2.5 km long. However, the road continues along its natural path after that and becomes Durbanville Avenue, though the entire stretch of 6.5 km is commonly referred to by Capetonians as Durban Road. The whole road also looked like a flower pot exhibition! Flower pots were everywhere along the route. We had to make do with Durban Road as the target instead of knowing a specific building on the 6.5km road. This slightly complicated things for us, as the road is a high-density target, with businesses and restaurants lining the entirety of the route. Given the technical coverage we had in place and the resources and ingenuity of the special task force we were able to deploy, we felt comfortable enough about the situation.

Upon our return to the office, we briefed Petros about our disappointing Durban Road expedition. By now, it was close to midnight. Petros said that he was too tired to continue working that night and would head home to get a night's sleep. Dramat, after sleeping in the office for weeks, decided to head home to shower. Given that I remained with Danie, one of my team members, we would be sufficiently covered on the monitoring side. I said I would call them in the event of any surprises popping up. All we needed now was for Petros to go past the special task force base en route to his house, brief them and ensure they deployed in the vicinity of Durban Road before five the following morning. As soon as I detected movement from the car, I would call him, and he would advise the task force that our targets were on their way, heading into a well-laid trap.

The night was quiet, with no additional source reporting, and our team's monitoring did not pick up anything unusual. At about three on the morning of 3 November, I fell asleep on the office floor, leaving Danie on monitoring duty. I woke up at five and checked with him. The target car had just started moving. It was heading toward Boeta Yu's house, with Waggie and Naziem Davids inside. They didn't have much to say to each other until they arrived at Boeta Yu's house. Clearly, they were there to collect the bomb and then head off to their target. After the brief stop, their conversation became more animated. One of them commented that the bomb was huge and smelly, too. I assumed this was the result of the diesel-fertiliser combination used in the bomb. We listened to their conversation and tracked their vehicle every step of the way. Time was on our side, and I was sure the task force was waiting on the other end of the trio's journey.

Once our bomber duo started moving, I called Petros to inform him. 'They are in the Ford Sapphire and have the bomb with them in the car. It looks like they are on their way to Durban Road. The live tracking shows they are about twenty minutes from the location.' I then asked him to alert the task force that our targets were heading into their embrace. Still half asleep, he told me, 'Sorry David, I was so tired when I left the office last night that I forgot to pass by the task force and request their deployment to Durban Road.' With Waggie and Davids now well on their way and no one to arrest them upon arrival, we decided that Petros had to pursue them himself and initiate the arrest as they were about to place the bomb. The fact that we were tracking the car now heading to Durban Road helped in that I could feed Petros their live location. In those days, GPS tracking did not have the accuracy it has today, but it was good enough to give a fairly decent indication of where they were travelling, and at this point, they were well ahead of him. Petros lived very close to the national road heading north, so it took him only a few minutes to get onto the N1 and commence his pursuit. He had no sight of them until he arrived on Durban Road.

At this point, and now rather desperate, I decided to call the police using the public 10111 emergency line. I initially called in a 'tip' as an ordinary member of the public, but the police officer on the other end of the line would have none of it. Given the detail I provided, he assumed my call was a prank, talking about a moving car with a bomb. 'Sir, you do know it's an offence to provide false information to the police?' and warned me to desist. Our targets were approaching Durban Road and within minutes of planting the bomb. With Petros still unable to catch up with them, I threw caution to the wind and told him who I was. I provided my rank and service number and said I was involved in the Pagad investigation. He insisted on an office number to call me back, something I obviously would not do, given that my number would trace back to a covert facility. In the end, I threatened that he'd be held responsible if he failed to act and the bomb went off. That got him moving, and he then communicated the information over the police radio network.

Petros was placing himself at significant risk by pursuing two armed G-Force members on his own, and I thought the support of the cops could help in case the situation turned confrontational. After my 10111 call, I returned to the line with Petros, who informed me that he had just arrived on Durban Road. From my tracking intelligence, I knew the targets had already planted the bomb and were heading back to Athlone. He had not received any backup from police units yet and informed me that he had stood down from pursuing Waggie and Davids and left their arrest up to the cops, who were alerted through the police radio network. While pursuing the bombers en route to Durban Road, he communicated with Riaan Booysen, who led the investigative team dealing with Pagad cases. He asked him to send police and investigators to what was shortly to be a crime scene. The two agreed to meet on Durban Road and manage the situation from there.

The two following hours resembled von Clausewitz's 'fog of war.' It was a combination of murky information flows, a poorly conceived narrative, and the need to protect the methods by which we obtained the detailed intelligence that led us to Durban Road. Given the unprecedented precision of the intelligence at our disposal and the forces we were able to deploy to arrest our targets in the act of planting the bomb, we had neglected to plan for simple human frailty. Petros could not pinpoint the device's specific location, and a rather lengthy search for it ensued.

On their way back to Athlone, Waggie and Davids were arrested in Epping by members of the police VIP protection unit deployed at the nearby Acacia Park parliamentary village. The news of their arrest and the thwarting of a bombing quickly spread up the security hierarchy. Just after seven that morning, I received a call from Williams, who said that he had taken for granted that we were behind that morning's success and asked that I congratulate the team on his and Selebi's behalf. I asked that the two of them come by in person soon and express their congratulations in person to what could only be described as an incredible team.

After some time, police sniffer dogs located the bomb inside one of the flower pots at the Keg & Swan pub on Durban Road. The device was timed to explode just after noon when the outside seating area would be crowded. It was a sunny November day, the last working day of the week for most people, and the pub was in the middle of a vast retail and commercial district. The bomb's construction and placement were intended to cause substantial fatalities, and its discovery saved many lives. That alone was a significant achievement and something worth celebrating. However, I felt deflated at the complications arising from a lapse that should never have occurred. The advanced presence of the task force at the scene would have resulted in an entirely different outcome. Exceptional intelligence was transformed into an average outcome due to an operational lapse, which I can only assume was due to fatigue.

There was still much for us to do while Petros dealt with the immediate situation on Durban Road. Our team had been monitoring the Grassy Park house where the bomb was constructed, and it became imperative that whatever evidence remained there be seized and the occupants arrested. Soon enough, the police raided the house, arresting the occupants, and found a veritable treasure trove of bomb-making material. The house was an investigator's dream, with lots of evidence, including fertiliser used in the explosive device, pipes, and fingerprints left behind. We could now forensically link the Keg & Swan bomb to the Grassy Park house, its occupants, and others who were involved in manufacturing the bomb. The occupants of the house, Fatima and Yusuf Enous, were arrested and swiftly agreed to testify for the state against Waggie, Davids, and others implicated in the bomb plot.

The arrest of the G-Force men made immediate headline news in Cape Town and across the country. Panic crept into G-Force circles as they realised the significance of the coup by intelligence. The SAPS in the province were even more surprised than the G-Force. We had informed no one of the operation until it was well underway. Given the history of leakages, this was the only way of ensuring the operation's success. A police spokesperson, when asked for comment on the apparent breakthrough in urban terror investigations, could only say that 'we don't know everything ourselves. We don't want to know because it could endanger our lives, or we might make a slip that could hamper the investigation.'

Friday afternoon prayer at Masjidul Quds in Gatesville was a gathering point for Pagad members. Logically, the latest arrests were the discussion point of the day. Other G-Force cell members and their commanders met to discuss the arrests and find ways to mitigate the damage. Matters were, however, well beyond their control. They were unsure whether any of those arrested would speak to the police.

Having tied up some loose ends, Dramat felt it was time to give the team a decent break. Having the rest of the day off, the team headed to Oudekraal Beach on the Atlantic Seaboard, where we indulged in the typical South African celebration – braaing meat on the coals while having a few drinks. The coincidence of my time in Crime Intelligence, mainly working on Pagad, being sandwiched between the initial integration braai in 1995 and this celebratory one at the end of 2000 did not escape me.

During the weekend, we met all our sources who had played a role in the most significant breakthrough in the years of working on Pagad. We congratulated them and expressed our warmest thanks for the service they offered us. These were the real heroes – working without the benefit of backup amongst people who attached no value to life. They all had experienced at least one death-defying moment where they risked exposure. They persevered with us for years, which bears testimony to their dedication. Many of our sources were people who cooperated voluntarily, with money being a distant second when coming to motivation. Our success proved the correctness of our emphasis on human source penetration of the G-Force.

The adage that 'when it rains, it pours' now came to define the G-Force's fortunes. The momentum was clearly on our side, and the quality of intelligence we produced was exceptional. In late November 2000, we created our own luck again, making probably the most significant breakthrough in impacting the G-Force's ability to continue operating as a cohesive entity. After a lengthy investigation by one of our teams headed by Amber, we identified a potential source in the G-Force. Riverside (pseudonym) was a recovering drug addict who was part of a rehabilitation program at the Pagad drug rehabilitation centre in Rylands. Ebrahim spotted him as a potential recruit, spent time cultivating him, and recruited him into the G-Force in 1998.

This is an approach Pagad used with many recovering addicts, premised on an assessment of the individual's vulnerabilities, their sense of obligation to Pagad for having 'rescued' them from drugs, and an often-fanatical hatred of the drug dealers who trapped them into a life of addiction. In the G-Force Riverside operated under the command of Boeta Yu and worked closely with Waggie and the Davids brothers. In the two years following his recruitment, he was involved in what can only be described as an orgy of unbridled mass murder. He directly participated in more than thirty murders. At least, that was when he forced himself to stop counting.

After discussions with Petros, we decided that we should develop a different approach to Riverside, approaching him with the option of becoming a state witness rather than a covert source. The scale of his involvement in murder made sustaining him as a long-term source impossible. We would not be able to obtain the legal authorisation for him to carry out any more acts of violence. In his position, it would not be limited to an attack that damaged property but would by necessity involve killing G-Force targets. The only practical solution was to run him as a very short-term source with the express intent of using him as a so-called Section 204 state witness, ideally in a conspiracy prosecution against leaders of the G-Force. A trial judge may grant such a witness immunity if he testifies truthfully against fellow conspirators or perpetrators of criminal action in support of the prosecution.

Obtaining such immunity for Riverside would be a very tall order, but we thought it was worth the trouble and decided to give it a go. Of course, we first had to convince him that his fate lay in our hands and that his interest was best served by working with us. Amber set up the first meeting with Riverside, where we presented our offer. The meeting required high-risk security measures, including making the initial contact in a public place where he'd have to walk through a security checkpoint with metal detectors to ensure he was unarmed. The entire team would be deployed to support Amber and me, who would meet with Riverside. On our way to a safe house where the meeting was held, he sat beside Amber, who was driving. I sat in the back directly behind him so that I could handle him in case he decided to attempt anything funny.

Our team observed the initial meeting point to check whether he had brought G-Force guests. They followed us once the area was cleared to ensure we were not being followed. This was our routine when meeting with Riverside. Apart from being a mass murderer, we were acutely aware of the psychological swings that a potential or actual source experiences when they have to consider betraying people close to them. The extraordinary value that a source like him could deliver did not detract us from being alert to this factor and the potentially fatal consequences a lapse in security could have upon any or all of the team members who engaged him. We were happy to smile with him and entertain some of his, let's say, eccentric requests, but he knew as well as we did that we were equally ready to act with extreme prejudice if he placed any of us at risk.

An example of such a lapse took place during the US so-called War on Terror, with devastating consequences, is the case of Jordanian Al-Qaeda member Humam Khalil Abu-Mulal al-Balawi. He offered his services to the CIA, who handled him from Camp Chapman in Khost province, Afghanistan. Al-Balawi provided the sort of intelligence we thought Riverside could deliver to us – unprecedented, direct access to leaders of a terrorist organisation. The type of intelligence that is so alluring that it sometimes blunts the alertness of an intelligence officer, especially the source handlers. On 30 December

2009, Al-Balawi was invited to a meeting at Camp Chapman with his CIA case officers. Due to his sensitive position, the standard security protocols at the base were relaxed for this special visitor. He literally drove into the base without being searched, and upon exiting the vehicle, detonated his suicide vest, killing himself and nine other people, including seven CIA officers.

At our first meeting, Amber and I outlined the case against Riverside, specifying the details we had and adding conjecture where such was missing. We made a good sales pitch, offering him the stark binary of a life in prison and a destroyed family or a life elsewhere, safe from the G-Force and able to watch his children grow up. He listened to our proposal, and although he initially declined, we closely monitored his movements and communications in subsequent days to see whether he reported the approach to anyone in the G-Force. We determined that he had kept quiet about our approach. This was always a good sign and indicator that a recruitment target had not settled on a firm decision, whatever he told us in the first meeting. Not everyone takes a bite when the apple is first offered, but many do at a subsequent opportunity. This gave us some confidence that a second approach might work. He agreed to meet again, and in this second meeting, we presented him with further evidence of his involvement in numerous attacks. Left with an admittedly inflated impression of vast volumes of evidence amassed against him, Riverside agreed to testify against those G-Force members who participated in attacks alongside him or of which he had direct knowledge.

However, he was quick to condition his cooperation on several factors. He demanded the relocation of his entire family. He specifically stated that he had no faith in the police witness protection programme and wanted a special arrangement in place to protect him and his family. Secondly, he wanted a guarantee of immunity from prosecution. As a third condition, he insisted that he was only prepared to testify if his father, as head of the family, approved his decision. The first condition was possible to satisfy, and we could negotiate an agreement with Williams and Selebi for a secure relocation. We knew that the existing witness protection program was hopelessly inadequate for a witness in Riverside's position and set up an entirely independent capacity to deal with his family's relocation. The second condition depended entirely on the NPA and, in this particular instance, the Scorpions. They were the only people who could make a potential witness an offer of immunity from prosecution in return for testimony. In the end, the immunity had to be conferred by a judge in the case where the witness testified. We explained that were he to testify truthfully and comprehensively about his involvement in urban terror, the judge would grant him immunity as agreed by the NPA. He accepted our commitment to meet the relevant prosecutors at the Scorpions and request an offer of immunity.

The third condition would be the most difficult to meet, almost leading to the undoing of the entire operation. After obtaining Riverside's consent, I arranged a meeting for Petros and the family at a safe house outside Cape Town. His parents had no idea what they were stepping into when they entered the well-concealed and well-furnished house in a quiet seaside suburb. I was essentially an observer at the meeting, with Petros taking the lead. We decided to dispense with long-winded conversation and get to the crux of the matter from the word go. Petros told Riverside's elders of our previous discussions with their son and our proposal to save him the pain of prosecution and likely life in prison. In return, he would have to testify against fellow G-Force members.

The parents were visibly shocked when we listed the litany of killings in which their son was involved. They simply refused to believe Petros. 'There he is. Ask him yourself,' Petros responded. Without saying a word, Riverside nodded that it was indeed the case, resulting in the expected tearful breakdown as his parents tried to come to terms with the fact that their son had just admitted to being a mass murderer. Once things calmed down, the father said that they obviously needed some time to consider the proposal and would get back to us with a response within a week. He was concerned about the religious implications of his son testifying against fellow Muslims and said he wanted to think about this.

At the next meeting a week later, Riverside's father said they had thought long and hard about our proposal and the situation in which their son found himself. The family patriarch, now clearly the only one deciding and speaking, said that their son 'made a mistake by doing what he did, and agreed to have their son testify in exchange for immunity and relocation abroad. They explicitly did not want him placed into the police witness protection programme, which they, like us, regarded as incapable of offering any serious protection. We left the meeting in high spirits, confident of another, more significant breakthrough than the one on 3 November.

By exploiting Riverside's access and pre-existing knowledge of the involvement of senior G-Force members in terrorism, we intended to roll out an operation that would gather evidence against and prosecute them. We had the advantage of time on our side. We did not need to rush anything and could execute the operation at our chosen pace. We immediately initiated the necessary processes to carry out the Riverside operation. First, we had to obtain the go-ahead from Selebi and Williams, which was, given the extent of Riverside's involvement in Pagad's murderous activities, as risky for him and his family as it was potentially controversial for us. The authorisation was obtained when Petros flew to Pretoria the following day to brief Selebi and Williams. Although initially shocked by the scale of our potential witness's involvement in G-Force violence, they agreed it was worth the risk and investment if he could deliver a significant impact on the G-Force.

We prepared a memorandum for the DSO prosecutor responsible, Gray, to deal with the immunity issue. We requested a meeting to present it and brief her on Riverside and our breakthrough in obtaining his cooperation. The conference, also attended by Adams, agreed that the evidence such a witness could provide was so crucial and held such significant prosecutorial potential that his involvement in numerous murders was of less importance. He was, after all, a cog in the G-Force wheel and had no command authority in the structure. We then went ahead and planned the takedown operation. We planned to arrest key members of the Security Council, several cell commanders and active hitmen in one fell swoop. Most of them were to be charged with murder, conspiracy to commit murder and related offences. Critically, we needed to ensure the secrecy and security of the entire operation.

Amidst our meticulous preparations, I was interrupted by an urgent call from Riverside one evening at approximately 8 p.m. He requested an emergency meeting. We met at a quiet cafe in Constantia about an hour later. Before meeting him, I alerted Dramat of the urgency in Riverside's tone during the brief call. It was a tone of panic, a rare occurrence for him. I assured Dramat that I would update him after my conversation with Riverside. My goal was to address any issues promptly so we could continue operational preparations for the takedown.

Riverside was accompanied by his wife. This was not only unusual but in contravention of our agreed meeting protocol. The presence of his wife could affect not only the freedom with which we discussed issues but also impact how we dealt with an unexpected security situation. As soon as we sat down, however, I realised that he was in a state of absolute panic and near meltdown. He was fidgety and spoke in a rushed manner. I asked him to take a few deep breaths and speak slowly. While he calmed down, I ordered his favourite chai tea. 'The whole thing has collapsed,' he told me, 'I'm going to run away now. My wife will go with me.' He then informed me of a meeting with his father earlier that evening, where the latter informed him that he sought the advice of an imam to obtain an authoritative opinion on whether it is permissible for him to testify against fellow Muslims.

I wanted to know who the imam was and when this engagement occurred. Regardless of the outcome of these consultations, it posed a significant risk to our entire operation. Riverside was hesitant to reveal the imam's identity but did mention that he was a Pagad sympathiser. I pressed for details on the engagement. 'I assume your present state is an indication that the imam's advice was not very positive?' I suggested. 'Of course not!' Riverside exclaimed, 'Otherwise, I wouldn't be in this state. He told my father it was not permissible for me to testify, and if I did, it would become obligatory upon all Muslims, including my family, to kill me.'

The father told Riverside that he would approach the Pagad leadership the next day to inform them of our approach to his son. He planned to explain that his son was confused but did not intend to betray the organisation. Riverside, who murdered a married couple to intimidate a witness against a fellow G-Force member, knew a bit more than his father about Pagad's tolerance for potential state witnesses. One who went ahead actually to meet the cops and then agreed to testify was a dead man walking. Whether he now testified or not, the G-Force would kill him and his family for merely considering the possibility of becoming a state witness.

Well, that's going to screw up our timeframe, I thought. *So much for doing things at a pace of our choosing.* First, I had to disabuse Riverside of the idea that he could get back into his car and drive off into the night, never to be seen by ourselves or Pagad again. 'There is no way,' I said, 'that you can tell me, a serving officer, that you will simply disappear after having committed the crimes you have. Also, to think Pagad won't track you is foolish. Your only chance of survival now is to recommit to our agreement. Otherwise, you and your family will be dead in no time. You know how the G-Force works, and you do not have the means to stay ahead of them.'

Riverside's wife was central in getting him to understand what I was saying. She would much rather take a risk with the state's resources behind them than try to independently eke out a living while hiding somewhere outside Cape Town. I guaranteed them that we would find a way of managing the situation, no matter how catastrophic it seemed at that moment. I needed them to trust us and our ability to ensure their safety. In the end, my threats and his wife's common sense got through to Riverside and he agreed to stick with us... if we could convince his father.

I told Riverside to go home and await further instructions. We had to act with speed. I called to brief Dramat and Petros on this potentially devastating development, and we met immediately to chart a course of action. Before Riverside left Constantia, I arranged for some team members to shepherd him home. We had to ensure he went home instead of trying his disappearing trick and that he'd be safe upon arrival. Simultaneously, we dispatched the rest of our team to take up discreet positions in the vicinity of Riverside's residence. This was complicated because he lived in the centre of a G-Force hornets' nest, but the team was authorised and equipped to act if any threat to him or his family arose while we got our ducks in a row. Our primary task was to reverse the perception the family now had of the impermissibility of him testifying. We would then have to bring forward the extraction plan and execute it immediately. We assumed the imam that Riverside's father consulted could not be trusted to maintain the confidentiality of the discussion and would leak it to Pagad, giving us no more than a few hours to execute the operation.

With someone like Riverside, they would act decisively and immediately. He was not a fish they would consider alternative ways to fry. They would not confirm the information or call him in to discuss the issue. Instead, they would rapidly deploy a hit team to kill him and, most likely, his entire family. The most sensible route would be to send a respected and senior religious leader to the family to discuss the question of testimony and provide a proper perspective on the matter. Using our extensive contacts amongst the Muslim clergy, we got hold of a leading Islamic scholar and imam.

Having explained the background and unfolding fiasco to the imam, he agreed to meet the family and put their mind to rest regarding testifying against Pagad members. We were not Islamic scholars and had no sophisticated understanding of Islamic jurisprudence; we, however, assumed that testifying against people who killed women and children in an undeclared jihad would not pass muster under Islamic law. This is precisely what the imam told us, and he volunteered to meet the family at their residence at 1 a.m. With the eminent Islamic scholar in the house, we reinforced our presence around the residence with the special task force. Their presence would be handy if any G-Force members stumbled onto the gathering, whether by accident or intending to harm the family.

The imam was a revered figure in the Muslim community and could have used his status to bludgeon the father into accepting his interpretation of Islamic law. This would have been the quick way, but he refused to adopt such an approach. He clarified that 'this family has a momentous decision to make, and my responsibility is to inform them properly, answer their questions, and put their mind at ease. This will take time.' Dramat and I excused ourselves from the conversation between the imam and family and patiently waited for their deliberations to conclude. When the meeting ended, he let us know and left without hinting at what was concluded. Riverside's father spoke to us. 'The imam', he said, 'took time to explain to us that it could not be contrary to Islamic law to testify against Muslims who had no authority to declare jihad and who indiscriminately killed women and children. As Riverside's parents, we are satisfied with and accept the imam's guidance. My son will testify as we previously agreed.'

Our focus shifted to the urgent task of extracting Riverside's extended family – his parents, wife and child, sisters and brothers, and their immediate families. The team flawlessly executed the extraction of 15 family members within thirty minutes of the imam's departure. By now, the covert unit could mobilise its members for rapid deployment, access substantial resources, and execute plans under the intense pressures of time and physical risk. It was a long way from the often-faltering manner in which we had operated a year or two before. By the time the sun rose, the family was on their way, escorted by our team to a safe house outside the Western Cape, in transit to permanent relocation abroad. Our CI colleagues in another province received and cared for them while Riverside was taken to a debriefing centre set up for the operation. Here, he was introduced to prosecutor Gray and two investigators summoned to an 'urgent meeting' without any prior warning.

The debriefing with the investigators lasted several weeks. Not only did Riverside have to provide written statements on his role in urban terrorism, but he also had to accompany investigators to physically point out places and people. This usually took place under cover of darkness and with maximum security. We had intelligence from other sources that the G-Force was now actively searching for Riverside to eliminate him. After the lengthy debriefing process, all the role players met to plan the sequence of arrests. We were the same set of actors who met under the leadership of Selebi and Ngcuka after the Mano's bombing almost exactly a year prior.

This time, there was no fumbling over empty case dockets, incompetent prosecutors and sabotaging police detectives. We were of one mind and had a goldmine of evidence, a credible witness, and a capable, dedicated prosecution team.

Frances and Boeta Yu, the most active and critical members of the G-Force Council, were the first to be arrested. They constituted the G-Force centre of gravity, and their removal from the operational equation had the paralysing effect we desired. Zacharia Albertyn, commander of the Retreat G-Force cell, and Shahied Jones, a prolific G-Force hitman, were also apprehended. Other G-Force members and commanders would later join them. In total, Riverside testified against twelve G-Force members.

Immediately after their arrests, two of the detainees made statements confessing to their involvement in the crimes with which they were charged. Williams and Jones admitted that they were members of the G-Force and that they participated in numerous murders, as alleged by the state. The arrests and subsequent confessions caused havoc in the Pagad structures. The Keg & Swan arrests and Riverside's defection dealt a significant psychological blow to the G-Force, in addition to the effect the arrests had on its viability. A terrorist organisation like the G-Force can only function effectively if it maintains a high level of trust in its ranks. Its members engage in hazardous activities and must have confidence that the people with whom they plan and execute criminal activities will not betray them.

The mysterious discovery of the Keg & Swan bomb and the subsequent arrests showed that the intelligence services had capabilities that the G-Force could no longer circumvent easily. Riverside's defection proved that the state had developed the persuasive power and intelligence to shift the loyalties of even the most hardened G-Force members. The arrests following his defection destroyed the G-Force's cohesion and neutralised its ability to carry out any sustained terrorist campaign. There was no need to arrest 200 people, simply the few who made the whole system tick. Just as we predicted, the structure had indeed imploded in on itself, and the instrument that made it tumble was concocted in the covert war room, deploying the right mix of ingredients.

The outcome of the Riverside operation was a welcome boost to the morale of the covert unit and the broader national security community. The unit had evolved from a peripheral entity meant to die a slow, barely noticeable death. Instead of its obituary, its exploits are now written in the annals of South African counter-terrorism intelligence. The German playwright Bertolt Brecht wrote, 'Intelligence is not to make no mistakes, but quickly to see how to make them good.' The unit was not flawless, and the Keg & Swan situation pointed this out in the starkest of manners. But we retained our cohesion and remained singular in our focus throughout all the challenges and disappointments. Mistakes did not affect our broader effort, as the exceptional Riverside operation following the disappointing Keg & Swan outcome showed. Dramat was a demanding commander, as was I with my team, but we never blamed any of our subordinates for failing whilst trying. We wanted to encourage a culture of considered risk-taking and innovation when it was not yet the buzzword so often devoid of meaning that it is now. We accepted that some failure would be the natural companion to our approach.

The emergence of the covert unit in a toxic institutional environment intended to eliminate it is a fascinating study of resilience. Had the unit been led by non-ANC officers, it would have been unlikely to survive or even attempt to do so. The trio of Petros, Dramat and myself refused to submit to the irrational and malicious efforts of the Smits and Trollips to close us down. It simply never occurred to us to let them succeed. We leveraged the access we had developed through contacts from my head office days or via the very supportive ANC leadership in the province to sustain and grow it into a potent team. Conversely, the faith they had in and the resources committed to the team by Williams, Selebi and Tshwete was unusual for such a small outfit. They saw through the machinations of those who tried to kill off a critical capability and saw in it the potential to achieve something spectacular.

Ultimately, it was only proper that the G-Force was undone by officers who had cut their teeth in the military underground and ANC intelligence. Pagad played a game we knew too well, and we had mastered to perfection during the national liberation struggle. As one of the veteran Afrikaner cops on our team told me long after, 'David, in my many years as a security policeman, I served under countless commanders, all white, until I joined the covert unit. If the Pagad operation was run by old white Security Branch commanders instead of you and Anwa (Dramat), we would still be hunting Pagad, and the death toll would have been much higher. The Branch people in Cape Town didn't have the skill set and attitude you guys brought to the operation. Your leadership was most clearly displayed by the fact that you and Anwa never instructed us to go and do stuff, but always to do things alongside you.'

The resilience, strategic nous and innovation that characterised the best the ANC had to offer, coupled with the institutional memory and discipline of former Branch staff we recruited, proved a potent combination and was ultimately the basis for our success.

CHAPTER 8

Home-Brewed: Developing a National Security Praxis

Victors who do not know how to build on their victories are no different from losers.
—Lüshi Chunqiu

Twenty years of reflection has provided us with sufficient perspective to properly understand the Pagad phenomenon and the work done to dismantle its terrorist infrastructure. It was challenging to think about them objectively while caught up in all the developments and turmoil that defined that crisis. This was more so in the case with my own involvement with Pagad, given that I accompanied the organisation as an adversary from its birth to its neutralisation as a terrorist threat.

The difficulty with instantly assessing the success of an operation such as the one against Pagad was whether we had sufficiently impacted its capability to render it sustainably ineffective. Given Pagad's resilience over the preceding six years, only a fool would have read the late 2000 and early 2001 developments as a decisive defeat, at the time. This uncertainty made an assessment difficult for fear of being premature in our judgments. Still, by early 2001, it was clear that we had inflicted a significant and potentially fatal blow against the G-Force. This deserved a comprehensive, if preliminary, assessment of our work over the six years. Yet, that would not happen.

Ultimately, what passed for an assessment consisted of a very short debrief on lessons learned. The exercise took place at a resort on the West Coast and had the air of a celebratory as opposed to a learning event. Percy Sonn chaired the gathering of police, prosecutorial, and intelligence structures. It could not have lasted more than two hours, and no preparatory work was done before the discussion. It did not even come close to doing justice to the years of labour that went into dismantling Pagad's terrorist infrastructure. Neither did it enable us to explore the innovations that emerged during this effort or the institutional blockages and sabotage that unnecessarily prolonged it.

Since then, the people central to the anti-Pagad effort have had the opportunity to reflect, and some have incorporated these reflections into their work within the state. I researched the phenomenon, taught about it, and developed intelligence and counter-terrorism training programmes that drew from the lessons of the effort. The excitement and astonishment I encountered abroad at the scale of our success and the operational innovation ran counter to how it was followed up in South Africa. Everyone got back to mopping up the remains of the G-Force infrastructure, moved on to new positions within the state, and assumed greater responsibility. Their rapid upward movement meant we lost their ability to reflect more deeply on what the Pagad operation implied for South African National Security, intelligence, and policing.

A question still asked today is why Pagad collapsed, especially considering the relatively low number of convictions. Many G-Force leaders remained free, and some of its cells retained both their human capability and some weapons they could use to continue their campaign of terror. In a sense, this is the wrong question to ask because it assumes the defeat of the G-Force could only be effected through the mass arrest of its members. On the contrary, our intention was not to collapse the broader Pagad organisation or prosecute the entire G-Force but to eliminate its ability to function as a cohesive entity. Prosecuting large numbers of G-Force members was neither desirable nor practically feasible. The amount of resources, time, and skills to do so simply did not exist in the police and prosecuting authorities.

Terrorist organisations like the G-Force need three prerequisite elements to function effectively. These are the lifeblood of underground paramilitaries. The first is operational security – the sense that you can conspire with others, communicate your plans and be relatively confident that the plans will not be leaked. What became clear to G-Force cells and commanders by the end of 2000 was that we had penetrated their command and control system, and the transmission of orders was no longer secure.

The second central element to sustain a terrorist organisation is legitimacy amongst at least a sizable section of the population. By the end of 2000, Pagad had wasted most of the political legitimacy it garnered during its earlier years. The balance between mass mobilisation and terror was heavily weighted towards the former. A militant organisation that loses its balance in calibrating consent and coercion is bound to become marginalised and easily isolated from its base. This is a lesson we ANC cadres involved in the Pagad operation knew well. We had built these politico-military capabilities in the 1980s and realised that denying the G-Force that umbilical link would be central to sustaining and compounding the impact that arrests could have.

The third prerequisite for success is freedom of manoeuvre. Paramilitary organisations thrive when they have operational freedom of manoeuvre. Such freedom encourages innovation in action, boldness and risk-taking. The G-Force operated with impressive swagger between 1996 and mid-2000, but by the end of the year, we compelled it to become more cautious, conservative, and risk-averse.

The element of surprise is critical in intelligence operations. By late 2000, the covert unit could execute its operations by exploiting the element of surprise. The thorough and deliberate work we had done since 1997 culminated in a short but decisive series of interventions, especially since the turn of the millennium following the 1999 Christmas Eve bombings. The precision of the operations towards the end of 2000 surprised the G-Force leadership in its scope, detail, and success in penetrating what they regarded as a highly secure and compartmentalised organisation.

Major-General Mick Ryan, an Australian strategist, posits that 'whether achieved through physical or virtual approaches, surprise generates a cognitive effect in one's adversary. This feeling of perplexity, shock, and uncertainty in individuals as well as in teams, is designed by those seeking to achieve surprise to undermine an enemy's cohesion and morale.' Pulling the three prerequisites for successful operational work out from under the G-Force's feet, coupled with the element of surprise, affected the organisation's ability to reconstitute or pivot, leading to its demise as an effective force for sustained violent action.

A distinguishing factor in whether surprise is temporary or sustained is the ability to create compound surprise, that is, to stack one tactical surprise upon another, ideally within a short timeframe. This ensures that momentum remains with the attacking agency, deepens the adversary's crisis and does not permit it space and time to reflect, fix breaches, and re-establish its modus operandi. At the level of morale, consecutive tactical surprises often have an effect that exceeds the sum of its parts. Like individuals, institutions can also become overwhelmed by the cumulative impact of constant surprise, shock, and disorientation.

The effect of this surprise was heightened because neither Pagad nor most of the police leadership had any idea of the capability we had been building in the preceding three years. The secrecy that could only work in the context of a covert operations unit went hand in glove with the speed at which surprise was effected. It was an example of what the Soviet strategist Alexander Svechin referred to when he wrote: 'Surprise, which is the backbone of the offense, is, according to Clausewitz, an eagle that has two wings – concealment and speed.'

The operation against Pagad took place at a difficult moment, just as the country transitioned from an Apartheid regime to a democratic constitutional order. The national security community was in the midst of an organisational and cultural transition. It struggled to find its place in the new constitutional order, adjust its modus operandi, and ensure the functionality of institutions constituted of formerly mortal enemies. The ability to function in this environment in the face of a growing threat required the twin elements of adaptation and innovation. The first is the ability to change course, ways of work, and targeting as the conditions demand. The other is creating new ways of conceptualising the threat (Vearey's intervention with the urban terror concept being a case in point), integrating disparate capabilities inside the police and across the intelligence community, and developing new modes of leadership. It was a time that the Palestinian philosopher Abdaljawad Omar calls 'an acute state of in-betweenness, where all former norms, rules, structures, and even emotions are thrown into contention.'

For those of us who came through the liberation movement, creativity and innovation were a core part of our political training and organisational disposition. While expected to deliver high-quality results, ANC cadres operated with limited resources and under constant enemy harassment. The best way to conduct a political or military struggle in this context was with creativity and innovation as a form of survivalist instinct. Later, as we settled into government bureaucracy, the requirement to innovate was less appreciated. Writing in the context of the post-revolutionary Soviet Union in his seminal work on strategy, Svechin posits: 'When a revolution starts, there is no need to worry about private initiative because it is everywhere. But in normal conditions, when there is no particular revolutionary enthusiasm, initiative is a very fragile phenomenon which must be carefully cultivated.' In our case, it was up to the covert unit's leadership to encourage and nurture such innovation.

Dramat, the quiet but effective commander of the covert unit through most of the Pagad operation, displayed a style of leadership that was essential to the team's success. This leadership style, which emphasised trust and delegation, was key to our success. We functioned as a mutually reinforcing team, with me leading the counter-terrorism unit and him the covert unit as a whole. This leadership style was defined by what in Russian operational art is called *nastavlenie* (a manual to guide action) instead of *direKtiva* (a directive). It meant providing a general disposition and line of march to our team and relying on their creativity, drive, and boldness to navigate the complexities of covert operations against the G-Force. This approach, an anomaly in the command-centric police, was the lynchpin of our success.

Building trust and a strong team identity were crucial for enabling this risky mode of work. Trust cannot be created by declaration and must be patiently constructed. The first step was constituting the covert unit itself and selecting the right staff. Petros started this process by appointing Dramat and then incorporating me into the unit. This gave him two subordinate officers he could trust and delegate responsibility to. When Petros was promoted and moved out of the covert environment, Dramat and I selected a small team of people we thought would meet the trust threshold. This included former Branch officers and ANC cadres we recruited from the police VIP unit.

The hours spent talking to and conspiring with my team strengthened our bond and gave everyone a sense of being part of planning instead of just functionaries merely implementing commands. Trust is most solid when team members feel they are entrusted with significant responsibilities and not just the execution of mundane or bit-part roles. Despite the media circus that accompanies the phenomenon when it becomes public, failure is a perennial feature in intelligence. Espionage is, after all, not conducted in a sterile laboratory but in the real world, sometimes combating highly capable adversaries.

From its formation in 1995 to its withering away from 2001 onwards, the G-Force had proven itself a capable, innovative, and resilient adversary. Sometimes, intelligence failures are minor tactical failures one can correct on the spot. Other times, they are strategic failures, such as adequately characterising Pagad in the first two years of its emergence. Mistakes are bound to occur in adversarial contests of will, minds, and resources, such as our struggle against Pagad. The adversary might outwit you, or you could miscalculate elementary factors. To trust our subordinates, we had to accept that they would sometimes fail, as we did. We operated by the Machiavellian maxim of making mistakes of ambition and not mistakes of sloth.

The success of our operation against the G-Force was only possible with the level of vertical and horizontal integration we had developed by late 2000. Within crime intelligence and the police service, the covert unit was singular in its level of access to the national leadership, with a particularly close relationship with Williams and Selebi. Their trust in us and the material support they provided enabled us to turn our usually unconventional plans into reality. Our partnership with comrades from KwaZulu-Natal and the assistance the experienced Lalla offered was invaluable. The expertise Lalla gained from years running intelligence and military operations against the Apartheid regime from exile and the driving ambition of his young sidekick, Moodley, helped the covert unit through a time when it was marginalised and its very existence threatened by the Western Cape police leadership.

What began as a budding partnership when Fraser arrived in Cape Town to head up the NIA's Western Cape office sometime in 1998 had turned into a full-blown integrated capability by late 2000. The timing of this partnership and its timely maturation exponentially increased the covert unit's capability and reach. The NIA's considerable technical capabilities significantly enhanced our own, often enabling minute-by-minute recalibration and deployment of resources. Fraser's arrival transformed the relationship between Crime Intelligence and the NIA from its mainly official footing to one of close operational efficiency defined by unprecedented sharing and joint exploitation of intelligence. Despite the high level of integration and mutual respect, a healthy competitive edge remained between ourselves and the NIA.

The last component of our partnership, and most critical from the prosecutorial angle, was IDOC and its later iteration, the Scorpions. We had unfettered access to their prosecutors and often sought their counsel in sensitive operational matters where we operated at the outer edges of the law. In this, Sonn, Adams, and Davids, their young star prosecutor, were invaluable resources. Later on, Eunice Grey added another sharp prosecutorial mind to that team, and we worked well together. The openness with which the Scorpions approached the cases of Jogger and Riverside, where they were state witnesses, reflected this appreciation and the uncompromising trust between the NPA-CI-NIA triumvirate.

Despite rapid technological advancements and the rise of Artificial Intelligence (AI) in the national security domain, the most valuable asset for an intelligence organisation remains a well-placed, well-managed human source. While there are increasingly important offensive and defensive ways to deploy AI in intelligence, policing and warfare, human sources have the unique ability to attribute meaning to activity, provide context to chatter, and link data points gathered through mass surveillance. As we saw with Pagad, when a human source provides a tip-off about an impending bombing a seemingly innocuous shopping trip to the garden centre to buy fertiliser can take on a completely different meaning. This is a testament to the unique insights that human sources can provide.

But the HUMINT-technology debate should never be a dichotomous one. Human sources excel in carrying spy tech into denied spaces such as secured meeting facilities, the residences of targets, or the vehicles used in terrorist operations. Knowing which spaces to target, when they are used, and who uses them is as precious as gold to an intelligence planner. This knowledge allows for the precise and optimal use of limited and costly technical resources.

Constructing an information network in a target structure is a complex and fraught endeavour, further complicated when the target runs a secure operation and metes out punishment with extreme prejudice to anyone suspected of collaborating with the state. The G-Force did not tolerate the slightest signs of collaboration and applied a very low threshold to making a 'guilty determination.' Once a decision is taken to recruit a source in a target organisation, the search for the right candidate commences. This exploration not only focuses on who fits the bill in meeting the information requirement and is a realistic prospect. The target must be a character who can endure the pressure of working clandestinely, manage their emotional state in adverse circumstances, and critically, be able to follow orders from their handlers.

What made otherwise committed Pagad members spy for us to the fatal detriment of their organisation? The traditional model of categorising an individual's motivation to spy against his state or organisation is codified in the MICE model – Money, Ideology, Compromise, and Ego. This rather crude model assumes singular motivations and ignores the complexity of human motivations and emotions. It also overlooks the fact that the motive to start spying often differs from the motive to continue doing so, even though the risk increases the longer the espionage game continues.

Recently, more comprehensive approaches to understanding motivation were developed. This breaches the wall between the motivation to become a spy versus the motivation to continue. The psychologist Dr. Robert Cialdini developed a recruitment and handling model called RASCLS – Reciprocation, Authority, Scarcity, Commitment or Consistency, Liking, and Social Proof. Most human beings need to *reciprocate* what qualifies as a good deed. The deed draws them into espionage, as they need to respond in kind. A simple act such as providing a warm halaal meal to Johnson after a week in cold police cells created instant rapport. It undoubtedly contributed to his willingness to cooperate as a source.

When approaching a potential source, we always spoke with *authority*, often stating that we represented a high office such as the presidency or Crime Intelligence headquarters. In the case of Riverside, his willingness to become a state witness was partially motivated by the evident *authority* with which we presented ourselves, bolstered by the fact that we could call on the head of the Scorpions and the national police commissioner to solve whatever he regarded as obstacles to his continued cooperation.

Being approached by an intelligence service is rare, and the opportunity it presents is a *scarcity* to which the potential source becomes privy. He would know that the offer could meet one or more of his needs, often in ways that no one else can, that it has a time limit, and that the scarce opportunity would be offered to someone else should he decline. The chance to achieve something great and unusual, such as contributing to the defeat of the G-Force, played a significant role in some people's decision to cooperate. They could sense the opportunity and the scarcity thereof and jumped at it. It motivated them throughout our relationship and drove them to deliver exceptional intelligence.

Once a source had made an initial *commitment* to collaborate, they often continued cooperating to rationalise their original decision. Even the most hardened G-Force members who crossed the cooperation threshold frequently just to get out of an immediate pickle turned into reliable long-term sources. Maintaining internal mental and operational *consistency* was a key driver in this type of loyalty. This is the intelligence equivalent of the sunken cost fallacy, where an initial decision and investment become embedded because the source would instead continue collaborating rather than admit the decision's wrongness (from his, not our, perspective). Our role as handlers was to embed commitment and consistency in the relationship as early as possible. Part of it was to break down any preconceived notions G-Force members had of the intelligence community and see us as usual yet assertive and empathetic individuals.

According to Cialdini, we like people who are like us. While a handler's relationship with a source is professional, both the initial recruitment and the quality of the handling relationship are enhanced by the source *liking* some aspect of the recruiter or handler's background or personality. Some of the Qibla sources we recruited liked that we came from a similar political background, having fought in the liberation struggle against the Apartheid regime. Others enjoyed a mutual interest in reading widely. The more touchpoints between the intelligence officer and their source, the greater the likelihood that a deeper trust can be built.

Given the intense relationship between our officers and their sources, *social proof* or informational social influence is a common and desired outcome from the officer's perspective. We sought to model behaviour and encourage ideas that would make our sources more likely to adopt these ideas or mimic said behaviours. This could include conversations about what is acceptable in cases of political violence, especially the controversy around killing women and children or innocent bystanders. With some of our sources, these ideas took hold and replaced their previously held belief that indiscriminate killing was both operationally and religiously justified.

Some sources are extraordinary, defined by their dedication, contribution, and willingness to adapt to the most trying circumstances. While working against the G-Force, I recruited and handled some exceptional individuals. They did not always produce the most spectacular results, but their absolute loyalty, creativity, and durability placed them in a league of their own. They were the sources who rose to the top if they felt their handlers had invested time, effort, and training in them.

Our victory over the G-Force was not a stroke of luck, but the result of a well-crafted strategy, innovative leadership, and the deliberate building of offensive intelligence capabilities. At the strategic level, the government initially struggled to comprehend the scale of the threat posed by Pagad. However, once this cognitive obstacle was overcome, a strategy with precise contours evolved between 1997 and 1999, leading to ultimate success.

The first element of this strategy was to defeat Pagad through an integrated political and security project. Not to minimise its effect, blunt its militancy or incorporate it into the more cooperative anti-crime initiatives in the Western Cape, but to defeat it. In effect, for the intelligence community, this meant the decimation of the G-Force's ability to function as a cohesive entity and the political marginalisation of Pagad as a political force and social movement.

The second element of the strategy was to design and implement a project centred on South African realities and disconnected from what was then an increasing Western obsession with 'Islamic fundamentalism' as the new global threat to US hegemony. Given our political history, we needed to retain our distance from the US and its allies, even though they offered unlimited assistance, training and intelligence sharing to support our struggle against Pagad. Such an association would have sucked us into the American narrative around extremism. It would have compelled us to invent imaginary links between Pagad and the 'global jihad'. It would have elevated American approaches to neutralising such threats at the expense of our own initiatives.

As it happened, none of the successes we achieved can be ascribed to American or other external assistance, and the innovation enabled by our self-dependence delivered more success than similar US projects on the African continent. Retaining our autonomy in dealing with the Pagad phenomenon also shielded us in the post-2001 world, where the 'global war on terror' became the primary lens through which the Americans viewed and practised their geopolitics.

Once the strategic direction was clear, the national security apparatus had to transform the executive's strategic guidance into concrete intelligence and policing action. When the writer Dorothea Brande stated that 'a problem clearly stated is a problem half-solved,' she might as well have been writing about the process of determining intelligence requirements, which now logically flowed from the government's characterisation of Pagad as an urban terror threat. The process of intelligence requirements is critical to developing the correct understanding of what the intelligence consumer requires, what the consumer's assumptions about the threat are, and what purpose such intelligence is meant to serve. This exercise would be conducted at Crime Intelligence headquarters in collaboration with partner agencies such as the NIA and Defence Intelligence.

The requirements had strategic, operational and tactical elements, and we produced a constant stream of analytic briefs dealing with all of these. While we had not conceptualised it as such at the time, the intervening concept of an operational level in intelligence was an innovation in doctrine within CI. Until then, two distinct levels of operation existed, strategic and tactical.

The effort to defeat Pagad would consist of multiple simultaneous tactical-level operations, all intended to achieve the strategic aims outlined earlier. To enable coherence between the numerous interventions and manage the focus and deployments of these multiple tactical efforts, a new level of thinking and acting had to be developed, creating what we refer to as 'intelligence operational art.' In the context of war, Svechin states that 'operational art dictates the basic line of conduct of an operation, depending on the material available, the time which may be allotted to the handling of different tactical missions, the forces which may be deployed for battle on a certain front, and finally on the nature of the operation itself.' As we transformed the executive's requirements into intelligence operations and products, we benefited from having a team of officers within the covert unit and Fraser's

NIA team who were at ease with converting strategy into tactics and managing at the operational level.

Given the undeniable success in integrating political, informational, and intelligence operations to achieve defined strategic aims, and the level of innovation displayed throughout the Pagad operation, it is logical to ask how these lessons can be incorporated into contemporary efforts to counter organised crime, subversion and instability in the country. It also raises the question of how valuable these lessons can be to counter organised crime, terrorism and destabilisation on the African continent. Perhaps it is time to show that we have lessons to teach the rest of the world instead of simply mimicking what we are fed from elsewhere.

South Africa now faces a polycrisis – a complex set of interlinked crises so embedded in our society and political economy that the effect exceeds the sum thereof. This phenomenon, which encompasses the entirety of the country's political economy, has a severe impact on our National Security. While it is premature to speak of a failed or failing state, this conversation and discourse emerging more frequently in the public domain should concern the state, national security professionals, and the broader public. In its 2022 Risk Assessment on Organised Crime in South Africa, the Global Initiative Against Transnational Organised Crime (GI) reported, 'South Africa faces a complex, hybrid criminal threat. Having originated in highly constricted conditions under Apartheid, in three decades, organised crime has spread across the country and forged links around the world. It has been quick to seize opportunities, robust in the face of (often weak) law enforcement pressure and assertive in protecting its spheres of influence.' Of the fifteen categories of organised crime the GI assessed, all were rated as stable at a high level or increasing. This pessimistic but realistic assessment reflects a country on the brink of irreversibility in our failure to deal with serious crime.

Of the five lessons I can draw from the Pagad operation, the first is about *learning and praxis* itself. The liberation struggle was defined by continuous learning, and knowledge acquisition itself was regarded as a form of struggle. At the ideological level, the liberation movement had to continuously learn, re-conceptualise and re-strategise. From the development of the concept of 'Colonialism of a Special Type' to characterise the South African political economy in 1963, the 1978 ANC study tour to Vietnam to learn about asymmetric People's War, to the study group established by ANC President Oliver Tambo to develop a constitutional model for post-Apartheid South Africa at the height of the South African conflict in 1986, the struggle was a showcase of learning and praxis.

National Security institutions can only be successful if they are dynamic learning institutions. In the post-Mbeki era, an anti-intellectualism crept into the nation's body politic, affecting our intelligence and security institutions. The virtues of learning and thinking are now dismissed as impractical intellectualism and are avoided like the plague. Yet, without learning, we cannot understand the world or develop and innovate intelligence tradecraft. These are all processes that require abstract study, integrated with an engagement with the practical realities of the world and the art of intelligence. A dynamic learning culture in the context of national security institutions must, by necessity, aim to develop intelligence praxis and not focus on the academic study of intelligence and security. Praxis does not claim the false neutrality mantle in which the academy wraps itself. It has a moral commitment and a history-making purpose. In the South African context, this means developing an Indigenous and decolonised national security praxis embedded in local traditions while drawing on a wide range of insights and experiences from across the globe.

Until a coherent strategy emerged, all the efforts to counter Pagad were more or less a series of rearguard actions doomed to failure. The centrality of *strategy as a prerequisite for building and maintaining national security* is the second lesson of the Pagad experience. Intelligence is an activity practised on a continuum of war and peace, and strategy is the process of finding our place on that spectrum, defining an optimal situation and determining policy. It is not a series of plans linked together and labelled 'strategy,' as strategy must, by necessity, precede planning. In recent years the South African national security apparatus has been disadvantaged by the lack of political imagination and leadership that has come to define South Africa's executive.

This poverty of imagination and leadership is writ large in the absence of a national strategy to determine the nation's purpose. Intelligence without strategy is the equivalent of deploying a missile without a guidance system. The construction of an intelligence architecture without a national strategy and national security strategy creates a bureaucratic apparatus with no sense of mission. It cannot develop a cohesive strategic or institutional culture, recruit the right staff, deploy them properly or resource them in a manner equivalent to their purpose, when none exists.

With a government prioritising bureaucratic processes above strategy, the intelligence and security community does not have a broad strategic purpose. In practice, it then finds itself aligning its mission, resources, and effort with the fluctuating whims of politicians or the vagaries of short-term developments. The National Security institutions can only insulate themselves from a rudderless political leadership for so long, after which they inevitably fall prey to the effects of an absence of strategy.

The necessity of a context-relevant National Security Strategy in South Africa cannot be overstated. Such a strategy has to take cognisance of the dynamic changes in the geopolitical environment, the revolution in military affairs occasioned by the deployment of Artificial Intelligence in the battlespace and the changing character of war itself. The concept of hybrid warfare that emerged in the contemporary strategic lexicon has profound implications for the conduct of strategic and intelligence affairs. The increasingly vague boundaries between war and peace and the weaponisation of information are factors that could be wielded against us at a moment when our lack of national cohesion and our institutional fragility most expose us to the effect of such measures.

The weaponisation of internal political conflict, the lack of consensus on building the developmental state, and our decreasing influence on the African continent will be worsened by an assault that deploys non-kinetic warfare yet achieves the same effect – a loss of sovereignty, social fracturing, and an inability to exercise any freedom of manoeuvre to advance South Africa's national interest. Both the content of our National Security Strategy and the form in which it is developed must consider these new realities. In the asymmetric power dynamic in which South Africa operates viz a viz the great powers, such strategy must be rooted in building national cohesion and the ability to deploy state-society capabilities in defence of our sovereignty.

What made the Crime Intelligence covert unit successful in its campaign against the G-Force was that we did not see the unit as merely a block in a large bureaucratic organigram but as a capability to be deployed in achieving national strategic aims. *Developing and deploying capabilities* in national security is a third key lesson from the work against Pagad. The intelligence services cannot be mere bureaucratic entities. They are specific types of capabilities, that is, instruments capable of doing things required to build and sustain our national security. In the end, intelligence structures do things: thinking, advising, disrupting and combating. The more capable they are, the more efficiently they can execute these functions.

We should build out National Security capabilities with the design perspective of modern architecture, that is, context-appropriate, resilient to shocks and sudden changes, sustainable and flexible in their utilisation, and absent of ornamentation. Intelligence capabilities are, importantly, precise instruments not to be wielded broadly and indiscriminately but to achieve specific aims, often under wickedly stubborn circumstances. From the covert unit and the partnerships with the NIA, the military, and the prosecuting authority, the lessons of smaller, highly skilled, and integrated capabilities hold a certain appeal. They could be emulated on a larger scale.

A fourth lesson is that developing intelligence capabilities requires *dynamic and committed leadership* at the political and institutional levels. Mbeki as president, his security ministers, Selebi, Willams, and Ray Lalla in the police, Vusi Mavimbela first as Mbeki's advisor and then as head of the NIA, Fraser and Dramat were all examples of such leadership at the strategic, operational and tactical levels. Too many mundane characters have since taken to the helm of both these levels. From politicians to bureaucrats, the few capable and dynamic leaders seem to swim in a sea of the average and stale. This reality is often reflected in the obsession with vacuous symbolism on the one hand and bureaucratic procedures on the other. While both have their place in government institutions, turning them into the raison d'etre of the institutions is self-defeating. It starkly contrasts the need to lead dynamically, with purpose and vigour.

Symbolism has become the purpose of some national security institutions, especially the police. The same lack of dynamic leadership is displayed in the perennial charge to 'go back to basics' instead of looking to the future. Of course, 'the basics' we are meant to go back to are those of a security community under Apartheid, detached from the population, imposing itself without legitimacy and unable to combat sophisticated security challenges without the use of violence and fear. This type of leadership thrives in the context of a collapsed transformative political project and the absence of strategy.

In *The 18th Brumaire of Louis Bonaparte*, Karl Marx makes two simple yet profound statements. These aptly capture the similarity of the 1799 Bonapartist coup in France with the unwinding of our own republic's transformative security and policing strategy. First, he states that the intention of *The 18th Brumaire of Louis Bonaparte* is to demonstrate how *the class struggle creates circumstances and relationships that make it possible for the hero's part to be played by a grotesque mediocrity*. The problem with some of our national security leadership is that it represents this kind of mediocrity, and realising this themselves, they live in constant fear of those who might think differently and, heaven forbid, speak and write about this.

Marx further states that 'every giant presupposes a dwarf, every genius a hidebound philistine.' According to him, 'the first are too great for this world, so they are thrown out, but the latter strike root in it and remain.' Rebuilding capable national security institutions would mean marginalising such characters and, in their place, supporting those leaders who display innovation, dynamism and a commitment to the national developmental project. It also means identifying and developing the younger echelon of leaders who will occupy these spaces in the next ten years.

The fifth lesson is that *strategic autonomy* in systems, infrastructure, and paradigms is critical to rebuilding our national security architecture. Strategic autonomy is closely related to *learning and praxis*, the absence of which compels one to operate through the copy-and-paste method of institution building, tradecraft, and capability development.

When the ANC embarked upon Operation Vula in the late 1980s, it required a secure communications system with which the external leadership could communicate with the commanders it had deployed inside the country. Having the required technological capability, the Soviet KGB offered to provide such communications for the operation. However, the ANC politely declined and developed its own communications system, deploying Tim Jenkins to build it from scratch. Such innovation, when more obvious and easily accessible options were available, enhanced security and control over the communications system but also ensured the ANC's strategic autonomy over its most sensitive initiative. Such autonomy must characterise our physical and cyber infrastructure, as well as our ways of thinking and working.

Apart from the broader political and institutional lessons, the experience of countering the Pagad threat so early in the life of democratic South Africa was personally exhilarating even as it was exhausting. It was a privilege to work with colleagues, many old comrades and former enemies, to build a capability operating with purpose. This unity in purpose allowed us to see the potential of what we were building beyond our pasts. The officers of the covert unit took a marginalised unit in shambles when Petros took command, redesigned it, developed innovative tradecraft, and forced their way out of the cold into the centre of South African national security.

Working against targets such as Pagad and its G-Force, which operated at a consistently high tempo, demanded that we do the same. The effects of this exertion are not felt in the moment, when adrenaline, the occasional sleep, and large doses of energy drinks keep you going. Yet, the delayed exhaustion catches you at some point and often in devastating ways, as I discovered when I left Crime Intelligence. Having spent six years in a constant now-secret, now-open confrontation with Pagad, I only felt the ramifications afterwards. The trauma made itself felt in broken relationships, struggles to adjust to everyday life, and an inability to live a life and find meaning detached from an all-consuming job. It took me many years to even consider the effect of this experience on my worldview and behaviour and some more years of therapy to start reflecting more deeply about it. Without this reflection, this book would have stagnated where I left it 20 years ago.

I am certainly not the only person to have experienced trauma or some other form of psychological effect from that experience. For everyone in the covert unit, the experience was physically demanding and emotionally exacting. We also had to take care of sources who risked their lives not just for the cause of defeating Pagad or the money we paid them but often for us, the individuals who recruited and handled them. Our wits and common sense were the only tools we had to manage the range of emotional issues they experienced, sometimes expressed and often concealed for fear of looking weak.

The psychological support provided by CI consisted of one therapist who serviced the entire division, more than one-thousand intelligence officers and a sizable number of deep cover agents. It was an impossible task. Developing strategy, building capabilities, and training your officers have limited utility if you do not make their psychological well-being an essential element of your institutional effort. Many officers, agents and sources are content to live a dangerous and anonymous existence in service of the nation, and the least we can do for them is to prevent them from stumbling and catch them if they ever do.

Key Personalities

Abdus Salaam Ebrahim, a Qibla member of long standing and founder of Pagad, was the charismatic and aggressive commander of the G-Force. He led the transformation of the G-Force into an offensive instrument that targeted gangsters, then the state and Western interests. He was convicted on charges of public violence for involvement in the incident that led to the murder of notorious Cape own gang leader Rashaad Staggie.

Achmat Cassiem was a veteran anti-Apartheid activist, imprisoned on Robben Island at the age of 17. Founder and leader of Qibla, Cassiem shaped the ideological foundations of, and exerted substantial influence over the Pagad leadership. He was an inspiration to many of the militants who came through its ranks. He died in July 2023.

Amber (pseudonym) grew up on the Cape Flats during the turbulent 1980s. She joined the police's Security Branch in the early 1990s and was recruited by Petros into the Crime Intelligence covert unit 1999. With a deep understanding of Cape Town communities and an extraordinarily creative disposition, she was a star performer at the covert unit.

Anwa Dramat hails from Cape Town's Bontheuwel township, where he became involved in the African National Congress military wing during the 1980s. In

1988, he was convicted under Apartheid terrorism legislation and imprisoned on Robben Island. Dramat joined Crime Intelligence as part of a team of ANC intelligence officers integrated in 1995. The soft-spoken Dramat led the covert unit to a number of spectacular successes in the critical 1998 to 2000 period. He subsequently rose to become the head of the Directorate for Priority Crime Investigation (the Hawks).

Anwar Frances first came to the attention of the police when he was arrested at Gatesville Medical centre following an explosion in which two fellow G-Force members were killed. Francis subsequently became a critical player in the G-Force leadership structure.

Arthur Fraser grew up in Cape Town and served in the ANC underground before integrating into the post-Apartheid National Intelligence Agency. He was seconded to the Truth and Reconciliation Commission to investigate Apartheid-era human-rights abuses. Fraser was the Western Cape head of the NIA at the height of the Pagad troubles. He served as Director-General of the State Security Agency from 1996 to 1998.

Attie Trollip worked in the Apartheid Security Branch and left the Branch in the early 1990s to work at a police station. He returned to intelligence as the provincial head of Crime Intelligence. After his tenure as the Western Cape head of CI he transferred to the police detective branch.

Chris Martin (pseudonym) grew up on the Cape Flats and was a prominent member of the Security Branch in the late 1980s, where he specialised in infiltrating progressive student and youth organisations. He was the first officer assigned to work with me on the Pagad investigation, and continued working on the operation until its conclusion.

Dawood Adam, formerly an advocate in private practice, was brought into the Directorate of Special Operations (a.k.a. the Scorpions), where he headed the Western Cape office. Adam was crucial to improving the quality of prosecutorial work against Pagad G-Force members, and a central cog in the Scorpions' relationship with the police and intelligence community.

Jeremy Vearey, a former Umkhonto we Sizwe (MK) combatant and Robben Island prisoner, led the team of ANC Department of Intelligence and Security (DIS) officers that integrated into the Western Cape CI structures. Vearey became the provincial head of intelligence coordination within CI, before leaving for successful stints elsewhere in the police. He rose to the rank of Major-General within the police.

Mzwandile Petros, a former teacher and political activist from Paarl, integrated into CI in 1995 and became commander of the covert intelligence unit that ran deep-cover operations against Pagad. Following the success of the unit, Petros rose rapidly through the police ranks, ultimately becoming police commissioner in both Western Cape and Gauteng provinces.

Percy Sonn came from a legal activism background and was brought into the prosecuting authority by then minister of justice Dullah Omar. Sonn led the Scorpions, where he brought together a talented team of prosecutors to pursue charges against G-Force members.

Rayman Lalla commanded ANC military and intelligence operations during the anti-Apartheid struggle. He integrated into the police in Kwazulu-Natal province, before succeeding Tim Williams as the divisional commissioner of Crime Intelligence. Lalla was a key support to the covert team leading the Western Cape operation against Pagad.

Tim Williams held senior positions in the ANC's exile machinery and joined the post-Apartheid police management services before his appointment as divisional commissioner of Crime Intelligence. Williams capacitated and strategically guided the Western Cape covert team's operation.

Willie Els was one of two deputy heads within CI, both of whom came through the Security Branch. He was Williams's point man with the covert unit and the national head of CI's intelligence gathering capability.

Organogram

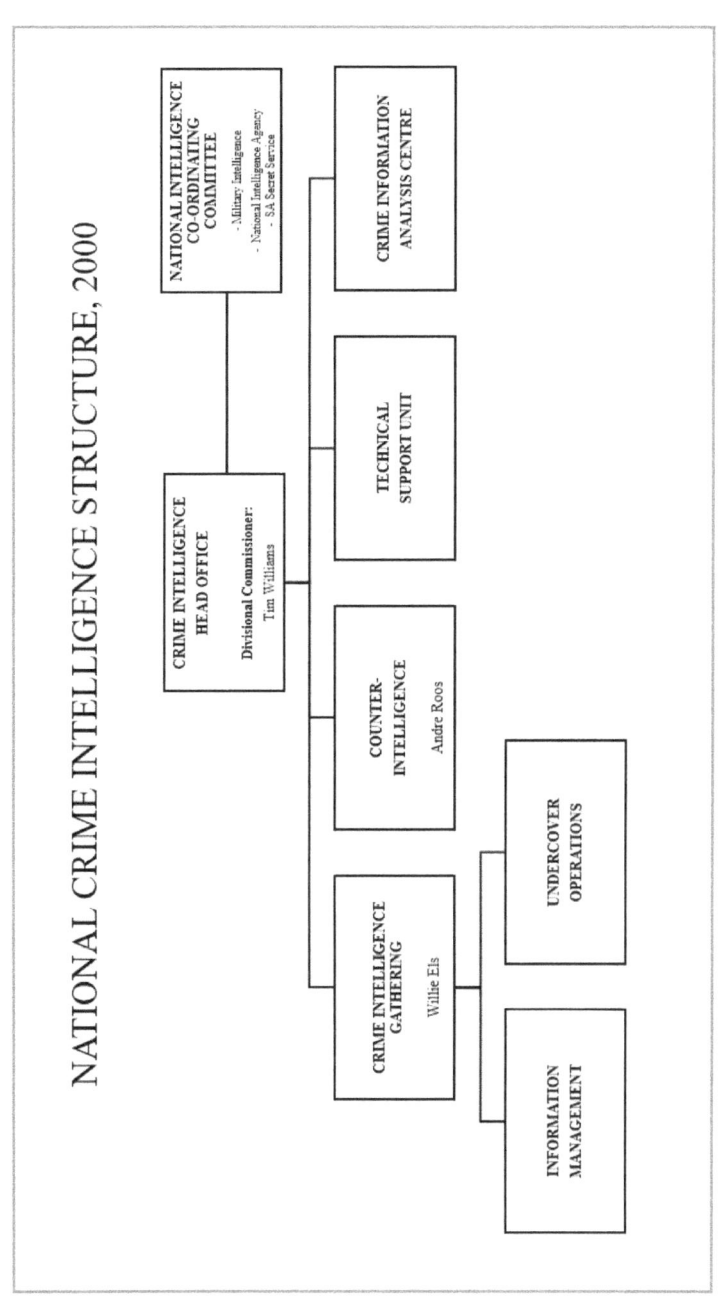

NATIONAL CRIME INTELLIGENCE STRUCTURE, 2000

NATIONAL INTELLIGENCE CO-ORDINATING COMMITTEE
- Military Intelligence
- National Intelligence Agency
- SA Secret Service

CRIME INTELLIGENCE HEAD OFFICE
Divisional Commissioner:
Tim Williams

CRIME INFORMATION ANALYSIS CENTRE

TECHNICAL SUPPORT UNIT

COUNTER-INTELLIGENCE
Andre Roos

CRIME INTELLIGENCE GATHERING
Willie Els

UNDERCOVER OPERATIONS

INFORMATION MANAGEMENT

Acronyms

NIA	National Intelligence Agency
SAPS	South Africa Police Service
CI	Crime Intelligence
Pagad	People Against Gangsterism and Drugs
IUC	Islamic Unity Convention
MJC	Muslim Judicial Council
G-Force	Gun Force
NPA	National Prosecuting Authority
IDOC	Investigative Directorate for Organised Crime
DSO	Directorate of Special Operations (Scorpions)
ANC	African National Congress
MK	Umkhonto we Sizwe (Spear of the Nation)
DIS	Department of Intelligence and Security
SB	Security Branch
NICOC	National Intelligence Coordinating Committee
PICOC	Provincial Intelligence Coordinating Committee
CIA	Central Intelligence Agency
KGB	Komitet Gosudarstvennoy Bezopasnosti (Committee for State Security)

www.ingramcontent.com/pod-product-compliance
Lightning Source LLC
Chambersburg PA
CBHW051101030726
47504CB00006B/1724